THE APOCALYPSE OF ENOCH

ASH FALL

AN END OF DAYS NOVEL

BEN REEDER

A New Babel Book release
381 High Point Drive

Holiday Shores, IL 62025

www.newbabelbooks.com

ISBN 978-1-63196-026-0 (trade paperback)
First printing.

Printed in the United States of America.

Acknowledgments

Ash Fall was an interesting book to write. It was my first venture into someone else's world, and I'm really grateful for the help in making it look like I knew what I was talking about! Many thanks to Shane Moore for the help with getting the zombies of your world right, and helping me keep the history straight. And doubly so for letting me play in your world. I wish I could have used all of the cool ideas we came up with in our brainstorming sessions!

As always, I'm so grateful to my family and friends who put up with the late night writing binges and the constant talking about the book. Thanks for being my sounding board and for not locking me up when I worked out dialogue out loud instead of in my head like I thought. Thank you, Randi, for being such a steadfast partner in all things with me.

Thanks are also due to James Fipps and Alexa Heart for letting me take so many liberties with the characters bearing their names. You two are as awesome in real life as I hope I made you in fiction.

Thanks to Ed Gehlert for turning my first draft into something workable, and for the thousand other things you do.

Thanks to all my cool brothers and sisters in the Brolo Nation for just being there like you always are. I went through some rough times outside of the writing of Ash Fall, and the constant upbeat attitude and pure awesomeness of the Brolo Nation always made those rough days dealing with a death in the family a lot easier.

Most importantly, thank you readers, for buying this book. You're the reason we do what we do.

"The Nephilim were on the earth in those days, and also afterward, when the sons of God came in to the daughters of man and they bore children to them."

Genesis 6:4

1

Ferals are a lot like pens, Jake Carter mused. *There by the hundreds if you didn't need them, but nowhere to be found when you're actually looking for them!*

If there had been one to be seen, it wouldn't have been hard to spot. The flat landscape around the small convoy was pretty much a uniform beige color, with dots of gray or green. Every now and then a hill would pop up out of nowhere. Looking off in the distance he could see a long line of them on the horizon.

Through the passenger window of his heavily modified Ford F-350 he could see for miles. He could almost see as far on his left except where his driver Danny Marcus blocked the scenery. In front of them the view was obscured by Red Devil's rig. The white Hummer with its black eagle flag was almost hidden by the massive third generation Outbreak Response Battle Suit it towed.

The newest generation suits were supposed to be faster and tougher then the first gen suits that Springfield's ZOD teams had put together four years before. Part of the reason they were on the road in the middle of the Texas Hill Country was to battle test the suits before they joined the units converging on Springfield.

Red Devil's ORB was painted like his support vehicle, but it also carried crates of unpainted ORBS parts near the front of the trailer. Jake's vehicle had several crates of its own, just like Ken Bowman's rig Ranger. Behind them was the massive armored bus that carried the team of engineers hand-picked by Peter Mayhew himself for this run. Led by one of Peter's countrymen by the name of Paul Blakefield, they represented the best field crew for the ORBS units.

"You missing Corpus already?" Danny broke Jake's concentration.

"Oh, sure. Nothing like sleeping in a barracks that's older than my grandfather and busting my ass in a hangar all day in hundred degree heat. And don't give me that 'dry heat' shit, either. That depot was right on the damn water."

Danny laughed. "Yeah, me too. But, better you than me, buddy. I'll take Ash Trooper training over being an ORB pilot any day."

Since he knew Danny had put just as much sweat into building the Spartan rig's bio-diesel support truck as he had put into helping build his own ORBS unit, Jake let that comment slide. "Tell me again why I volunteered for this gig?"

"Because you aced the pilot tests and the alternative was working on more ORBS units in hundred degree heat."

"Right, instead of sticking my ass out on the front lines of the feral fight in Springfield."

"Hey, they made the first of the battle suits. That's pretty hard core."

"Gentlemen, you may wish to open your windows or stick your head out of a hatch for a moment," Paul's slow, deep voice came over the radio. "We're picking up gunshots back here on the microphones. It may be that it's time to test your armor out."

Jake rolled his window down, smiling at Paul's hybridized accent. Most of the time the faint traces of his native British accent were there, but some words sounded like he'd been born and raised in the South.

Sure enough, the soft but distinctive pop of gunfire reached his ears after a few seconds.

Jake pressed the transmitter on his mic. "This is Spartan, confirming gunfire."

"Very well, then. Get suited up and prepare for battle."

"You heard the man!" Danny called over his shoulder. "Get

your butts in gear and get Spartan ready to roll!" Jake climbed through the opening between the two bucket seats and into the back of the modified truck. Bunks lined the wall on the left, with a cramped table at the end.

On the right was the radio and operations station, with the compact toilet and galley taking up the rear of the back cabin on that side. The other three Ash Troopers had already opened the armored rear door and were moving across the tongue to the trailer that held Spartan. The first two across were Bobby and Dean Harper, siblings from Missouri. Both had been going to school in Rolla. They had been down in Houston when things went to shit five years ago and decided they'd stay to lend their engineering skills to the ZOD teams.

Bobby opened the front of the ORB and climbed inside, letting her brother power up the systems externally while she loaded up the bolt-gun mounted to the right 'arm' of the suit. Trooper Hirota had grabbed Jake's harness and holsters. Hirota took care of the weapons, both on *Spartan* and on his person.

"Okay, the Glock is loaded up with the XTP rounds I told you about, and I loaded the Judge with buck shot rounds." Hirota slipped the harness and assault vest onto Jake's shoulders. She quickly strapped a Glock's holster to his right leg and grabbed the side of the trailer as Danny hit a curve.

"Here's hoping I don't have to use them."

"Your mouth, God's ears. I went with the wave blades on the knuckle saw. Pneumatics are good on the spikes and everything else is good to go."

"Batteries are good," Dean called out. "You should have a few hours of juice."

"Bolt gun is loaded with spike rounds," Bobby added. "Secondary mag has the explosive core. Don't matter which one you use, nothin' short of a car is gonna stop 'em."

"Got it."

The leg covers folded in when he put his boots into the foot harness and twisted into the locking mechanism. He grabbed the comm set and slipped the ear piece into place, then grabbed the hand controls.

Bowman's voice crackled over the radio. "Ranger, ready to deploy."

"Red Devil, ready!"

The steel mesh of the cage was broken by a two inch gap that gave him good lateral vision, though the mesh itself was also pretty easy to see through. Though it wasn't visible from his side of the cage a red lambda was painted below the ZOD unit logo on the front of the cage, with matching symbols on each shoulder. He reached down and grabbed the arm controls. The one on the right was much like a fighter pilot's stick and the left appearing more as an oversized glove.

Both arms sported a heavy blade welded to the underside so even if the other weapons were somehow destroyed or disabled, the arms themselves were still pretty formidable weapons. Jake flexed his left hand, and the left arm's thick steel claws closed and opened in response. The right arm's weapons mount swiveled left and right to match his movements on the stick.

"Spartan, ready to rock and roll!"

The pops of pistol fire and the crack of rifles became easier to tell apart. Shadows fell across the windshield as buildings of a small town blocked the light. The truck slowed to a stop. The green van with the Ranger tab painted on the front of it pulled to the right and stopped almost parallel with Spartan's black and red truck. Bowman had been a Ranger in Iraq and Afghanistan. He had the records to prove it, not to mention the battle scars. If he hadn't, ZOD would have vetoed using the unit insignia.

"Bison Four to ORBS, I have folks fighting creepers on two sides of the street. Looks like a horde of the fuckers!" Caleb Jackson's voice shrilled across the radio. Red Devil's crew chief was more excitable than usual as he continued. "One group of survivors is in some kind of uniform or something."

Paul's voice flooded the trailer. "ORBS, you may deploy. Let's avoid any... local entanglements if we can."

All three ORBS operators acknowledged the order as the support clamps released. The three Ash Troopers were already behind Spartan as Jake walked it forward. The step off the trailer was a bit of a challenge for him, but he managed to do it without stumbling. The delay meant he was the last one to the corner.

Red Devil and Ranger were already advancing on the horde of creepers, Ranger's chainsaw blade spinning and Red Devil's pneumatic axes pulled back and primed. Jake struggled to catch up and stumbled for a moment as his right foot hit the ground a half second late. Servos whined as he struggled to keep his footing and only managing at the last second to raise his left foot a little higher to catch himself on the third step. He could see that his misstep had brought him about a yard further forward than the other two battle suits. His heart was pounding and his throat felt like hot asphalt as he tried to swallow.

"Okay white boys, let's see if you kill these fuckers better than you can walk."

Without waiting for any acknowledgement Red Devil waded into the mass of infected, leaving the other two to follow. Jake's first step sent a body flying, then a feral was clawing its way up his leg. He pulled his left arm up and bent his elbow back until the snarling face on the other side of the mesh was between the claws. He closed his hand in the control glove. The head deformed and one eye erupted, sending a gooey stream of clear liquid into the cockpit. Jake straightened his arm and opened his hand, sending the now permanently dead man flying into the crowd like a cannonball.

He stepped forward and kicked anther creeper then thrust his right arm forward while he squeezed the control under his index finger. The pneumatic system drove a double edged blade forward with hundreds of pounds of force, skewering a monster's head. As he pulled his right arm back he closed his left fist and punched the one closest to him. The angled edges of the claw collapsed the skull beneath them. Number three dropped. Once he'd cleared the ones next to him he started swinging at any creeper that came close and a pile of small, twisted-bodies started to grow in front of him.

"This ain't much of a challenge." Bowman's voice sounded tinny in Jake's ear.

"Don't worry," Paul's voice chided over the radio. "A pack of the larger ones is on its way from the west. You'll get ample chance to test your suits out shortly."

"Hoo-ah!" Bowman called out. Jake swept his arm in front of him and let the blade slice two creeper heads from about the nose up. Once his immediate vicinity was clear he turned his head to look west and saw the half-dozen ragers running their way. Fifty yards short of the horde, three more slammed into them.

"Come on! Hit 'em while they're fighting each other!" Red Devil turned and started to wade through the gathered creepers, sending them scattering with each step. Jake followed suit, extending his arms so that each step brought his blades through the crowd of the twisted children around him. More than a few fell with their skulls split never to rise again. In his peripheral vision he could see Ranger outdistancing him, but he kept his pace. Falling wasn't fatal in an ORB suit, but he knew he'd never live it down if he did.

"Fire in the hole!" Red Devil called out an instant before a puff of smoke came from his right arm. A micro-second later, an explosion flung two of the ragers apart in a spray of blood and body parts. One was missing everything from the ribs up, but the other was rapidly regrowing the flesh on its chest and face. It got to its feet and shook its massive head. The one eye that still seemed to work zeroed in on Red Devil. It let out a roar before it leaned forward and started to run at the offending ORB unit.

The ORBS pilots knew their enemy's tactics. They had specialized training and equipment to counter them. As the rager took its first step Red Devil pivoted his left leg back and turned his feet so that they were both pointed directly at the oncoming beast. When its foot hit the ground the third time metal spikes shot out at an angle from the housings in the lower leg and buried themselves deep in the asphalt. The ORB leaned forward slightly with the arms extended, right hand over the left. Jake knew that Red Devil was aligning itself to divert as much of the impact as possible in a straight line that ran to the support spikes. He kept wading forward, but his eyes were on the charging behemoth and his fellow ORBS.

The rager hit Red Devil at full speed with a loud *clang!* Servos and hydraulics whined and Jake saw the ORB recoil slightly as joints flexed under the enormous weight that had just slammed into it. Before it could bounce off the nearly immovable barrier it had struck the claw on the left arm closed, sending curved steel talons between the thing's ribs to close around its breastbone. Almost in the same instant the pneumatic axe that lay against the right arm activated and sank into the thing's head again and again.

As the rager's skull turned into a red and white ruin Ranger and Spartan passed on either side, both headed for their own targets. Two of the newcomer ragers were still locked in combat with the ones that had been approaching. Jake maneuvered Spartan to the left and came to a stop as the pair he had targeted rolled toward his feet in a snarling mass of fists and flying blood.

He lifted his left leg and planted it on the bottom rager's chest. Reaching down he grabbed for the larger rager's head. Between the rolling and biting he was forced to settle on snatching it by the shoulder. Once he got a good grip he began closing the claw. Bone crunched under his foot as he put his weight down and lifted the other rager into the air. It roared in his face as it grabbed the robotic arm.

Steel bent under its thick fingers and Jake's eyes went wide as hydraulic pressure alarms began to sound. He twisted his right arm toward his left, and drove the double edged blade through the thing's eye.

More alarms sounded as the one beneath him sank its fingers into the armor of the leg on top of it sending the suit tilting to the right. With the gyros protesting, Jake pressed his thumb down hard on the stabilize button on the right stick. The spikes extended with a wet sound and the suit's slanting stopped. Jake leaned forward and let the dead rager's weight right him before he disengaged the spikes and stepped clear. A distant roar rattled the cage as he dropped the rager's body in the suit's left hand. His comm suddenly went wild.

"Spartan, brace yourself!" Bowman called out.

"Your spikes!" Red Devil was yelling to him from feet away. "Fire your spikes!"

Jake pressed the thumb button, but the only response he got was a red flashing light on his overhead control panel. He glanced up to see the warning light for the stabilizers flashing. *The spikes haven't finished retracting or the pneumatics aren't fully recharged,* his mind screamed as he looked out through the opening in the cage to see an oversized rager charging him.

Ten feet of flesh slammed into Spartan. For a moment the

world was a crazy blur. When he could see again the rager was stepping into view with both fists raised over its head. The cockpit rattled and multiple voices sounded in his ears as the gigantic beast took a step forward. The red light stopped blinking on the overhead control panel.

By reflex Jake lifted his right leg and caught his humongous attacker in the chest. He bent his left leg to bring his foot down flat. Red lights flickered on the control panel as he caught a ton of rampaging monster against his suit's foot. He hit the stabilizer control button. Three spikes slammed into its chest and the deafening roar turned into a burbling cough.

"Stabilizers... Good idea."

The suit whined in protest as he straightened his left leg, slowly bringing Spartan upright and planting the impaled rager on the asphalt. As the weight of the ORB crushed the thing's chest its struggles weakened. They stopped entirely as Jake fired the bolt gun and sent three feet of steel through its skull. The last rager was charging forward and Red Devil stepped into its path.

"Fire in the hole."

This time Jake could hear the soft *bloop* of the M32 grenade launcher being fired. He saw the forty millimeter hole the round punched in the rager's chest an instant before the round detonated and vaporized everything from the waist up. Both legs went spinning as Red Devil let out a victory cry.

"Don't try that shit at home, kids!"

"Trained professionals and all that." Jake added.

Paul's voice echoed in their ears. "Well done, gentlemen. Return to your vehicles if you would and let's see about getting your suits patched up, shall we?"

"Yeah, that might be a little...complicated."

"Oh, dear. Local entanglements?"

"Pretty much."

Red Devil groaned. "Looks like we've got our choice of rednecks to choose from... the local Confederate good ole boys club or the cast of *Deliverance*."

"There's Union blue in there, too." Jake offered as he scanned the two groups emerging onto the street. On his right, he saw blue and gray uniform coats, with the kepi hats almost universally associated with the Confederate Army and the Hardee or 'Jeff Davis' hats favored by Union troops.

The men and women in the mixed uniforms held an equally eclectic mix of guns. Everything from assault rifles to bolt action hunting rifles was represented in the mob. The other side was mostly wearing ragged jeans and t-shirts. They carried guns, blades, or blunt objects in hand. None of the latter group looked like they'd so much as combed their hair since the world went to shit.

"I think these folks are a historical group. The other guys... I'm with Devil. I'm hearing 'Dueling Banjos' over here."

"We're pretty much entangled here." The speakers clicked as Bowman switched his radio transmitter off. "Okay folks, we're not looking to start any trouble here, but as you can see we can end it pretty damn fast if we have to. Just let us on through and we'll leave you folks to whatever you were doing."

"Ya'll are pretty good against infected," one of the men in uniform said. "But I'm thinking you're not so hot against folks with guns."

"I don't think it's a question we'll have to answer today."

Bowman lifted his left arm and extended one of the claws toward the rear of the group that was facing them. The leader turned to look over his shoulder and most of the people with him followed suit. To the rear of both groups the gray clad Ash Troopers had spread out and were now covering everyone from cover with assault rifles and a couple of M 240B squad automatics. The leader nodded and held a hand up.

"Can't blame a fella for trying! Those suits would come in awful handy. Especially against these scavs." He pointed with his thumb at the ragged group facing them.

"Get 'em!" someone from the less organized mob yelled. The group on the left surged forward in an uneven wave.

"Fall back to cover by squads!" the uniformed leader yelled as he brought his gun up and fired a shot into the charge before heading for cover. The uniformed crew leaped into action, with most firing a shot or two into the advancing crowd as they scrambled for cover. A few shots rang out from the group on the left as they ran forward. One round sent sparks off the top of Spartan's cage. A group of ten scavs made a run toward Red

Devil. They got an HE round from the grenade launcher for their efforts. People and body parts went flying. Ranger stepped to the right.

"Concentrate fire on the scavs!" Bowman called out over the radio. The M-240B mounted on his ORB chattered as it sent 7.62 rounds into the group. Red Devil matched his movement taking their line of fire away from the Ash Troopers who were busy firing into the scavs from their position. The tactic created a shallow crossfire with only one avenue of escape. Jake moved his ORB right as well. The bolt gun on his right arm was better suited to single targets so he didn't waste rounds on the over-matched scavs.

"A Squad, B Squad," he heard the uniformed leader call out over the din of gun fire. "Volley fire on my command! Ready arms! Fire!" Nearly a dozen rifles opened fire in a single fusil-lade that ripped through the few scavs that seemed intent on continuing the fight. The rest broke.

"Hold your fire!" Bowman called over the radio. "Cease fire, cease fire! Save your goddamn ammo!" A few more shots came. Soon the only sound was the moans of the dying and the clatter of feet through the abandoned streets.

"Squads, stand to!" the other man called out. Jake watched as rifle barrels were raised to point almost straight up. The man stepped into the open and approached Ranger. His rifle was slung and a broad smile splitting his beard.

"Thanks for the help." Bowman called out from inside the armor.

"Likewise! I'm Sergeant Nate Bradley with the Texas Con-federation, Second Platoon, Regiment B. You folks must be with ZOD."

"Yes, sir. ORBS Division."

"Recognized your symbols. Heard some good things about you folks."

"Unfortunately, I can't say we've ever heard of the Texas Confederation."

"Not surprising. It took us all awhile to find each other. Most of us are from Mountain Man or Civil War historical recreation groups. We're in contact with some groups out in Mississippi, Georgia, and Virginia. Heard through them it's hell east of 'Ole

Miss, but they're holding out."

"Good to know! If you ever need to get in touch with us, I'll have one of our techs give you the HAM radio frequency we're usually on." More of the Confederation members had stepped into view and Jake could also see other faces peering at them from inside a nearby building.

Jake whispered softly over the radio. "I'm seeing kids here. These folks were defending their families."

Paul's voice crackled back. "Perhaps we should stop and say hello after all."

"Believing that they were driven out of the land of Jerusalem because of the iniquities of their fathers, and that they were wronged in the wilderness by their brethren, and they were also wronged while crossing the sea; and again, that they were wronged while in the land of their first inheritance..."

-Mosiah 10:12–13

2

"This is taking too long." Red Devil groaned.

He watched the group of Confed kids grouped around Paul. Inside the Confederation compound Fort Hope the rest of the ORBS teams were perched enjoying barbeque ribs, corn on the cob, and potatoes in various forms.

"Tell that to him." Jake gestured with a rib bone at the leader of the engineering team. A group of children and nearly half the adults were surrounding him as he told stories of his friend Peter. As he suspected, Red shook his head. Paul was one of the few people who commanded the Ojibwa's respect without question, which only made Jake respect the man even more.

"Hearts and minds, Devil... hearts and minds. Besides, I think he likes this part better than running the ORBS development teams. I don't think I've ever seen him smile this much." Bowman sputtered between bites of his own barbeque rib.

"Don't think I've seen this many kids all smiling at once. At least we got lunch out of it." Red Devil grumbled.

"Always an optimist, aren't you Red?" Bowman got up and tossed the bones on his plate to the pack of lean dogs.

"When are you going to tell us your real name? I keep feeling like I'm being rude or racist by calling you Red Devil." Jake took another bite.

"I chose it, white boy. That *is* my real name. In English. You have to *earn* the right to hear it in Ojibwe. Bet you didn't have a problem with the Redskins or the Chiefs."

"Hey, I have some Cherokee family. Guess that's why it bugs me."

"You keep calling me what I ask you to and we're good. It isn't an insult to me, so don't go giving me all that white angst and shit."

"If you're good with it, then that's cool. Just letting you know what I think." Jake held his hands up and shook his head.

Of the three ORBS operators Red Devil was easily the biggest. He stood an easy six feet and a few inches tall and was almost as broad across the shoulders. The aluminum camp plate was more like a saucer in his hands.

Standing next to the Ojibwe ex-cop, Ken Bowman gave up a few inches in height. The former Army Ranger was an example of a different kind of strength, however. Where Red Devil was bulky, Bowman would have been better described as 'ripped' by comparison. Neither of them seemed to lack for attention from the ladies, either.

Jake gave both a wide berth as he took his own plate to the mess area that the Confeds had set up in the old community center, tossing the bones aside as he passed the lounging quartet of dogs. A few inches shy of six feet tall, he knew he was lean only because the world had gone to shit over the past few months. By no means wimpy, he also acknowledged he was nowhere close to the same league as his fellow operators. He had some decent muscle, but he was not nearly as bulky or as ripped as Red or Bowman. The best way to stand out with those two around was to not stand too close to them.

The Confed group seemed to be mostly families. So aside from a few furtive glances, neither of his comrades was getting anywhere near the attention they were used to. As Jake turned from the mess area he saw Paul getting to his feet. Across the open floor Red Devil and Bowman also climbed to their feet, taking their cue from their leader.

"Well, I think we've made some new friends," Paul told the three operators as they made their way back to the vehicles.

"Though I doubt we'll see them very frequently."

"One less thing to worry about, I guess." Bowman mumbled.

"Who was the goddamn optimist?" Red Devil feigned shock.

Peter motioned toward the operators. "If you would be so kind as to join me on the bus we'll debrief and see what there is to learn from today."

Jake felt like his brain had been put through a wringer then jammed back into his head through a tube. The other two operators and Paul sat in front of a video screen on board the bus in a video conference with Peter back in Corpus Christi.

"Dipshit here just needs to learn better situational awareness. If he'd had his eyes open or if he'd been listening, he never would have ended up on his ass." Red Devil pointed at Jake.

"Perhaps we could be a bit more constructive." Peter pinched the bridge of his nose and shook his head as he spoke.

"I'm just sayin'! He got too focused on the two he was dealing with. He forgot there were more out there. If he'd set his stabilizers it would have knocked that rager on its ass."

"I *tried* to do that! But the warning light started flashing, like they hadn't reset or something." Jake crossed his arms and leaned back in his chair.

"I think he might be right. There's a four second delay in the pneumatic system to recharge and it doesn't start until the spikes are fully retracted. It's a safety feature to keep them from being prematurely fired before they're fully seated. If he'd just fired the stabilizers and retracted them, he might not have been able to redeploy in time." Peter offered as he looked up from a thick manual.

Paul nodded his head. "Then we'll have to see about addressing that. Thank you for being so diligent and patient, gentlemen. We'll stop and let you get back to your own vehicles. Get some rest. We'll most likely be in Springfield by sunrise."

"What is this bullshit?" Sergeant Heart roared. Behind her,

the three new ORBS operators went stiff. When she turned to face them, she sized their reactions up. The Indian dude's stony expression told her he was going to try to be a hard case. The guy next to him faced her with the blank expression of a seasoned vet. The smallest of the three gulped and actually looked worried. He'd be the easiest to bring into line. The Indian was going to need a little convincing. The soldier already knew what was what.

"They're kill markers, ma'am." The Indian sputtered. He was the only one of them who was taller than she was, but he wasn't acting like he was feeling his height.

"Kill markers?! They're fucking ego boo, mister! I have exactly zero room for ego in my unit! It's bad enough you took advantage of Mister Mayhew's generous nature to decorate the crap out of your armor, but do you honestly think anyone in *this* unit is going to give a flying *fuck* how many ragers you put down? These ORBS are fighting machines, not race cars! I want this pansy ass decoration off my armor on the goddamn double! Understood?"

"Yes, ma'am!" The Indian and runt called out.

"Do not *ma'am* me. Do you see any brass on this uniform? Do I *look* like an officer to you? I *earned* the rank of sergeant and you will address me that way. Am I perfectly clear?"

"Yes, Sergeant." The Indian growled.

"I can't hear you, recruit!"

"Yes, Sergeant!"

"Say it like you gotta pair, recruit!"

"*Yes, Sergeant!*"

"That's a little better. Now get those power sanders and get to work, recruits! I want those battle suits cleaned of all that froo-froo crap before lunch!" She left the grumbling trio to their work and headed to the pair of straight black ORBS on the other side of the converted convention floor.

The Ash Troopers that had come with the three new operators were crawling over the suits, installing new components and replacing most of the original internal wiring. The recruits ran to their trailers for the tools they needed. Heart cast a look over to the doors leading to the rest of the convention center. A few faces in black uniforms were peering through the glass at the new guys, but most of them disappeared once they caught sight of her actually looking. She shook her head. A lot of ZOD members had some military background and recognized the need for a chain of command, even an informal one. Every member was a volunteer and for most of them the discipline of a military unit was second nature after almost five years of fighting ferals.

Most members of ZOD handled the discipline well. Those who didn't... well, they were just about all dead now. As always, she was amazed by the commitment the average member had showed even before monsters had become a real thing. But being an ORBS operator had required a completely new level of dedication, one that the brass had wanted to be as much like boot camp as possible.

The highly trained Ash Troopers had been the guinea pigs for it and the operators were reaping the benefits of their experience. While the rest of the Springfield contingent slept and lived in the safer underground part of the convention center and staged out of the parking garage nearby, the newly recruited ORBS operators camped out on the main floor. Away from everyone else, where they would be broken down and built up to be what ZOD so desperately needed.

"Having fun?" Sergeant Fipps asked when she stopped beside him.

"Depends... How high did they jump?"

"The big dude with the mohawk and the little guy just about shit themselves. That Ranger, though ... he's a pretty cool customer."

"That's Bowman, he's got his shit together. Red Devil and I are gonna have to go a 'round or two before he gets with the program."

"What about the runt?"

Heart lit a cigarillo. "I don't know about him. He looks like he's just as likely to break as he is to get his shit together. I haven't read his file yet, so I'm not even sure how he got into the ORBS program."

"If he does get up to speed he might make a decent operator."

"That's a big goddamn if!" Heart took a long drag from her

smoke.

"What about their trucks?" Gray smoke escaped her lips as she spoke.

"Leave 'em. They're more the techs' babies. Besides, the Ash Troopers already earned their stripes. But we've got to get some uniform regs in place. Every trooper we've seen from somewhere else does something different, even now. It's been five years since the ferals showed up and we're just now getting to the point where we aren't losing more people than we kill. We've got to start playing things a lot smarter, Alexa."

Heart took another drag off her cigar before she spoke again. "Well, maybe having a nearly full ORBS squad here will help us start to make a difference. Between us and Nevada to the west, we might start to do more than just hold our own."

"Don't forget Corpus. Hell, they make 'em better down there than we do."

"It's too far from anything to be worth much. Any further south and they'd need gills."

"So long as they keep giving us new toys to play with they're as good as gold, if you ask me."

A little after 15:00 hours Bowman trotted up to the two sergeants with his undershirt stained with sweat and a handful of dark spots on the fabric.

"Sergeant Heart, we've finished sanding our suits down."

Heart looked at him from behind the knee of her ORB and nodded.

"Are your suits those shiny things over there looking like a chrome tribute to someone's inadequacy?" Sergeant Fipps pointed toward the freshly sanded machines.

"Yes, Sergeant."

"Let's go take a look." Bowman led him over to their suits. Fipps walked around them with a critical expression on his face. Ranger showed the obvious marks of the disk sander in a precise rectangle where anything unofficial had been painted. Red Devil bore heavy marks in broad arcs across the front, the metal showing where the sander had been pressed hardest. On Spartan the spot that had shown the Lambda symbols was a smooth, shiny patch.

"Bowman, you were a Ranger, right?"

"Yes, Sergeant."

"What did you do before the apocalypse, Devil?"

"I was a cop in St. Louis. Before that I was in the Army, Eleven-Bravo."

"What about you, Carter? Who were you before shit hit the fan?"

"I was a construction worker, Sergeant."

Fipps blinked a couple of times. ORBS operators had to have either some kind of military or police training or extensive combat experience post apocalypse.

"How the hell did you get into the ORBS program with no combat training, son?"

"I was in the SCA, sir. And I was a heavy equipment operator. The ORBS work a lot like a backhoe or a crane."

"Don't *sir* me! What the hell is the SCA?"

"Society for Creative Anachronisms, Sergeant. Middle Ages historical group. I was a fighter down in Texas."

"Sword fighting and shit like that?"

"Yes, Sergeant."

"That's all well and good, but you're all part of ZOD now. That means your battle suits are ZOD battle suits. Do you notice anything distinctive about ZOD since you joined up?"

"Everything is black or red." Bowman offered.

"Everything is black or red," Fipps confirmed. "Now, tell me, boys... are your suits black with red markings?"

"No, Sergeant." All three answered in unison.

"Then maybe you'd better fix that. Head over to the tech group and get the gear you'll need. And help each other out. I don't wanna' see your paint jobs looking as different as your sanding. I want uniform coverage and I want the markings exactly like the ones on the other units. You copy?"

"Yes, Sergeant!"

"Grab some chow, then get your asses to—"

The building violently shook.

"What was that?" Carter's eye darted around.

"Tremor. We've been feeling minor rumbling since Yellowstone erupted five years ago. Could be from there or it could be the New Madrid fault. Either way, it's done. Press on."

Lunch was basic, sandwiches and salvaged bags of potato chips with bottles of filtered and boiled water. From there, the three recruits spent the rest of the afternoon wearing facemasks and trying to give an even coat of black paint on their battle suits. By sunset, they had all three painted and were waiting for Sergeant Heart to finish her inspection of their work.

"It'll do. Now, go get your night vision gear and suit up. We're doing night maneuver training."

"We've already put in a full day, Sergeant." Red Devil groaned.

"And you're going to put in a full night, too! And what the hell is that look about, Carter?"

"Just tired, Sergeant."

"Do you think a rager gives a good goddamn about how you feel? Hell no! He's going to attack whenever he can and he *will not stop* until he's dead or you are! Now get your NVGs and suit up!" She turned on her heel and marched across to her ORB. Paul was sitting at the table in front of the two veteran battle suits, a set of blueprints spread out before him.

"You're going to run those poor lads ragged." His usual good cheer and smile unaffected by the screaming.

"That's the point. We need to work the bugs out of both the people and the suits."

"I'm sure there are plenty of both to keep us occupied un-til—" he trailed off, then chuckled. "I was going to say until the end of the world, but that's already happened, hasn't it?"

"Depends on who you ask. Do you mind running overwatch for us? Fipps needs the rack time."

"Delighted."

Twenty minutes later, Heart was leading the three new ORBS down a broad street with their main lights off. Inside Spartan Jake wiped away the first beads of sweat as he trudged along. The ORBS were hard enough to keep upright, much less spend more than four hours walking around in. His upper legs were starting to burn and he was beginning to feel a rasp in his lungs. The bulky night vision monocle over his right eye wasn't help-ing things, either.

"Spartan, you're 'stepping' too forcefully," Paul chastised him over the radio. "Remember the battle suit does everything you do, only harder. Take it easy when you lift your legs... like that, yes."

Jake tried walking normal and it did seem to take some of the work out of the process. It was still gratifying to hear Red Devil huffing and puffing beside him.

"Why the blackout, boss? It isn't like we're not a match for anything out there." Bowman whispered.

Jake scowled. The man could at least have the common courtesy to *sound* out of breath.

"You ever hear of Steven Tibbs?" Heart quipped.

"Rapper out of LA, right?" Red Devil asked.

"Yeah... someone blew his head off a few years ago. Or some*thing* did. High powered rifle at an insane range. Only one person we knew of who could do that and we'd heard she was turned, but we're still not sure what she turned into. So we're not taking any chances. Any other questions?"

Silence was the only reply the others could muster, so she led them further into Springfield's downtown. After a few hundred yards she could tell that staying together wasn't going to be the hard part for the new team members. It was going to be staying in a good formation that they were going to have to work on. She led them through the narrower streets and taller buildings, then through the uneven terrain of the square. When she reached the west end of the open area, the four found themselves faced with a new obstacle: a three foot drop. Heart switched her radio to a closed channel for herself and Paul.

"The suits can handle a small drop, right?"

"In theory up to ten or fifteen feet. Possibly more. The legs can handle the impact, it's the servos in the knees and hips that are susceptible to damage. Just trust your gyros to keep you upright." Paul's voice crackled back.

After switching back to the main channel she stepped to the edge. "What are you waiting for? A hand down?" She took a step off the ledge and flexed her back foot to propel her.

Bowman walked Ranger to the edge and angled his feet so that the battle suit slowly slid off, leaving a trail of sparks as he went.

Jake approached the edge and tried to emulate Sergeant Heart's step off, but his back foot didn't come off in time. He found himself plummeting headlong toward the ground. He got his front foot moving and landed on the other with most of his weight too far forward. As he stumbled, he put his arms out and caught himself against the side of a burnt out van. Sparks flew as the bare rims scraped across the concrete. He pushed himself upright, cursing silently as a yellow warning light came up on his overhead panel.

Red Devil bent both legs then straightened them suddenly, sending his battle suit a few inches into the air and forward. He also landed with his weight too far forward, but a couple of quick steps got his suit back under him.

"Sergeant, I have a servo warning light on. It'll probably hold for the rest of the patrol, but I don't know if it'll handle anything more than just walking."

"Damn it, Spartan. If you screw up my suit, I'll hand you your balls in a box. All right, Red Devil, Ranger, go north and follow the roundabout back to the road we came in on, where the theater is. Spartan, you're with me. Guess I'm gonna have to hold your damn hand all the way back."

Jake followed Sergeant Heart's battle suit as she skirted the square and followed the road back to the south until they met up with the other two ORBS.

"Did you see that, Sergeant?" Red Devil asked as they cleared the next cross street.

"Talk to me."

"It was some kind of flash, off to the right there, on top of that building…"

"I got nothin'." Bowman scanned the area.

"Same here. Get moving just in case. Spartan, keep up." She set a brisk walking pace.

Jake did his best to keep up. About fifty yards from the entrance Jake saw the steady yellow warning light change to flashing red, but he made it into the main staging area without it getting any worse.

"Carter, I want that busted servo replaced right the fuck now. Wake up a tech if you have to, but get your damn suit battle ready!" Heart barked at him.

"Now, Sergeant?" His eyes were tired as he glanced at his watch.

"Ragers don't give a fuck if you're suit is ready. They don't give a goddamn if you're ready, they're just going to try to eat your fucking face. So you will always be ready to fight. If that means skipping evening chow to fix a busted servo, then it means you skip chow."

"Yes, Sergeant." His shoulders slumped. It was shaping up to be a long night.

"Only that the generations of the children of Israel might know, to teach them war, at the least such as before knew nothing thereof;"

-Judges 3:2

Integrity brought her rifle up as the four battle suits passed below. The four new abominations bore the same markings as her former comrades, the red symbol of treachery that was ZOD.

She watched as they passed out of her view, then followed them again as they crossed back into her field of vision and traversed the square. The third one nearly fell. She considered sparing him until last. Better that he die alone, knowing what a fool he was while better men died around him. Maybe the bigger one, with the mohawk... no, there was something about him... his death should be at another's hands. They passed back out of sight as they returned along their original path. Integrity steadied the big rifle once more.

No, child. There is no time to toy with such as these. The Beetle Queen requires your help. Go west, to the place you once called Joplin. She awaits you there. The nebulous voice inside her head commanded.

"I need to kill them! They betrayed me!"

It has been but four years. You have many more before you. Your vengeance must wait, my child. Go to the Beetle Queen.

Integrity scowled and raised her head, feeling the cool air where her cheek had touched the stock of her rifle. Perhaps it was better not to let them know she was there just yet.

"I'll go. Damn you, I'll go."

Jake decided it was easier to list the places where he didn't hurt. A full week of training under Fipps and Heart had taught him that there was no such thing as "good enough shape" for an ORBS pilot. His upper thighs burned from the morning and evening runs, his arms and shoulders ached from constant maintenance on the ORBS. Every place else felt like a massive bruise from constantly being tossed around in hand to hand training or in the ORBS. He reached up and slowly put a hand on the heavy left arm of Spartan.

"At least today it'll be you beating the crap out of me."

Over the past week Fipps and Heart had made them cycle through every other ORBS unit. That had been bad enough, but they'd also forbidden the pilots to change any of the harnesses. Moving around in a battle suit he was used to tended to make him feel a little bit like a ping pong ball. Doing it in an unfamiliar one without being strapped in right made him feel more like a ping pong ball in a dryer.

"Hooo-wee!"

The unfamiliar voice came from near the front of the convention center. Jake stepped to his right to put Red Devil between him and the sound. Instinctively, his right hand dropped to the tactical holster on his right leg.

"You boys move like old men!"

A new ORBS unit stood on the back of a trailer. A young man in jeans, a black t-shirt, and a baseball cap stood beside it. As Jake's eyes became accustomed to the light streaming in over the barricade, he made out more details. The man's shirt bore a large number three on it and his cap had a stylized red A in a circle. Behind him the ORB was decorated with a Confederate flag across the front and emblazoned with American flags on the shoulder of each arm. A group of people in gray Ash Trooper uniforms were gathered around the battle suit, all looking busy.

"Who the hell are you?" Red demanded.

"Name's Jimmy Sams! This here's Samson. I'm your new

ORBS pilot." The young man's smile never left his face as he spoke.

"Where the hell did he come from?" Bowman muttered to his friends.

There was an audible snap as the retaining strap on his firearm closed. Jake turned to look over his shoulder at the sound of boots on concrete. Sergeants Fipps and Heart had emerged from the smaller conference rooms they bunked in and were stalking toward Sams and his ORB.

Jake leaned against Spartan. "This ought to be good."

Bowman and Devil nodded, all three of them united for once. The two senior ZOD members approached the shiny ORB with the same grim determination that Jake remembered seeing his first day in Springfield. He heard Fipps take a deep breath to start the verbal tirade.

No words left his mouth.

In the moment when he should have started to speak, the world tilted. When it tilted back the other way, Jake realized that the world wasn't just tilting. It was shaking. He took a step in the direction he was falling and put his hands out to brace himself. Cool concrete met his palms a split second later, even as a deep rumble and cries of alarm from elsewhere in the convention center reached his ears. Glass shattered around him. The floor vibrated under his fingertips as something impacted nearby. When he could focus, he saw wide gaps in the barrier facing the street. The light was different in the room and he looked around quickly, seeing no new holes in the wall. A momentary glance up showed him a chunk of roof missing.

"Perimeter breach!" he heard someone say. His gut went tight with fear.

"Saddle up!" he called as he scrambled back toward what he hoped was *Spartan* and pulled the exterior access panel open. A single gunshot sounded in the distance followed by a scream. Nearby, he heard another ORB open with the customary hiss of the hydraulics pushing the main cage upward and forcing the leg openings out.

His fingers bounced across the numeric keypad, his access code coming as muscle movement more than number recall. The front of the battle suit opened. In a split second he was up in the cockpit and turned around, his communication set already in place. One heartbeat later, the cage was dropping and lights were flashing green above his head and on the narrow display across the front. Without bothering with the four-point harness he slid his feet into the oversized boots and pushed his arms into the limb controls.

"Spartan, on the move!" He walked the battle suit toward the front of the building.

"Spartan, get over to the atrium and clear the barriers! Red Devil, on me!" Heart ordered through the radio.

Jake turned and strode to the prone Ranger. Bowman and his team were struggling to get the suit flipped over. "Move!"

Both pilot and Ash Troopers scrambled to either side. Jake reached down and grabbed the ORB under one arm. In a deft move he lifted it upright. It rocked in place for a moment but Jake was already headed for the glass doors separating the main convention hall from the eastern annex. Without slowing he charged through the glass and aluminum door frames, right into chaos.

Ferals were swarming through two holes in the barriers about twenty yards apart. They were being met by black clad ZOD members with shields and melee weapons. One particularly brave trio had grabbed a padded bench and was pushing a group of the beasts back toward the hole closer to him.

The break in the barrier wasn't complete. The wall sagged inward, funneling the monsters at an angle. Two ferals figured out that there was an end to the thing pressing against them not far away and reached around to grab the two men on the outside. Only the legs of the bench saved them from being pulled into hungry maws.

An infected fell as they pressed the horde back. It reached out and grabbed the ankle of the man on the right. He staggered and fell to one knee. The bench went forward without him. Jake stepped on the feral as it pulled the man closer. Spartan's massive metal boot easily flattened the infected man's skull with a crunch.

Another feral started for the intrepid duo still carrying the bench. Jake brought his right arm up and looked at the gun camera feed. When the beast's head near the middle of the image he triggered the bolt gun.

A foot long projectile covered the short distance and speared the creature through the face, exiting the back of its head and slamming into the shoulder of the one behind it. The first feral dropped, but the second found itself pinned to the inside of the barrier. The trio on the bench took advantage of the respite and shoved forward with new enthusiasm, bracing the breach with the bench.

Jake took a swing with his right arm at a stray feral. The impact from the blow sent it flying back against the barrier with a sickening crunch. It slid down the metal wall leaving a thick, chunky smear of red and gray in its wake.

A quick kick and step brought down another beast. The weight of Spartan squished the monster like a bug. The breach was temporarily plugged by the width of the bench. Arms reached for warm flesh, but more ZOD members rushed forward with saw-tipped bats and machetes. The press of infected let up long enough for Jake to push the pinned zombie outside. He grabbed the sagging part of the wall and shove it closed.

"I need a damage team here!" one of the ZOD troopers yelled, and a pair of men ran up with pieces of sheet metal and nail guns in hand. Behind them, a man and woman carried a heavy beam. Jake stepped back to give them room to seal the breach and brace it, turning to his left to help with the next breach. The sound of nails being fired into place was briefly overshadowed by the *clang* of the heavy steel beam hitting the wall.

The next breach was worse. The invaders were close to overwhelming the thinly spaced defenders and more were joining the ranks of the infected every second. The fact that some of the new zombies wore black ZOD uniforms made the defense that much more desperate.

"Make a hole!" Jake called out as he stomped toward the rear of the massed defenders. Several defenders stepped aside when he was a few yards away and he strode into the gap they left.

"Close it up!" someone yelled behind him and he heard more voices join the line behind him. The semi-circle of black was at his back now, with nothing between him and the barrier but dead people who hadn't taken the hint yet.

Like the previous breach, this one was a section of wall that leaned in. Overlapping sheets of steel had separated, leaving a jagged line. With deliberately long steps and wide motions with his arms, Jake walked the Spartan through the middle of the dead. Stomping a few flat and crushing the skulls of more with his arms before they pressed against him and made forward progress difficult. After a couple of steps, his forward momentum was halted. With a frustrated snarl, he brought his right arm up and activated the sword blade. Four feet of steel shoot out of the arm's weapons pod. He turned at the hip and brought his arm out to the side and down.

When he brought his arm forward the blade sheared through the tops of skulls for a few feet before it dropped to neck level. Entire heads were sent spinning into the air. The pressure against the front of the battle suit lessened and Jake took a few steps forward before he had to stop and do it again. This time he found himself at the end of the torn barrier wall.

He reached forward with his left hand and grabbed the loose end of the wall. He did another sword sweep with his right before shoving the edge of the wall toward the other side of the gap. Steel groaned as the distance dwindled by inches, the relentless press of the dead being overcome by the Spartan's massive hydraulic arms for a good seven feet. Then the wall stopped moving, though the metal still bent and screeched as zombies pushed against it.

"Need some help here!" Jake grunted into the mic at his cheek as the zombies took back a couple of inches.

"Ranger's almost to you." Bowman's voice came over the radio. Jake could hear the heavy tread of a battle suit approaching.

"Let me see if I can thin the herd a little for you." Jake looked to his right to see Ranger stop behind the ZOD line and lift its right arm. The barrel of the M240B was over the heads of the ZOD fighters, but not by much.

"Don't miss!" Jake said in the split second before Bowman opened fire. Jake fought to keep from flinching too badly as 7.62 rounds slammed into dead flesh just feet away from him. He could feel the impacts of bullets hitting bone. The pressure against his left arm let up for him to gain another step.

"I'm not doing enough damage," Bowman said a couple of seconds later. "And you're too close for a HE round from Devil."

"But not an explosive bolt!" Jake let go of the stick on the right arm's control surface, locking it in place until he grabbed it again. He hit the ammo select button by his middle finger. The bolt gun's status light went yellow then red as the magazine holding the solid steel rounds was disengaged and the magazine cartridge rotated to put the mag containing explosive bolts in line with the mag well. Jake felt the cartridge slide into place through his forearm then the lights went to yellow and finally green. He leaned forward and angled his arm around the edge of the wall. He pointed down and pulled the trigger.

Zombies flew in all directions when the bolt impacted the floor and went off. The concussion was like a kick in the chest, but hardly fatal. He fired three more times then pushed forward. The metal wall scraped against concrete and snarling ferals still tried to fill the void, but he finally got the wall back in place.

"Spartan, we can't get a team to you to secure the barrier!" Bowman called over the radio.

"Don't worry," Jake said back, suddenly calm. "You keep doing your thing, I've got this!" The metal wall shuddered under the impact of dozens of fists, but Spartan was more than a match for them. Jake put his left foot against the wall and leaned Spartan against it. He activated the stabilizer spikes. With the wall as secure as it was going to be against his battle suit, it was time to do what he did best: fix things. The switch back to standard steel bolts seemed to take an eternity, but the bolt gun's status light eventually went green. Remembering how it had pinned a zombie to the wall earlier, Jake pointed the missile weapon at the wall's overlapping break and pulled the trigger.

Six inches of steel was left sticking out of the wall. Jake aimed a little lower, leaving another six inches of spike protruding below the first. He repeated the process five more times until he was reasonably sure the temporary repair would hold.

"That ought to do it," he said as he retracted his stabilizers. "Now, let's do some more ass kicking."

There was a moment of stillness as Spartan's blade popped back into place. The ferals turned to the enemy in their midst. Jake activated the saw blade on his right arm for good measure and stepped forward.

Twenty minutes later, the last of the zombies was sporting a machete through its cranium. Spartan and Ranger were called back to the ORBS section. ZOD members made way for the two battle suits as they walked across the blood-slicked floor. More than one of their comrades had fallen at the hands of the relentless horde and risen again, only to die for good at the hand of the ORBS. It was quiet as Spartan and Ranger ducked back through the hole Jake had made.

Back in their own area, Jake could see that the damage hadn't been as bad. There had been only one breach and the new ORBS unit's transport had almost filled that. Heart's battle suit and Red Devil were stationed on either side of the newly repaired hole. Toward the back, Fipps and a few techs were looking his armor over. Jake walked Spartan back to the yellow painted square it had been assigned. He pulled his hands free of the controls and opened the cage. His shoulders and hips were sore from the constant impacts against the side of the cage from not having his harness on, and he fought to stay upright as he walked toward the front of the expo center.

"Man, that's a red sky! Glad we ain't sailors. Red sky at morning, sailor take warning, right?" The new guy stepped up beside Jake and looked out over the barrier.

"It's a sword day," Jake answered absently. "A red day, ere the sun rises."

"Hey, I know that one," Jimmy said, his accent fading a little. "Isn't that from one of them Lord of the Rings movies?"

"Yeah," Jake said. "*Return of the King*."

"What do ya'll think that was? Did someone drop a nuke or somethin'?"

"More like a hundred thousand nukes." Jake numbly responded as Red Devil and Bowman joined them.

"That's a lot of bombs." Red Devil whistled.

"Or just one really big volcano." Jake pointed to the north. A giant column of smoke was rising and spreading. Flashes of light illuminated details of its structure, but no thunder reached their ears.

"It'd have to be one huge ass volcano! There's a couple of nuke sites north of here. Hell, even McConnell should have a few, but they're mostly east of us, but if someone got a plane off—" Red Devil began.

"Not after all this time," Bowman said. "Jet fuel goes bad even faster than regular gas. No way anyone got a plane off the ground."

The four ORBS operators stood and watched as the cloud spread, slowly darkening the sky north of them.

"Yeah, it's a pretty cloud," Fipps joked as he approached. "Now it's time to get to work. Get your asses something like presentable and be in conference room two in half an hour. We got us a mission. Have your teams get the suits ready to transport by morning."

Twenty-five minutes later, all four operators were in fresh blacks and seated in the conference room. Outside, the main floor was a flurry of activity as the Ash Troopers worked to get the ORBS onto the trailers and the transport vehicles ready. Breakfast was reduced to lukewarm coffee and tepid pastries filled with either sausage and gravy or strawberry filling. The best thing anyone could say about either was that it filled the empty spaces in their stomachs. A wide screen monitor had been set up on a table at the far end of the room, with an array of equipment on either side of it. A woman Ash Trooper was putting the finishing touches on the electronic jumble.

"Okay, Sergeant," she said to Heart. "I've hooked this up to the dish the exhibition center had on the roof. It's not perfectly compatible with our gear, but it's in better shape right now than the dish we put up there. Sorry about that."

"There was nothing wrong with your work, trooper. That whole section of the roof came down."

The ORBS operators exchanged glances at that, since none of them knew exactly how much damage had been done by the initial tremor. Cracks were visible in the walls and floors, but they hadn't seen much more than that. The trooper left the room. Heart turned her attention to the table. She tapped a few keys on the laptop attached to the set up. The screen came to life, showing a blue curtain in the background.

"Sir, Springfield has just reestablished their uplink," a disembodied voice said. Moments later, a man in a black uniform sporting a pair of silver eagles on his collar sat down in front of the camera. His hair was an iron gray, cropped close to his head. His faced was lined and weathered, but his gray eyes were clear and intense.

"Sergeant Heart, good to see you still alive and kicking. How did you fare?"

"Good to be above ground, Colonel. Our losses were considerable. We lost forty-nine all told, about a fifth of our total force. If it hadn't been for the battle suits that number might have been a lot higher. These are my ORBS pilots. This is Mister Bowman, Mister... Devil, Mister Carter, and our newest arrival Mister Sams. We have a full squad with Sams arrival this morning, though he hasn't completed the training program."

The colonel on the screen nodded as his eyes scanned something on his end. "Well, Sams is going to have to learn on the job. With this morning's event, our agenda has changed considerably. We have sporadic contact with several teams in Nevada and Utah, but nothing in Wyoming or Montana. Our first guess is that the Yellowstone Caldera erupted, but we haven't been able to confirm that. For now, that's going to be our working theory. Yesterday, we got word from ZOD Iowa of some unusual activity up near Sioux City. They were sending a scout team into the city yesterday, but we've lost contact with them. I want you to take a contingent north to Sioux City as part of your overall mission and try to make contact with them. But that is only part of your mission, Sergeant. With this morning's event and the subsequent damage it appears to have caused nationwide, as well as the more widespread long term effects that we fear will come about if our working hypothesis is correct, your greater mission will have a higher priority." He paused for a moment and gestured to someone out of sight of the video feed. Moments later, something beeped on the laptop.

"If you joined ZOD before the zombie outbreak, you'll remember that our primary mission was preparation for the zombie apocalypse. The theory was that if you're prepared for a zombie apocalypse, you're ready for almost anything. In fact, the CDC pointed that out in *their* zombie plan. We took our plans seriously and now we're one of the few groups that is making a difference. But zombies weren't the only potential world ender we prepared for. Drastic climate change was another. And as big as this cloud is getting... drastic climate change is likely to happen. Our fear is that many communities are *not* prepared for it. They also have no idea *how* to prepare for it. The information I've sent you will help you get ready to deal with the probable changes to the weather. In addition to implementing these measures locally we want you to take the ORBS units and as many ZOD units as you can spare north. Go through Missouri and up into Iowa. Offer what aid you can to the local populace, including suppressing the local zombie threat. I believe you have some members there who specialize in greenhouse gardening?"

Heart nodded her head. "Two, Colonel. Doctor Kelly Linh and Doctor Cheryl Rasmussen. They're running our greenhouse and gardens."

The colonel continued. "Take one of them with you. I've sent some specific data for greenhouse gardening in cold weather for them to review and some other large scale survival info. Have them review it and get what specialists you can spare learning this stuff. You're going to need it."

"Yes, Colonel. We're sending a scout team to check on them, since we only just got radio capability back."

"Good. Get them up to speed on your mission and get ready to move out. I want you on the road first thing in the morning. Your overall mission brief is in the data I sent. Good luck and God speed."

"Thank you, Colonel!"

Heart shut the feed down and turned back to the ORBS team. "All right, men. You heard the colonel. This is exactly what we've been training for. Starting now, I want one ORBS on alert status and a second pilot and suit in on-call mode. Sams, since your suit is fresh you're taking first alert. Devil, you're his back up. You pick up alert status from him in eight hours."

"Yes, Sergeant!" Jimmy hustled out of the room.

Bowman turned to Heart when the door snapped shut. "Sergeant, about Sams and his ORBS? The rest of us couldn't help but notice the uh… non-standard paint job."

"His ORBS is out of regs? Now, I can't say I've noticed it officially. As his squad mates it would fall to you to help your fellow squad member *get* his suit up to standards, wouldn't it?"

Bowman nodded his head. "He does reflect on the squad as a whole."

"And we do want to help a brother out!" Red Devil had a

tight smile as they made their way toward the door.

All three men stopped when they were clear of the doorway and could see their ORBS. Clearly painted on all three of the black suits were the individual emblems they'd originally chosen. The Ojibwa eagle and the Spartan Lambda were done in red, while the Ranger tab on Bowman's armor was done in its traditional yellow. The paint on the new symbols was so fresh it still glistened and the Ash Troopers were still climbing down off the ladders beside the suits.

"Congratulations, gentlemen," Sergeant Fipps said as he approached. "You earned your marks."

"Damn straight we did!" Red Devil beamed.

Bowman stared at his ORB. "Thank you. It's nice to have my tabs back."

"No one can take those away from you. Technically, you boys are Specialists Three now. In the absence of a full corporal, you're it." Heart smiled.

"Now get your shit together! We got a mission to prep for." The three men jumped as Sergeant Fipps barked orders at them.

"For thou hast girded me with strength unto the battle: thou hast subdued under me those that rose up against me."

-*Psalm 18:39*

4

Integrity approached the field of beetles cautiously. The Beetle Queen hadn't responded to her presence and her children were unusually aggressive, even to one of the Chosen. The smell of death was strong on this field, which also struck her as wrong. Her beetles should have devoured all carrion, but the smell of rot and death remained.

The Beetle Queen sat on her throne in the middle of what was once Joplin. The hospital nearby still smoldered and half-devoured bodies lay sprawling out of windows and doors. Integrity could feel the handful of humans still inside. Her mind rebelled at the conclusion she arrived at. Her steps quickened toward her fellow Nephilim from behind. As she feared, she was greeted by sightless, unblinking eyes. A third opening was evident in the center of her forehead. The back of the Beetle Queen's head was missing, the wound covered by her long, black hair. Her top was ruined by a large hole just left of her breastbone. Bone shards pointed outward. Thick stripes of rusty brown emanated from the hole in her chest. A pulped red mass lay in her lap and something glinted in her left hand. Integrity plucked it from the lifeless hand with a snarl. It was a 7.62 by

51mm round, the same type her rifle fired.

'I am become Death' was etched on the brass casing. Her glowing eyes narrowed at the insult. *Who would dare to even touch one of my kind? Who dared kill a Nephilim?* Her eyes turned to the hospital and the infestation of mortal flesh it contained. She would seek her answers there. The humans would pay for their transgressions. She could smell the reek of their fear as she turned toward the building. Relishing the aroma, she started walking.

"God damn it! I paid a lot of bullets for that paint job! Ain't no one gets to mess with my armor!" Jimmy flung a wrench across the room.

"Stand down, Sams! That is not your armor! That is ZOD armor, issued to you as a pilot! You personalize it with *my* permission. I don't care how much you've paid to get an unauthorized paint job on ZOD equipment. Now, unless you want to hand over your ORBS certification and walk out that god damn door, you will settle the hell down and follow orders. Otherwise, I'm gonna put you on report for defacing ZOD property. So what's it gonna be?" Sergeant Heart bellowed at the irate man.

Jimmy glared at the sergeant for a moment before he spoke again. "I ain't takin' no orders from some bitch who couldn't cut it as a man."

The other three ORBS pilots looked at Jimmy with wide eyes, then at Heart.

"What did you just say to me, mister?" Heart's voice dropped low.

"You heard me, but I'll say it again. I ain't takin' no orders from some tranny bitch. You ain't man enough to be a man and you ain't woman enough to tell me what to do."

"And I suppose you think you're man enough to put this tranny bitch in her place, is that it?" "I don't hit women."

Jimmy swallowed hard, but his expression didn't change.

"According to you I'm not a woman. And I'm pretty sure you would hit a woman if she got uppity. So, here's the deal. I'm gonna take my stripes off, and I'm going over there. For the next ten minutes, I'm not a sergeant, I'm not your supervising NCO within ZOD. Hell, none of this is official anyway. Now, if you think you're a bigger man than I am, you're welcome to try and put me on my ass." As she finished, Heart took her hat and blouse off, then walked over to the open floor in her pants and undershirt. Jimmy walked after her, muttering under his breath.

"Shouldn't we help Sergea—"

Bowman cut Carter off. "This is between them. Let her deal with him. Then we say something."

"So, you're good with her being a guy before, right?" Carter's gaze went back and forth between his fellow pilots.

"Doesn't matter," Bowman shrugged. "She does the job. That's what counts."

"I didn't notice," Red Devil chuckled. "Don't really care, either. We got bigger shit to worry about than this, anyway."

"She sure as hell looks woman enough." Jake glanced at Sergeant Heart. He let his brain digest the new information as they followed the two over to the open area behind the ORBS transports.

Jimmy stripped off his blouse and hat as he approached the open area then rushed toward Heart with his fist back. The sergeant turned a split second before he was in reach. Her fist snaked out. Jimmy's head snapped back and his feet went out from under him. He fell on his ass. He sat there for a moment before shaking his head and trying to get to his feet. Heart stepped back and put her arms down at her side, standing in profile to him.

"I'm gonna kick your ass, bitch!" Jimmy slurred when he found his footing.

He stepped forward and feinted a couple of times with his left, but Heart didn't react. The third time he made a more serious jab, which Heart slapped aside. Her fist snapped forward and hit him in the chest, knocking him off balance. She walked forward and caught his right jab against her forearm, this time snaking her arm around the arm and trapping it against her side. Jimmy tried to throw a punch with his left, but Heart knocked it aside and slapped him before she stepped back. He stepped in with a right hook that she ducked under before delivering a sharp upward jab to his ribs.

"Come on, kid! Quit holding back. Fight me like you'd fight a guy. Hell, fight me like *you're* a guy for Christ's sake." That seemed to hit home. Jimmy stepped in and threw a right and a left hook in rapid succession, both of which Heart danced back from.

"You fight like a bitch!" Jimmy's face was bright red.

"You call this fighting like a girl? This isn't fighting like a girl."

Jimmy swung again and Heart leaned out his reach. Quickly reversing she lunged in and pinned his arm against his chest. "This is how a bitch fights."

Her knee came up and caught him between the legs. Jimmy deflated. She brought her left fist into his midsection as he bent forward then sidestepped and brought both fists down across the back of his shoulders. He landed with his arms and legs splayed. After a brief moment he rolled onto his side and threw up on the floor. Heart knelt beside him so she could put a hand on his shoulder and rolled him forward.

Heart sat next to Jimmy and motioned for the others to leave. "This never happened. The world has bigger problems than my gender. So, get over it."

"Yes, ma'am." Jimmy moaned softly.

"Most troopers I tell not to call me ma'am. I figure you earned it, though." She got to her feet and held a hand out to him. After a moment Jimmy took it. She pulled him to his feet and watched him for a second to make sure he was going to stay upright. When she was sure he wasn't going to collapse again, she turned and picked up her hat and duty blouse.

A few minutes later, Jimmy hobbled back to the staging area to find the other three operators waiting for him.

"Welcome to the team. You usually earn your marks around here in feral blood." Bowman gestured to the newly painted symbols on the other three battle suits.

"Was it you fellas that fucked with my suit?" Jimmy asked.

Red Devil stepped up and glowered at him with a humorless smile. "We didn't want you to feel left out."

"Since all the good battle suits were black." Jake added.

Sams looked at the other three for a moment, sizing them up. Only Carter seemed an even match for him. Bowman was a Ranger and Red Devil looked big enough to snap him in two without a second thought. One look at their faces was enough to tell him that he would never face only one of them. Momma Sams hadn't raised her son to be a fool.

This wasn't just three men he was looking at, it was a single unit. One he was supposed to be a part of. And between one man and a team, he'd learned the smart money was always on the team.

Jimmy looked at his ORB and smiled. "Looks like Dale's race car that way. Maybe I'll paint a big 'ole three on it."

Rasmussen and Linh showed up around sundown, just as the Ash Troopers had all six battle suits loaded up on their trailers. Sams' suit was on a converted fifth-wheel trailer that was towed behind a Chevy Silverado. Sergeants Fipps and Heart's battle suits were pulled by a pair of black Ram 3500s. The two scouts that had gone to retrieve them pulled in as Fipps' battle-scarred suit was being locked into place. No sooner than the two vehicles stopped the doors on the lead vehicle were opened and a pale-skinned woman with a strawberry blonde pixie cut emerged. Her round face was set in a frown. Her clothes hung off of her like they had originally been made for a bigger woman. Black showed at the cuffs and collar of her stained coveralls. Her boots bore a patina of scuffs and scratches.

"Why was I pulled off my duties and dragged all the way across Springfield in the middle of the busiest day I can remember since... well, since the world went to shit?" she demanded as she approached.

Behind her, the other vehicle's doors opened and a tall woman with slightly darker skin emerged. Her dark hair was longer, but its true length was hidden by the bun she'd imprisoned it in. Her eyes had a slight epicanthic fold and her cheekbones were slightly higher than her companion's. Most striking about her was the somewhat less severe expression she wore.

"We understand that there was some damage to the greenhouses, Cheryl." Fipps started.

"Some damage? *Some* damage? They're a mess! No, they're a

hot mess! It's going to take us a week to get things put back to-gether, and in the meantime, we have to keep the plants alive."

Kelly spoke up. "And the people you sent to help are going to make sure we get everything fixed as quickly as possible. But I have the same question. What do you need a pair of botanists to do outside of an agricultural setting?"

"Not exactly the same question." Fipps smiled.

Sergeant Heart stepped up. "But better phrased. One of you is going to act as a mission specialist on a sort of... goodwill trip. The other is going to stay here and make changes to our greenhouses and whatever to deal with some new environmental developments."

"I can't possibly leave and I can't let Kelly go, either. We're both too important to the greenhouse here and getting it back in order— Wait, what environmental changes?"

"The kind that happens after a massive volcano blows up." Fipps interjected.

"You mean...what happened this morning..." Rasmussen sputtered.

"Yeah. Headquarters wants us to send out a group to help and spread the word along with them." Fipps smirked.

"I can go." Kelly shrugged. Heart suppressed a smile at how quickly she volunteered.

Rasmussen looked at Kelly. "But...we'll have to concentrate on our own survival."

"And that will be your job," Fipps said as Heart led Kelly away. The taller botanist seemed to relax as she left her com-panion behind, her shoulders dropping a couple of inches and her back straightening.

"You're going to be in good hands," Heart said as she led her toward the ORBS. "Not only are you going to have a full contin-gent of troopers, you'll have a squad of our new battle suits with you to protect you from things like ragers."

"Those look... impressive." Doctor Linh eyed the black com-bat frames.

Heart couldn't help but notice that her eyes strayed to the gathered pilots as often as they did to their suits. They weren't a bad looking group and between them they represented most of what a woman might find physically attractive in a guy. Red

Devil covered the larger end of the spectrum, looking like a younger Arnold if he'd been born a Native American. Sams on the other hand, had the boyish good looks, lean frame, and easy innocence of youth. Bowman and Carter seemed to cover the everyman range. Both were average height and size, but obviously in good shape. The former Army Ranger leaned toward the dark and brooding type and Carter the more open, blue collar look.

She led Kelly past the pilots to the area set aside for the expedition's mission specialist, basically a table with a laptop and a thick binder. While thumb drives were convenient, they required power and a working computer to be accessed. Running a printer took a lot of power, but the finished product was durable and more easily accessed.

Heart motioned toward the binder on the table. "Okay, get yourself familiar with the cold weather protocols. You're going to have to teach this to laymen, so look at it with the intent of simplifying it for folks who have a hundred other things going on."

"Right. Results, not data. A technical seminar, not a scientific lecture." She nodded and went to the table, everything else apparently forgotten about.

The next four hours were the last stages of a nightmare of logistics for almost one hundred troopers and the resulting support they required. Vehicles, food, shelter, and ammo were only a fraction of what had to be wrangled, to say nothing of the people themselves. By the time lights out was called dawn was too close and sleep was in short supply.

"And ye came near and stood under the mountain; and the mountain burned with fire unto the midst of heaven, with darkness, clouds, and thick darkness."

-*Deuteronomy 4:11*

Sunrise saw a convoy of black vehicles pull out of the nearby parking garage. Scouts led the way with a pair of heavily armed and armored Zombie Response Vehicles behind them. The designation of ZRVs for these vehicles had most members of ZOD affectionately calling them Zervs.

The rig for Mauler along with Ranger and Samson followed, with a pair of black buses, three converted panel vans and an armored RV behind them. Thunder led Red Devil and Spartan, with a pair of ZRVs and a Rattler behind them. Every vehicle had music playing at maximum volume. The Rattler deployed its chains as soon as they hit the end of the ramp.

Immediately, every feral in the area started toward the convoy. They turned east as soon as they left the parking garage and kept going at a slow enough pace for the monsters to keep up until they got close to National Street. The lead vehicles started to speed up, each taking the left turn onto Glenstone without stopping. The Rattler bringing up the rear didn't speed up. Keeping its pace steady it was just fast enough to keep its infected pursuers in sight.

The rest of the vehicles made the turn several hundred yards ahead of the Rattler and kept gaining speed as they crested the overpass. By the time the tail car was at the top of the overpass the rest of the convoy had already made the next turn and were out of sight down Chestnut. The Rattler kept its pace and was still drawing infected down Glenstone Street.

On board Spartan's rig, Jake kept his attention on the radio. His mind was more on the team that was playing decoy than on the highway. The plan was for Rattler Six to draw them off about a mile, then speed up and make their getaway down another side street and lose the horde by breaking line of sight and going quiet. The convoy turned onto the highway and followed it to the junction of US 44 which would take them to the first stop in their tour, Fort Leonard Wood.

As they made the turn east Scout Three sped up and left the rest of the convoy behind. The Zervs took up a slight lead and covered both lanes, one slightly in front of the other. As they got close to the range for the vehicles' radios, the words Jake had been waiting for came over the air.

"This is Rattler Six, contact broken. We're heading back to base. Good luck and God speed!"

With that Jake turned his attention forward. Even after the end of the world Missouri was beautiful country. He allowed himself to enjoy the rolling terrain and lush, overgrown fields. The contrast to west Texas with its open, stark landscapes and dusty colors.

They drove through St. Robert without finding any sign of living human beings. They turned south to check out Ft. Leonard Wood. Aside from a few skeletons and a handful of stalled cars on the road itself, it looked like even the dead had abandoned the area. The convoy slowed to a crawl as everyone scanned the side of the road, looking for anything worth checking out. Suddenly the convoy lurched to a stop.

"First and second squads, get ready to disembark to check the strip mall on the left. Third and Fourth squads, set up a perimeter. ORBS pilots, you're on standby." Sergeant Fipps voice snapped over the radio. "First and Second Squads, concentrate on that Oriental grocery store, see if there is anything worth salvaging inside."

Jake scrambled to the back of the rig and then spent the next couple of minutes trying to stay out of the way of his Ash Troopers as the prepped Spartan. Black clad ZOD members jogged toward the store front, their gun barrels down and heads moving left and right. When they made it to the door of the store they ranged out to either side to form a cone with the widest part closest to the entry. The two in the lead flanked the door. The one on the left pulled her machete from its scabbard then nodded to the man beside her, who pounded on the door several times.

For a couple of minutes silence reigned supreme. The man slammed his fist against the door a few more times and waited another few seconds, but didn't get any reaction. He gave a hand gesture to the woman and she sheathed the machete. She pulled a small crowbar from her belt and proceeded to pry the door open. The lock popped free and she stepped back, but nothing came out. The crowbar went back into her belt. Drawing her pistol she led the way in.

The rest of the team went in by twos behind her. Fifteen minutes later they came out in pairs, one carrying an armload of boxes and the other covering. One of the panel vans backed up to the store and started loading up, but the process was finished all too quickly. Nothing else in the shopping center seemed to promise anything useful. A tax preparation place and a title loan company were the only other neighbors the market had.

Further down the road the teams repeated the process at a pair of pawn shops. The first one was as empty as the market, but the second was occupied. As soon as the team advanced on the place a rager threw itself at the door. As the double glass doors bowed outward at the impact of the thing inside, the squad advancing on the door raised their guns. Moments later a face appeared against the glass and the lead man pulled the trigger on his shotgun. The face disappeared in a spray of red and pink. All was quiet. Neither pawn shop yielded much in the way of useful guns or tools, though the second did have a generator in the back. Once that had been muscled into the back of a van the convoy headed for the base proper.

"Our job here isn't a supply run," Fipps announced over the radio. "If we find weapons or ammo loose we grab it, but we're her to see if the armories are intact. It's been five years, so we don't have our hopes up. If by some strange chance they are still untouched, it's someone else's job to crack 'em. ORBS pilots, stay on alert status."

For the rest of the afternoon Jake rode in the back of Spartan's rig, waiting for a call that he hoped would never come and watching as other men and women took risks scouting the base. As the sun began to cast long shadows across the roads Fipps finally ordered the teams to load up and head back to the base's entrance.

A few miles northeast of town they turned off the highway. The convoy followed a side road that crossed the Gasconade River and curved through a small town called Jerome. A mile or two past Jerome they found their campsite for the night, one of several spots that the scouts had reconnoitered while they were busy at Fort Leonard Wood.

The black scout vehicles were waiting in an open field on the right side of the road. The bigger vehicles followed the dirt road until they came even with their waiting comrades. The armored RV turned and found a spot first, then the two buses turned and alternately pulled or backed into position across the front and back of the RV so that all three vehicles' doors were pointed inside of the 'U' they formed. Two of the panel vans parked nose to nose to create the other end of the rectangle. The remaining vehicles parked facing away from each other in a double row just past the vans. The vans left a narrow gap between their front grills for people to come and go.

Once the vehicles were in place, teams went around the outside and pulled down the heavy iron sections of fencing that had been welded to the buses and the vans. The black iron pieces swung down into place with a squeak. The teams padlocked them into place to prevent crawlers from finding a way under the buses, especially since the ends of the sections buried themselves several inches in the dirt.

By the time the outside was secured, the team in the RV had finished taking care of their job for the night: making dinner. The heavily armored vehicle had been converted to a mobile kitchen inside. A thick stew seemed to be the night's main dish, with a huge tub of mashed potatoes and another filled with corn sitting next to it. The food wasn't fancy, but it was filling. Big vats of tea and lemonade were the drinks of choice.

Jake eventually found himself standing at the end of the line with a full plate and bowl. Very few friendly faces were looking his way. While no one had been rude or even hostile, he still felt less than welcome in any conversation he tried to take part in while he'd waited in line. The other ORBS pilots were seated on the ground at the far end of the temporary yard. He made his way to join them and sat down in an open spot in the circle.

"Is it just me—"

Red Devil cut him off. "No, it isn't. I can't tell if it's hero worship or if they think we're cursed."

"An ORBS operator's average lifespan is about a minute. We're running face first *at* ragers and anything else that's bigger, meaner and uglier than a basic feral. That makes us either crazy or stupid. No one is certain of which." Heart explained.

"Yeah, we ain't sure either!" Sams opened on an old coffee can with his knife.

"Jimmy, since you and Jake can stay with your suits, you two have alert status. The rest of you are out of the guard rotation in case we need you to suit up."

"I'm sure that made us a lot of friends." Bowman chuckled.

"Making friends isn't our job. We're all here to make dead things deader." Heart stood.

"What's that?" Jake asked Sams as Heart headed back for the bus.

"Hobo stove," Sams answered. "Good way to stay warm at night when you ain't got a girl beside ya'. I also don't have to settle for that watered down crap they call coffee in the mess tent." Jake moved closer and watched as he worked.

Once they'd finished eating, Jake and Jimmy made their way back to their vehicles while the rest of the ZOD troopers took their turn on guard duty or amused themselves until lights out. Just before lights out, Danny came out and climbed into the truck. Jake had racked out in the back, with a paperback in hand.

"Figured this was where the party was." Danny took a seat at the radio.

"Yeah, the strippers'll be here any minute and they're bringing a keg." Jake glanced over the top of his book.

"Well, I figured I'd use the radio to take a listen, see if we can pick anything up."

"Hate to tell you this but pretty much everyone's off the air, man."

"Except *Conspiracy Now*. Seriously those dudes are total whack jobs, but they're still there. And some nights when the skip is good, there are still some HAM radio operators on the air." Danny half-joked.

"Good luck getting anything with that big ash cloud in the air."

"Yeah the ionization is gonna be bad, but you never know." Danny pulled the headphones down from their hook and clicked the HAM radio on. For about an hour he slowly cycled through the frequencies, listening for a couple of minutes before moving on. Finally, he stopped and leaned forward.

"Jake, you asleep?"

"No. Why, was I snoring?" He fumbled with his book and slid a makeshift bookmark between the pages.

"Listen to this." Danny pulled the plug from the headphones and the low hiss of static filled the camper.

Then a soft, crackling voice cut through the static. "This is Knox County Sheriff. We read you, Cardwell Farm. Do you have an emergency?"

"We sure do!" another voice came over the line. "We got dead folks wanderin' around our fields. And not just the normal kind, either. There's some of those real big ones. They've already killed six cattle and our dog."

"Understood, Cardwell," the Knox County voice came back. "Are you familiar with the blackout procedures we've been broadcasting?"

"Uh, yeah, my daughter says she knows what to do."

"Okay, institute blackout procedures right away. We're dispatching a guard unit to help you. Tell us where you are and how to get to you from Edina." Danny wrote frantically as the man from Cardwell Farm gave directions.

"Here's hoping I'm being redundant!" Danny finished scribbling the directions down. Jake crawled forward and pulled the collection of maps from the glove compartment, then came back and opened the Missouri map. After a few minutes, he put his finger down on a spot and looked up.

"They're a ways north of us."

Danny nodded, then got on his personal radio. "Heavy One, this is Spartan Two. Reporting radio intercept. Did you pick that up too?"

"Spartan, this is Heavy. Confirming affirmative on that. Knox County?"

"Heavy, Spartan. Affirmative for Knox County."

"Spartan, Heavy. Good catch and thank you for confirming. Heavy, out."

"Guess we'll know tomorrow what the plan is." Jake headed back toward his bunk.

"Guess so. I'm going to keep my ear to the sky for a little longer, see if there's anything else to hear."

"I'm going to get some sleep." Jake climbed into the bunk and turned the overhead light out. "Some of us still need that."

"Silly little mortal."

After breakfast the next morning Fipps and Heart called everyone into the rectangle formed by the vehicles. They stood on either side of Paul Blakefield. The man wore the black uniform of ZOD with captain's bars on his collar.

"Good morning everyone!" His crisp voice carried across the small enclosed space. "Last night we intercepted a radio transmission from a small town somewhat north of us. It sounds as though they could use some help dispatching ferals. We'll be turning north later today and offering what aid we can. So, are we all ready to kill some ragers?"

The loud and energetic response brought a smile to his face. "Well done. Let's be about it then."

In half an hour the convoy was back on the highway, the scout vehicles once again ranging ahead. As they approached Rolla, the radio came alive.

"Scout One to Heavy One!" they heard. "Heavy infestation on the road! We're heading back your way. I see at least two ragers in the bunch. Scout Two is damaged but it looks like they should make it."

"We copy, Scout One. We're sending the ZRVs and the ORBS to assist." Paul's calm voice responded.

"Thanks, Heavy!" Scout One sounded relieved.

The ZRVs and the ORBs surged ahead. Less than two minutes later, they passed Scout One. The smaller black vehicle skidded to a stop as they zoomed by. Scout One turned around to fall in behind them. Further ahead Scout Two was visible. Its right rear quarter low to the ground, with black shreds of the right rear tire flopping around as it slowed to a stop.

For a moment nothing seemed wrong, until the horde they had been trying to outrun crested the hill behind them. Ferals ran at a full sprint, their regenerative abilities allowing them to maintain the breakneck pace almost indefinitely. The ORBS rigs pulled to a stop, their pilots already strapped in during their approach. Meanwhile, the ZRVs sped up and rammed the first wave of zombies. The front of each car had been fitted with a pointed scoop, making it look like a murderous snowplow. Atop each of the black cars was a boxy contraption that had four arms attached to it. As they drew nearer the arms on each car started to spin. Heavy iron rods welded together to form eight pronged spikes along its length deployed at head height for an average human being. The initial impact was spectacular. Ferals went flying in either direction as the plow in the front sheared off legs and the spiked chains scrambled zombie brains.

With the first wave blunted, the ZRVs pulled back to cover Scout One's crew while the six battle suits entered the fray. Red Devil, Ranger, and Thunder started off with high explosive and high velocity party favors. Red Devil unloaded all six HEDP grenades in his launcher, while Ranger and Thunder poured bullets into the target rich onslaught in short bursts.

Where shrapnel and lead didn't do the trick, skull busting overpressure often did. The remnants of the first wave hit them and it was all blade work. Heart activated Thunder's chainsaw and swung the heavy katana blade into place on her right arm. Fipps led Samson and Spartan into the fight with the jackhammer primed, and the heavy blade on his right arm deployed. Another wave appeared behind the first, and in it, they saw the four lumbering forms. Only three of them looked humanoid, though. For a moment, all six ORBS pilots were spell bound by what they saw.

"Is that a—" Jake asked.

"It can't be—" Jimmy balked.

"I think it is—" Ranger offered.

Heart moaned. "It's a feral elephant."

"Was the goddamn circus in town or somethin'?" Red Devil murmured astounded.

"Thunder, your team gets the three big guys," Fipps ordered. "We'll take care of Samba the Great over here." He led Samson and Spartan to the right, letting the other three battle suits form up into a wedge of their own.

"How are we going to take down an elephant?" Jake waded through ferals and made their way clear of the other half of the squad.

"First, we're going to get its undivided attention... or at least you are. Who knows, maybe you'll get lucky and kill it with the first shot."

"If only." Jake muttered as he lined up the gun camera on the massive gray head. He shifted his aim up a little for distance. The picture shifted a little when he pulled the trigger, but his eyes were on the rest of the world. The massive metal bolt flew in a blur and the next thing Jake saw, it was stuck in the elephant's head. The beast went down with a trumpeting roar and Jake let out a yell.

"Spartan, for the win!"

"Headshot!" Jimmy intoned, mimicking a video game. The roar faded to silence, but the horde kept coming. "Next time, save something for the rest of us, man!"

"No promises." Jake laughed as he started forward again. Then the roar thundered into the sky again. Jake stopped in his tracks. "Uh, guys... I don't think it's all the way dead." Ahead of him, the massive gray form struggled to its feet, blood trickling down the front of its broad face.

"Looks like it's only mostly dead," Jimmy added.

"Which means it's still slightly alive," Jake shot back.

The beast turned its head toward Spartan. Fipps registered its attention and shouted a warning. "Spartan, *do not* use your stabilizers."

"What?" Jake blurted.

"They're not strong enough to stop a charge from something that big. Take the hit if you have to, but get out of the way if you can. Samson, cover his right flank, be ready to move in on this thing after it makes its charge." Fipps moved to one side of Spartan.

"Roger that, Mauler!" Sampson moved to Spartan's right.

Ahead of them, the infected pachyderm was tossing ferals to the side as it charged. Even through the legs of their suits, the three ORBS pilots could feel the impact of its platter sized feet on the asphalt. Jake watched it thunder toward him. His hand was loose on the stick and he fought every urge to fire his stabilizer spikes and meet the charge head on.

"Roll to dodge, roll to dodge," he whispered to himself as it got closer, close enough to see that one of its eyes wasn't looking where the other one was. At about twenty yards, it veered to Jake's left and bore down on Mauler. At the last second the thing lowered its head and tossed the battle suit to the side of the road, just as Mauler had started to move.

"Crit fail!" Jake screamed as he tried to move out of the way of the elephant. The beast stopped in place, turned, and started moving in his direction. Realizing he'd never get out of the way in time he brought his right arm up and locked the elbow. He activated the sword blade.

It hit the blade. Jake watched the steel shatter right before the tusks caught the cage and threw him straight back. He hit something solid and came to a stop mostly upright, with yellow and red lights flashing on his control panel. His right arm and left leg hurt, but in that distant way he'd come to associate with fading shock.

"Jake!" Danny's voice came over the Spartan's internal speakers. It was thick with static, but it worked. "Talk to me buddy. You're lit up like a Christmas tree."

"Still here! Damn that hurt."

"Okay, you've still got arms and legs. Your weapons are redlined and you've got maybe ten minutes of fight left in you. If you go full power, probably less."

"Sword's busted, too!" Jake struggled to his feet and looked around. He'd hit a tractor, which had taken the brunt of the fall and kept him mostly upright.

"Do you have anything left to fight *with*?"

Jake looked around. His eyes fell on the attachment hooked to the tractor. "Yeah, cunning and a fighting spirit."

Forty yards away, Fipps got Mauler to its feet with the help of a minivan that he left a little shorter in the middle. He turned to see Samson at the elephant-feral's side desperately shoving against it. It appeared he was trying to knock it over. The elephant tried to back away and turn. Samson kept moving forward and turning along with it. With Spartan out of the fight, knocking it over seemed as good a plan as any.

With his ears ringing, Fipps stomped toward the bizarre dance and waited until an opportunity showed itself. As the massive animal tried to spin away from its tormenter, he advanced and caught it just behind the back legs with his left claw. The steel pincers closed and locked into place. The elephant bellowed out an agonized call. Its hind legs buckled, dragging Mauler down with it before Fipps could unlock the claw. He bent at the waist to keep from being pulled down on top of the animal, but he was still off balance. Instead of disengaging the claw he pulled straight back, leaving a huge wound for the creature to heal.

"Go for the spine!" Fipps yelled, not even bothering with his radio. Samson's right arm came up and slammed down just behind the shoulders of the great animal. The beast's front legs folded.

In front of them the metal pole barn style building that Spartan had disappeared into erupted in an explosion of green. Spartan emerged with five feet of steel gripped in its claw. Like a slasher in a horror movie, it raised its arm and brought the heavy blade down on the elephant's head. There was a crunch of bone, but the thing kept thrashing. Its wounds kept healing.

"The bolt you hit it with!" Fipps called over his radio as he punched his claw back into the thing and activated the jackhammer on the other arm at the same time.

"Hit—" he started, but Spartan was already winding up for a backhand. The blade slammed into the butt of the metal projectile and drove it the rest of the way through the bone of the skull and into the thing's brain. With one final spasm, the infected elephant went still.

"—the spike!" Fipps finished.

"Spartan, for the win." Jake panted.

They turned to head back to the fight. The crews in the ZRVs and the Scout's had held their own, leaving a ragged circle of feral bodies around their vehicles. The other three battle suits had dispatched the three ragers and were mopping up the last of the ferals as Fipps and his team approached.

"You look about like hell." Red Devil commented as they got closer.

"I feel like it, too," Jake answered. "At least there is symmetry."

"Jake, get Spartan to the rig!" Danny's voice came over the internal speakers. "Before it goes offline on its own."

"Yes, Mother." Jake turned and headed for the trailer.

"All right people, get Scout Two mobile again and let's press on!" Fipps called out as the rest of the ORBS started back to their own vehicle rigs.

Jake turned Spartan around on board the trailer with his display lights flickering and the battery power warning light blinking fast yellow. It went to a solid red a few seconds before he powered down. Bobby and Dean rushed forward to help him wrestle the cage up. Bobby let out a low whistle as she pried the left leg cover open. One side of it had a narrow streak of blood.

"Want a souvenir?" she asked, holding up eight inches of elephant tusk. Jake looked down to see his pants torn and a thin gash on the inside of his thigh.

"Missed it by that much," Dean said, holding two fingers a couple of inches apart. Jake stepped out of the armor on shaking legs.

"Holy crap!" He took the shard of ivory.

Kim and Danny stood on the railings next to Spartan to take a look at the rest of the damage. "Well doc, give it to me straight. Will it ever play football again?"

Kim quickly surveyed the damage. "Gun mount's busted, but the bolt gun looks okay. I think it's just the mounting plates. We should be able to fix those and replace the bolts. We can patch the armor and beat the dents back out. Looks like the sword blade completely shattered, though. I'm not sure we can forge a new one in the field."

"Use that." Jake pointed at the makeshift blade he'd used on the elephant. "It's thicker than the blade we used and it didn't break when I smacked that damn thing in the head with it."

"Barely bent it. What the hell is it?" Danny looked at the makeshift sword.

"Blade from a brush hog. I had to snap the bolt holding it on."

"It'll do," Danny said with a sigh. "Okay, you're driving while we try to fix some of this. I just hope we don't run into another fight today."

"You and me both!"

Jake walked to the end of the trailer and knelt down. His body was stiff and sore. He felt every ache and tight spot with each step along the way to the cab. He started the truck and fell in when the rest of the convoy started moving. Once they were safely on the road the radio crackled to life and Paul's voice came over the air.

"Spartan, please go to channel 2." He acknowledged the message and switched the channel.

"Spartan, go for Heavy."

"What is the status of your battle suit?"

"Out of the fight for today."

"That is unfortunate, but understandable given the foe you faced. Likewise, Samson is temporarily out of commission as well. One of the crew in Scout Two was lost today and the driver is injured. I want to assign you and Mister Sams to Scout Two and put their crew in to drive your rigs. We'll stop once we're out of Rolla and make the change."

Half an hour later the convoy stopped and Scout Two drove back to the rear of the column. Jimmy hopped out of the truck pulling his rig and trotted up to Jake's window.

"Man, what the hell's he thinkin'? We're battle suit pilots, not taxi drivers." The younger man stomped back and forth as they waited for the crew of Scout Two to grab their gear.

"Not sure, but you're about to get your chance to ask him." Jimmy looked to where Jake was pointing to see Paul's lean frame coming their way. Jake reached behind him and grabbed his black assault vest and field pack. He got out of the truck to stand beside Jimmy.

"What in the hell is that thing?" Jimmy asked as Jake slung his gun belt across his left shoulder. Jimmy was pointing at the hilt of his sword, an odd S-curved design.

Jake smiled. "It's a falchion. Kind of like a machete and a broadsword, all in one."

"Sweet! Where'd you find that?"

"My study. I owned this before things went to shit. I had this with me all the way from El Paso to Corpus Christi. Killed a lot of ferals with it."

"Damn, that's pretty hard-core. Me, I like a good ole fashioned machete. What's your long arm?"

"Pump shotgun. Never was a very good shot. You?"

Jimmy turned to show the weapon slung barrel down across his back. "M4 carbine. If it's good enough for the US Army, it's good enough for me. Red dot sights zeroed in at a hundred yards."

"If it's that far away, I don't think I want to bother it."

The crew of Scout Two made it over to them as Jake finished speaking. They exchanged the keys to the vehicles. Paul ambled up as the exchange was concluded and motioned for the two ORBS troopers to walk with him.

"I want the two of you to know this is not a punishment detail. Rather, I prefer to keep men like yourself as close to the thick of things as I can. Sitting in the rear echelon while other men went forward into action doesn't suit you. It's part of why you were selected to be ORBS pilots."

"I dunno'," Jimmy drawled. "I may not laugh in its face, but me and danger ain't really all that close, either."

Paul put a hand on Jimmy's shoulder. "Nonsense! When the base breach alarm went off in Memphis, you ran toward the breach site."

"Hey, how'd you know about that?"

Jake piped in. "Because they did the exact same thing down in Corpus Christi! But it turned out to be a drill, didn't it?"

"Yeah, somethin' about testing reaction times or some shit."

Paul smiled at the pair. "All part of the evaluation process. An ORBS pilot has to be ready to face dangers the average trooper could not survive without armor such as your battle suits and do so without flinching. Men such as yourselves, who run toward danger, not away from it. So hop in, gentlemen and enjoy the ride."

Jimmy leapt in the driver seat. "I'm drivin'"

"Knock yourself out."

Jake headed for the passenger side of the black Mustang. His sword was stowed beside the seat and the shotgun fit into the scabbard that was mounted under the dash. The tactical holster on his thigh wasn't as easy to access as it was in Spartan, but the Glock in the tactical vest was still a simple draw. He strapped himself into the four point harness and slipped the crew helmet on as Jimmy turned the engine over and revved the gas a few times.

"You want me to get out and paint a big number three on the side there?" Jake joked.

Jimmy grinned. "Naw, just hang on!"

He hit the gas and the car leaped forward, pressing Jake back into the seat. They rocketed toward the front of the column, but slowed as they saw the two ZRVs. Once they passed them Jimmy brought the car onto the road and hit the gas again. They did not slow until they caught up to Scout One a mile or so down the road. After that, their pace was much more sedate.

"Hell, we ain't broke thirty miles an hour since noon." Jimmy grumbled three hours later as they wove through a small group of cars.

Jake pointed at a sign that promised the next town was only a few miles away. "I'm sure we'll be able to open her up after we pass through Hermann. You might get up to forty, really feel the wind in your hair."

"Ain't you just a little ray of sunshine."

"Wait, do you see that?" Jake's smile and jokes were suddenly forgotten.

"Movement, looks like several ... uh, people up there."

"Hard to tell, isn't it?" Jake grabbed the radio to call the contact in.

"Advance and observe, Scout Two," Paul's voice came back. "Scout One stay close and be ready to assist Scout Two if the encounter goes hostile."

Jimmy eased the Mustang forward. Jake pulled the binoculars from their case in the center console. In the magnified view, he counted nine people. Worn and battered suits and skirts hung off their bodies. Each carried a briefcase or computer case in one hand, with a weapon of some sort carried or slung. All of them sat in a circle and all eyes seemed to be on the only one who was on his feet. An occasional nod would break the absolute stillness of the group, or a furtive glance down.

"What are they doing?"

Jake put the binoculars down and turned to him with a bewildered look on his face. "If I didn't know any better, I'd say they were having a business meeting."

"And he said, Let us take our journey, and let us go, and I will go before thee."

-*Genesis 33:12*

Jake had seen business meetings happen, but they were mysteries to him. Every suit he knew complained about them and considered them a huge waste of time. He'd seen execs spend hours sitting around tables, talking, taking notes or whatever it was they were doing, but none of them ever looked happy going in or coming out. He'd also heard tales of ferals doing things they used to do in life, but he'd never actually seen that happen. And he'd seen *lots* of ferals.

As he got out of the car, he figured it was a pretty safe bet that the nine people he was walking up to really *were* people. Even the infected weren't dumb enough to hold a business meeting after the apocalypse. Humans? Not so much.

Jimmy got out on the other side and leveled his M4 at the circle of people while Jake buckled his blade on. Once the falchion was secured at his side he grabbed his shotgun. He started to walk forward slowly in the combat stance he'd learned from Ken Bowman. As he got closer he could hear the standing man's voice, which told him more effectively than anything that at least that guy wasn't infected. When he got within twenty yards of the group, one of them stood and started to head in his direction. As the man approached, he held up a plastic badge.

"That's far enough!" Jake pointed the shotgun at a point a few feet in front of the man's feet.

"Lance McClowsky," the man said firmly. "I'm the VP of Financial Operations. We're having our quarterly planning session here, and we would appreciate it if we weren't disturbed." Jake stopped for a second. He stood up straight with his brow furrowed, but the shotgun never moving an inch.

"Excuse me?"

"If you can wait until the meeting is over, or maybe just come back later," the man said, letting the sentence fade into silence as if the implication was clear. The man leading the 'meeting' approached them. The rest of the group stood, milling about just a few feet away from the area they'd just been in.

"It's okay, Lance," the other man said with a confident smile. "We had reached the end of today's agenda. I'll talk to this gentleman." Lance nodded and headed over to the group. Once he was a few feet away, the newcomer let out a sigh and seemed to deflate a little.

"Who are you?"

"Larry McCoy," the man said. "I'm the head of 'HR' here." He brought his hands up to do air quotes when he said 'HR' and gave Jake a knowing smile.

"I'm not sure I follow."

Up close, he could see that while the man's suit was battered and threadbare, it didn't have the look of a garment that had been worn since the world ended.

"Human Resources. Back before, it was the workforce. Now... it's the group. Back before, my job was to optimize and enhance the value of the human asset segment through training and development. It isn't all that different now."

"What was that about a quarterly planning session?"

"Oh, that's exactly what we were doing," McCoy said with a broad smile. "You've caught us during a leadership retreat. We're trying to decide if we need to come back across the river to start looking for untapped resources, or if it's better to stay on the other side. Resources are more plentiful over there, but there are a lot more ferals. It's been quite a spirited discussion. We have some good ideas from our leadership and we're all recharged and ready to get back to what we do best."

"Who exactly are you leading?"

"Oh, we have a workforce in the hundreds back home. They look to us for leadership and development. We're going to lead them through this to a profitable new quarter."

"Then what's with the retreat thing? Don't they need you?"

"Most of them are self-directing and we did leave a few team leaders in charge to handle day to day operations while we handled the big picture issues. I mean, if it weren't for us and missions like this," McCoy said as he reached into the pocket of his coat. Jake tensed and raised the barrel of the shotgun, but when his hand came out of the pocket, he held a fistful of pens and markers. "Our human assets would revert to total savagery."

"Pens? You left your people behind to get pens?"

"And paper!" McCoy said quickly. "And we had to recertify for our leadership programs. This year, we rediscovered the heart of leadership in this region: the Capitol itself. Lost since the end of the world, we found it and held our recertification ceremony in the Governor's office!"

Jake shook his head as he started to understand what was going on. Overhead, a rumble of thunder reminded him of their basic mission. "Look, do you have someone who handles farming or gardening?"

"Rick Hodgekins is our VP of Agribusiness. It's a new division, only a couple of years old but it's got a lot of potential for positive growth."

"Do you see that?" Jake pointed at the gray cloud cover. "That's going to change the way Rick's division works. We've got a specialist who can tell him how to handle the changes that are coming."

"Oh, good! Rick's a positive learner; he'll be glad to have some new ideas to take back home with him." Jake nodded and headed back to Jimmy.

"So, what's up with the suits?"

Jake looked over his shoulder. "If I had to guess these people have gone tribal, but they're using a corporate sounding structure for it. The 'chief' is their head of Human Resources and their head farmer is the VP of Agribusiness. But get this... They just went on a pilgrimage somewhere to get *pens*."

"And paper. I heard that part. But what were they redoing?"

"They were recertifying in their leadership programs. If anything it *sounds* dumber now than it did back in the day, but it also seems to be working. I'm gonna ask Paul if we can get Doctor Linh to talk to their Agribusiness VP."

A few minutes later Kelly Linh was being sent forward in one of the ZRVs and a plump, balding man came forward from the group of 'executives.'

"Larry mentioned there would be a certificate," the man said as they waited for Kelly to arrive. "Will you be sending that to us, or will I receive it at the end of the course?"

"The certificate," Jake stammered. "Um...well...it'll be ready for you by the end of the course!" The black car was approaching, and Hodgekins beamed his appreciation of the news.

When he had gone to meet Doctor Linh, Jimmy turned to Jake. "What certificate?"

"The one I'm gonna make," Jake started toward McCoy. A couple of minutes later, he came back with a few sheets of paper and a couple of markers. "Here's hoping my calligraphy isn't too rusty."

"Your cal-what-ery?"

"My fancy printing."

Jake said as he pulled the cap from one of the pens and started making a few experimental strokes with the marker. "Chisel tip, perfect. Okay, it's kind of cheating, but see how the pen makes different widths of mark if I hold the point steady but move the pen in different directions? That's all calligraphy is. Fancy printing with lots of little decorations."

"I wouldn't know about all that. My folks never did cotton to that fancy joined up writin' none. Seriously, how do you know this stuff?"

"Back in the day I was in the SCA, squired to a knight. My knight required all of her squires to learn calligraphy and chess, among other things."

"That's that medieval group. Joustin' and stuff, right?"

Jake took a breath as he prepared to explain, then thought better of the effort. "Yeah, kinda like that. A lot of the arts and stuff from the Middle Ages, too."

Jimmy smiled and gestured at the certificate Jake was making. "Like calligraphy. Why go to all the effort, though?"

"Guess I'd rather make an honest deal with other humans than have to deal with a hostile takeover later on."

"You got a point, there. We've got enough things trying to kill us. Guess we don't need to be gunnin' for each other, huh?"

That night, Jake found himself onboard the converted bus designated Heavy One. Most of it was dedicated to troop seating, but the first four seats behind the driver had been removed and converted to a small command post. Blakefield, Fipps, and Heart were seated across the aisle from Jake and Jimmy.

"So near as I can tell, they figure that leadership generates some kind of... I dunno, like radiation or vibe or something that they can soak up. Makes 'em better leaders if they sit in other executives' offices long enough."

Paul slowly stroked his chin. "I understand them taking the pens and paper. No corporate entity seems capable of existing without memos and directives and other endless paperwork. But the significance of the plaques and certificates eludes me, I'm afraid."

Jake thought a moment. "Have you ever heard of counting coup?"

"I've heard the term, but the meaning is lost on me. After all, I'm an engineer, not an anthropologist."

"It was something the Plains Indians used to do in battle, to show how brave they were. A lot of things were counted as coup. But the big ones were being able to touch an enemy with either your bare hand or with a coup stick and get away without getting your ass handed to you. Those certificates, they're coup. They're proof of their leadership. It's their way of saying 'We went to the holy place and sat where leaders sat.' Just like most Americans buy souvenirs to show where they've been."

Paul nodded. "Medals and campaign ribbons."

"Yeah, only on a more primitive scale. This crew is nowhere near as civilized and sophisticated as the Plains tribes."

Fipps gaped at Jake. "How is it you know this kind of stuff? Your file says you were a construction worker in El Paso. You only listed a couple of semesters at a community college, but you sound like you could teach history."

"History was sort of my hobby. I did the Mountain Man rendezvous and a few other living history things until I got involved in the SCA."

Paul shook his head. "Back to the topic at hand. This corporate tribe seems fairly benign. I'm not inclined to view them as either a threat or a potential asset. You lads have spent the most time with them, does that sound right to you?"

Jimmy nodded, but Jake was slower to respond. "Their HR guy, McCoy. It's like he knows that they're a tribe. He knows what they're really doing, but he's.... he breaks the fourth wall, if that makes sense."

Paul's eyes sparkled in understanding. "Yes, I believe it does. He's seen the fire in the cave, but no one else around him has. Very well gentlemen. Again, thank you for your diligence. Your crews tell me your suits should be fully repaired by tomorrow. In the meantime I believe it's Red Devil and Mister Bowman's turn to take alert status, if only by sheer necessity. You lads get some rest."

The next morning was heralded by more gray than black in the sky. The overcast now touched the horizon all the way aroun, and was punctuated by streaks of lightning every few minutes. The convoy broke camp with spirits as gloomy as the skies and continued north.

Jake and Jimmy were back with their rigs, both dozing in the early morning light after helping their teams finish repairs on their armor. Jake roused himself as Danny brought the Spartan rig in behind Red Devil and Thunder's rigs in the lead. The convoy moved forward slowly, with the Scouts staying in sight of the lead vehicles. Static ruled the airwaves and only line of sight communication seemed to work.

Scout Two broke the silence just before noon. "We've got something ahead of us. I count three, four... make it six motorcycles ahead, all heavily armed. Looks like we might have a fight on our hands—or not."

As the rest of the convoy topped the hill, Jake could see the group of riders Scout Two was talking about. Four more had joined them. When the other vehicles came into view, he could see them stowing their rifles. Moments later, they turned and rode back down over the hill.

Scout One's driver laughed. "Looks like they didn't want any of this!"

Paul's voice clicked to life over the radio. "A bit outmatched were they? Carry on, Scout One and Two."

The terrain turned flat as they went further north, with once cultivated fields now strewn with high grass and weeds as far as the eye could see as the followed Route 19 toward Mark Twain Lake. They crossed the Clarence Cannon Dam around three and the ground started to slope upward gently. Twenty minutes later they doglegged west for a little bit, then headed back north just outside of Monroe City.

As the sun was beginning to get close to the horizon, Paul called them to a halt. "Ladies and gentlemen, I believe we have the attention of the local authorities. ZRVs and Scouts, take up positions forward and to the rear. ORBS, mount up and take positions at the front."

Jake hustled to the rig and climbed into Spartan's control cage, with Red Devil and Thunder lumbering down from their trailers almost in unison with him. The rigs for Ranger, Mauler and Samson pulled up and their cargoes were dismounting within the minute. All six battle suits were arrayed across the road when the first flashing lights came into view. The red and blue strobes were visible for a long time before they resolved into individual vehicles. As they drew closer, Jake could see that not all of the vehicles were police cruisers. Some were military Humvees with light bars attached or flashers mounted.

Red Devil looked grim. "If there was a rager within ten miles, it would be on its way here right now!"

Jimmy laughed over the radio. "At least they don't have their sirens going."

"Can the chatter! Look sharp." Fipps ordered.

The first vehicle pulled up. It was a silver sheriff's department vehicle with the Knox County seal on the hood. The Humvees pulled in behind him while more sheriff's department vehicles covered the rest of the road.

Once the vehicles stopped, doors opened and gun barrels were trained on the ZOD column. From inside Spartan's cockpit Jake could see a few pistols, a couple of mounted machine guns, and a lot of assault rifles.

Bowman let out a low whistle. "That's a lot of bullets pointed our way."

The driver's side door of the lead car opened. A burly blond man in a tan uniform got out and raised a bullhorn. "I'm Sheriff Dave Holder. You all have about ten seconds to identify yourselves and explain to me why you're bringing an armed force across Knox County lines."

"Sir, I'm Alexa Heart, and I'm with ZOD Midwest, out of Springfield," the speakers on Thunder crackled. "We're not here to do anyone any harm. We've actually come to offer our help."

"We've heard you all on the radio. You're an awful long way from home."

"Yes, sir, we are. But our mission is important. I'm going to open my armor and step out so I can explain it to you face to face, if that's all right."

"Just a second, ma'am."

He turned and gestured to his troops. The gun barrels went from aimed to ready positions. None were holstered or slung, but no one was in direct line of fire. Once his people had all complied, he turned to Heart and nodded.

The front of Thunder opened up and Sergeant Heart stepped out. As she drew closer to Holder it was apparent she was easily as tall as he was. He seemed to find her size surprising, if his expression was any indication.

With an ear toward the conversation, Jake looked at the force facing them. About half were in police or sheriff's department uniforms and another quarter were in military camo. The rest were in jeans and t-shirts, carrying hunting rifles and shotguns.

Bowman clicked his transmitter on. "That's odd. Those men in camo are National Guard. They should be answering to the governor, not a local sheriff."

"And I *should* be building a golf pro shop on a golf course in El Paso! But 'should' doesn't mean shit any more, does it?"

"Ain't that the truth. Lots of civilians in the mix, too. Wonder if it's a volunteer thing."

"Wouldn't they be in uniform if they were conscripted?"

Bowman's gaze turned to things only his mind could see. "Maybe. In Iraq and Afghanistan the bad guys didn't wear uniforms. When they forced farmers to fight the closest thing to a uniform was a fucking bomb vest."

"This doesn't look like an insurgency to me."

"True. The first thing you want to do is separate your conscripts from the locals. Uniforms, distinctive haircuts, things like that. So, I'm guessing it's a volunteer militia thing. Could be a good thing."

Sergeant Heart turned and headed back to the line of ORBS. Once she was back in her suit, her voice came over the radio. "Listen up, folks. Sheriff Holder is willing to work with us and let us operate here in Knox County with a few conditions. First, he wants us to work out of Edina. His people will provide us with power, water, and sanitation while we're there. But anytime we send people out on operations, he wants his people to go out with us. Side arms are authorized for open carry only outside of our camp when we're not conducting ops. No concealed weapons. We've agreed to send teams to handle any incursions of infected elements, especially the big fuckers. I want to make it very clear, each of us is representing ZOD every second we're here. You follow those rules or I will personally kick your ass all the way back to Springfield. Heart out."

"And the man wondering at her held his peace, to wit whether the Lord had made his journey prosperous or not."

- Genesis 24:21

7

It didn't take long for their first assignment from the Knox County sheriff to come. The first of the tents that they had packed were still being laid out when a deputy pulled up to the encampment in a patrol car. Within minutes, Red Devil, Spartan, and Thunder's rigs were following the deputy's vehicle down a two lane road marked as Missouri Highway Six. Jake fought the urge to start singing a Van Halen song from a tornado movie as they sped along under gunmetal skies.

The deputy explained over the radio as they travelled. "The Howards contacted us about ten minutes ago. Said they heard their cattle bellowing and… well, screamin' is the word they used. Bill Howard, he said he drove out to the pasture and saw this group of big zombies was killing and eating the cattle. Of course the steers ran toward the farm house and Bill's afraid them big ones are gonna follow 'em. We've been having problems with them, because they're too hard to hit from a safe distance, but once they get close enough that you *can* hit them… that's all she wrote."

Sergeant Heart's voice sparked across the radio. "We copy,

Deputy Richards. We'll take care of them. Our battle suits have handled bigger things than ragers."

"What in the hell is bigger than one of those rage zombies?"

"Mister Carter helped bring down a zombified elephant yesterday. So, I think we can handle whatever Mister Howard saw. Did he get an accurate count of how many there were?"

"He said he saw three or four, but he couldn't be sure, since they were so far off."

"We can definitely handle that."

They sped down Highway Six until it curved south, and then about a mile later turned north on a gravel road. The dust kept them from seeing much of what was in front of them, but the darker shapes of the vehicle ahead kept them from running into each other.

Suddenly, the radio crackled to life and a woman's voice came over the airwaves. "Knox County, this is Howard Farm. Is that you coming down 164?"

The deputy answered her. "Affirmative, Howard Farm. We're almost there."

"Thank God! Bill Junior and Carl went out to look for themselves, and Bill Senior went back out after them. I've been hearing shots from the woods for a couple of minutes and… oh God, who was that?" A piercing scream cut across the background.

"Jake, go—" Danny started to say before he realized he was talking to an empty cab. Moments later, Jake was coughing on dust as he climbed into the control cage on Spartan and hit the automatic close button. He could see Red Devil's rig behind him and he was guessing Devil was doing much the same thing. The rigs were slowing to a stop. Gunshots and rager roars reached his ears as he flipped the switch that withdrew the mounting brackets on Spartan's sides. No longer braced into the rig, Jake guided Spartan to the edge of the trailer and stepped off.

"Spartan, clear!" He turned to his left and started to move in the direction of the screams. Thunder and Red Devil called clear on his heels and the rigs sped off. Thunder strode into the woods without waiting. The other two battle suits followed, crashing through the underbrush without slowing.

"Make some noise. Get their attention." Heart ordered

"You got it!" Red Devil let out an ululating call.

Taking his comrade's cue, Jake started singing an SCA battle song. Heart belted out a simple three note call that she repeated. She added another series of seemingly nonsense syllables to. Jake stopped his song and let out a deep laugh. When she picked up the next verse, he joined in.

They emerged into a long clearing that ran parallel to the road and discovered their attempts to make themselves known had worked better than they had expected. Two men stumbled toward them, the larger of them carrying a third over his shoulder. The second man turned and pointed his rifle at something behind them. He fired then turned to catch up with the other. Heart turned Thunder and moved toward them, with Spartan and Red Devil flanking her.

The taller man staggered past the battle suits and dropped to one knee. Slightly behind Thunder, Jake could see that the bigger man's shoulder was covered in blood when he lowered the person he was carrying to the ground. Probably Bill Senior he guessed, from the amount of silver in the hair that stuck out from beneath his Royals baseball cap.

Jake turned to focus on the far end of the clearing. He saw a pair of ragers emerge from the trees at a run. Both howled the deep roar of their kind, a sound he was getting all too used to hearing. He stepped forward and heard the hiss and thump of Thunder's stabilizers activating. Firing his own, he rolled his shoulders and brought his suit's arms up. His left fist closed and Spartan's claw responded, turning the three pronged "hand" into a solid ball of steel and bringing a thick, seven inch long metal spike attached to one of the claws around to point forward.

Thunder and Red Devil deployed their punch spikes as well, and set themselves to receive the incoming charge.

The first one barreled straight toward Thunder, the ground shaking with their combined tread. It drew out in front of the other, bellowing as it came. When it hit, it had a ten yard lead on the second rager. The fight was short. It slammed into Thunder and stopped in its tracks. The monster staggered back with blood pouring from rapidly closing wounds on its thick chest.

Even though Heart's suit had been rocked backwards, its operator was still unfazed. Even as the ORBS gyros corrected its stance, she brought up her right hand. Like Red Devil, her suit had been fitted with an M32 grenade launcher. When she pulled the trigger the six-shot weapon discharged an anti-personnel round, sending twenty buckshot pellets across the four feet between the barrel of the MGL and her attacker. The attack blew away everything from the neck up.

The second rager showed a much faster learning curve. It veered right, aiming for the gap between Red Devil and Thunder. With his battle suit unable to move and reset to handle the charge, Red Devil stuck his right arm out to the side and deployed the suit's pneumatic axe. The blade caught the rager across the bridge of the nose, shearing off the upper half of its skull. It ran a few more steps before it pitched forward and tumbled.

"That was easy." Red Devil intoned.

"That ain't all of them!" Heart shouted.

The other two turned to see two more ragers emerge from the trees. Then three more followed them. More and more stepped out of the brush, until ten stood at the far side of the clearing.

"Ya' had to say something." Jake quipped as the ragers approached more cautiously.

"He said three or four! Not ten or twelve." Red Devil protested.

Heart watched the massive zombies start to spread out. "Suck it up you two! Mister Howard, are you still with us?"

"Yes, ma'am! I can't leave my boy to these things. Carl... son you need to go."

"Negative! He can't outrun these things. If you want to survive, your best bet is to stay behind us. You hear me, Carl?"

"Yes, ma'am." Carl sounded weak.

Heart switched to radio communication. "Shoulder to shoulder, gentlemen!"

Jake disengaged his stabilizer spikes. "Old school."

"The oldest." Red Devil responded, a grin obvious in his voice.

They pivoted so that there was about a foot between the shoulders of their battle suits. The pilots reset the stabilizer spikes.

Heart barked orders. "Red, go with canister rounds if you're not there already. Spartan, stick with standard bolts. If you use them. We do not move from this spot while a single one of these bastards is still standing, you got that?"

"No retreat!" Red Devil snarled.

Jake nodded his head. "There is no try."

"Damn straight. We win or die. Bring it!" Heart roared.

The ragers circled for a few more moments. The largest raised its fists and gave a thundering bellow before charging at Red Devil. Jake found three closing in on him and waited until they were too close to dodge before he activated the new version of his sword blade. The brush hog blade had been long enough for two swords and Kim had added a new one to the left arm.

The pneumatic blades shot forward and caught the rager on the right in the throat, but the left hand blade went wide and tore a shallow cut in its target's shoulder. Jake opened the claw hand, which automatically retracted the blade. The returning edge made the cut deeper, opening the wound to the bone.

The beast's momentum brought it into reach of the claw. Jake closed his fist, puncturing the rager's cheek and left eye in a stainless steel grip. The third rager started pounding the cage with its ham-sized fists, but only succeeded in making a few dents in the spring steel structure. Jake silently thanked the engineers who figured out that by giving the cage more spring, it would absorb the shock of a blow better and disperse the impact before much damage could be done. Every punch made the cage flex as it also recoiled on the rubber shock cushions, reducing the rager's blows to a fraction of their effectiveness.

As the left hand rager struggled to pull the claws from its face and middle, one of the monsters beat against the cage. Jake glanced at the bolt gun's camera. Though it shook like crazy, he could see the eye of the one he'd speared through the throat. It made a good enough target. He pulled the trigger. There was a wet, meaty sound, and the left side of the armor stopped shaking. But where he'd solved one problem, it seemed the middle rager had figured out that brute force punching wasn't going to work. There was a screeching sound as Jake watched part of the cage peel back along the right side. Then a massive face appeared in the widening tear in the battle suit's armor.

Jake retracted the sword blade and fought to bring the right arm around, but the massive rager was deep inside its reach. With a growl, he let go of the arm's control stick and pulled the Glock 22 from his holster and brought it up toward the opening. The rager opened its mouth to utter another yell, but Jake shoved the gun between its teeth and pulled the trigger three times. Brass bounced inside the cage. Jake's ears rang from the shots going off in an enclosed space, but it wasn't enough to completely cover the choked sound the rager made as it went limp and slid down the front of the armor.

Jake relied on the internal safeties of the Glock as he tucked it into the front of his assault vest and grabbed the right hand control stick. The rager he'd grabbed was still struggling with the left hand claw, but like its leader it had decided to try whatever was attached to the claw. The outer armor buckled under the thing's grip, then it got a fingerhold on the edge and started trying to pry the vambrace off.

"Not today, you son of a bitch!" Jake jabbed the thicker blade under the bolt gun into the rager's side. He extended the sword blade as well. Four feet of spring steel punched through the rager's ribcage and the point ended up sticking out the other side of its body. Blood burbled through the claw as the undead giant brayed its anger.

"Shut," Jake yelled at the creature as he locked the right arm. "The Hell," he continued as one eye glared at him over the claw. "Up!" he concluded as he pulled back hard with the left arm.

As the front of the thing's head came away in the claw, Jake felt his stomach revolt. He opened the claw and shook his hand to dislodge the gory product of his improvised move. When he retracted the sword blade, the rager dropped like a sack of potatoes. A gunshot sounded from behind him and he saw blood spray off to his right. To his left, a rager fell with the left side of its head blown away. He heard Red Devil's pneumatic axe activate behind him.

Silence fell for a moment punctuated by long, labored breaths and the low moan of one of the men inside the protective triangle.

Jake looked around. "Clear on my side."

Red Devil and Heart echoed him. He released his stabilizer spikes. When he turned around, he found himself witnessing a gut-wrenching moment. The man Bill Senior had been carrying was missing his right arm below the elbow. Someone had made a tourniquet with a belt and a thick stick, but it was only delaying the inevitable. Already, the flesh surrounding the stump was red and inflamed.

"Devil, you're on overwatch." Heart opened the cage on Thunder. "Call the rigs, have them come back to where they dropped us off."

Jake opened his armor up and stepped down, joining Sergeant Heart as she knelt by the younger Howard.

The younger man looked up at his father. "It's okay, Dad. I know what's up."

The older man's eyes were red, and his cheeks were wet. He shook his head as his lip trembled. "Son, I'm sorry. I should've been there faster, but I didn't know you were out there... I didn't know—" His face contorted with grief and he let out a choked sob. Jake and Heart shared a quick look, and both were surprised at the sadness they saw in the other's eyes.

Heart placed a hand on the old man's shoulder. "Mister Howard, There's nothing we can do. Once the tourniquet is released—"

"Some of them don't change, right?" Bill Senior asked, his voice breaking.

Heart shrugged. "Very few. One in maybe a thousand? I don't know exactly. I've only ever heard of one. He was never the same."

"But...there's a chance..."

"No, Dad. Please, no. You know what they said at church about people who get infected. That they don't have a soul anymore. I'd rather die good with God than lose my soul."

"No, Billy. We've done lost your sister. I can't lose you, too."

"If I turn, it won't be me anymore, Dad. I don't want to do that. I don't want to be that. Just give me your pistol and walk away."

"Suicides go to Hell, Billy!" the youngest man's face was wet with tears, and his voice wavered as bad as his father's did when he spoke.

Jake gritted his teeth. "I'll take care of it."

Billy looked him in the eye and nodded. Sergeant Heart put

her arm around Bill's shoulders and turned him away. Carl glared at Jake and leaned closer.

"How long would it be once you let the tourniquet go?" Billy asked once they were alone in the clearing.

"A few hours. Most of the massive changes would happen near the end. It... it'd hurt a lot."

He looked up at Jake and smiled, then grabbed his hand as he pulled the Glock. "Then I guess you ought to do it fast. You know you don't have to put your soul on the line for me like this, right?"

"I figure I'm about as damned as anyone."

Billy smiled and pulled the pistol down so it was under his chin. The young man offered Jake a calm smile.

"I'll put in a good word for you with God when I see Him."

Jake clenched his jaw and pulled the trigger. "I'd appreciate that."

Heart approached Spartan's rig. "Never figured you for a sci-fi geek."

Jake had the Glock disassembled, the pieces laid out precisely on a small folding table. He looked up at her as he ran a swab through the barrel. "What with me being a construction worker and all. Guess I could say the same."

"What with me being a girl and all?"

"Nah, it's just the way you're... well, you. It's like you were born wearing sergeant's stripes or something."

"News flash for you, I used to be a cosplayer. Serious fangirl."

"Is that how you knew the fight song from the first episode of *The Lexx*?"

"Yeah, it was playing in one of the video rooms at the last con I went to. It's one of the last good memories I have before things went all Armageddon. So, what about you?"

"It was like required reading in the shire I was part of in Ansteorra. *Monty Python, Doctor Who, The Lexx, Red Dwarf*, and *Blake's Seven*. If fighter practice got rained out, or sometimes we'd just get together over the weekends and watch DVDs."

"Maybe that's where it comes from."

"Where what comes from?" Jake asked as he began reassembling the pistol.

"Doing the right thing. Even when it's hard."

"Is that what I did today?"

"Yeah, you did the only thing that *could* be done for that kid. Don't you ever doubt that."

"Is that an order?"

"Do I need to make it one?"

Jake shook his head. "I just needed to be sure who was doing the talking."

"You see any stripes on my sleeve, Carter? No, ya' don't. Just one trooper to another."

"Yes, ma'am."

"What did I tell you about calling me 'ma'am'?"

"I don't call my sergeant ma'am. But my momma raised me to treat a lady with respect. I hope you don't mind."

Heart smiled at that and nodded. "That I'll let you get away with."

"And before him shall be gathered all nations: and he shall separate them one from another, as a shepherd divideth his sheep"

-Mathew 25:32

The best part about operating on ferals was that they almost always survived. As Doctor Martin Kilgore straightened from his latest acquisition, he weighed the added benefit of an un-complaining patient against the near perfect survival rate. The feral on the table stared up at the ceiling, its eyes fixed on some unknown point. The control module had long been in place; to-day's modifications were purely for convenience. He lifted the right arm and inspected the stump where he'd fitted a pry bar. The flesh was already healing around it, attempting to grow a new limb in place of the hand he'd removed.

"The secret is in the bones, you see," he said aloud. "By iso-lating the end of the bone from the blood, I can keep the muscle tissue from growing back. It has no attachment points and the bone itself cannot regenerate either. Add in the insulated inser-tion point for the prosthetic and you have a combination pry bar and stun gun."

"You know I could care less about all this science shit," his audience dryly stated. Kilgore turned and held one hand up, his fingers and thumb brought together over his palm.

"Couldn't care less, Miss Argent... The correct term is *couldn't* care less. As in it is not possible for you to have less care than you currently do... er, don't. You know what I mean."

"Yeah, I don't give a fuck, and it isn't possible for me to give *less* of a fuck about all the science shit."

The obnoxious woman wore black from neck to toe, with a pistol holstered on her right leg and under her left arm. A pair of knives rode on her left hip and the handle of one was visible at the top of her right boot. Kilgore had stopped speculating whether he'd seen all of the weapons she carried or not. The second most important thing about Patricia Argent was that she used her weapons well. Far more crucial was that she used them for *him*.

The lesson in semantics was interrupted by an alarm from one of the computers he'd set up. He rushed to it, his brow furrowed. "That is *not* a good sound."

"I'll say," Miss Argent agreed. "Sounds like a cop car humping a tornado siren."

"Colorful comparison, but hardly apropos. It is the cause for this particular alarm that should make you worried."

"Yeah?"

"Yes," Kilgore shot back. "It's the failure alarm for the control module... rather, the feedback from their nervous systems indicate that they are not consistent with the commands issued by the control module. In particular, it is the failure alarm for the larger of the infected. What we've heard referred to as 'ragers' and hulks."

"You've lost control of one of those big fuckers?" Argent looked around nervously.

"Three or four, to be exact."

Another alarm went off and the only rager still in the building stirred from its dormant state. "Make that five."

His voice was calm and his pulse unchanged as he watched the beast stir. The restraints he'd made would hold even the largest of the raging beasts. This one only seemed intent on being elsewhere. If a dormant subject was no longer under his control, then someone was actively overriding his commands. He meant to find out who it was.

"You want me to do the brain splatter thing with him?"

He shook his head, his hand hovering over the release button. "No, Miss Argent. I'd prefer that you arm yourself with the tranquilizer rifle and prepare to follow this one to the source."

She bounded over to the makeshift armory she'd set up and grabbed the large rifle. "Okay, I'm good."

"Excellent! And Miss Argent... good hunting." His hand fell on the release button.

She had sent him north, because the voice told her to. Integrity had sisters to the north. Little sister? Sisters that weren't as strong as she was. Funny how he could remember her name, but not his. She had written it down once, but he could no longer make sense of the marks on the scrap of cloth.

C O R E Y. He had no idea what it stood for, but sometimes he could look at it and remember that he was Corey. He smiled as memory returned. For a moment, he was a little bit himself again. He had to find Integrity's little sisters. She had put a special mark on him so that they would know she had sent him. But first... someone had been playing with Corey's little brothers.

He sat holding the limp body of the little brother he'd found. Someone had stuck metal into him and when Corey had pulled it out, he'd stopped being alive. He knew he shouldn't do that again. But they all listened to him, even if it was a little harder sometimes to reach them and get them to do what he wanted.

Integrity would understand. The other brothers all had the metal on their heads, too. They didn't like it. It hurt all the time. He looked up as two more joined him. One hand no hands. Instead, someone had put a big knife on one arm and a big hammer on the other. They also had bolted steel plates over its chest and back. The other had large baskets wired onto its back and metal plates with rings attached to them. A fourth brother was on his way, but the fifth he hadn't felt move.

He closed his eyes and concentrated on the fifth one. He felt it coming closer. There were others farther away and they were coming, too. But the important ones, the ones who had the metal in their heads, he had to help them. The voice told Integrity that he had to bring them to her, but his own voice said he had to help them. His own voice told him to break whoever had put the metal in their heads.

He looked west, but the fifth one wasn't coming from there. There were people to the west. People in black, like the ones Integrity hated. He didn't know why she hated them. Or if he had known, he'd long forgotten. Just like he'd forgotten what C O R E Y on the cloth he held meant. He just knew it was important. But like she had told him... was it Integrity? Someone had told him if the ZOD people saw more and more of his kind, they would call more to come help them.

For some reason he remembered that might be bad. But they were small and weak. He had more of his little brothers coming and his friend the bull. He would kill them all, he knew.

McCarran Airport, Nevada.

Integrity frowned. This group of humans had resisted and they had survived. From what she knew of them, they should have been at each other's throats. Military, law enforcement officers, common citizens, and criminals all stood on the other side of the hastily built wall. They had repulsed the first wave of her horde with gunfire, shields, and blades when it came to it. They had fought, bled, and died shoulder to shoulder... when they would have turned on each other months ago. It was their nature. The humans around her had turned on her. People she had mistakenly called friends had been ready to kill her because of what she was, what she had become.

She paced along the concrete, her rifle in hand. Behind her, more ragers and more ferals were joining her army. She remembered how mortals would band together against a common enemy. That made sense. If she had come upon them in disarray and seen them find common cause against her in their dying hours, the world would have been right. Movement on the wall caught her eye and she brought the rifle up by reflex. Her finger stroked the trigger a microsecond later. Her target had been spotted, range and wind compensated for and her aim point moved appropriately in the time it would have taken a mortal's reflexes to respond. A spray of red followed the kick of the rifle butt against her shoulder. The report echoed back across the quarter mile of open space. Bullets hummed past her, a few chipped concrete nearby. Then she heard the whistling of an incoming mortar round. It detonated only a few yards short of her. She turned and walked away at a diagonal as another round was launched.

Her thoughts returned to the oddities of this group of humans. Unlike the two small groups she had destroyed on the way here, this band had been united before she arrived. With no common enemy to make them set aside the petty differences that they held so dear, they had still managed to fortify the airport with a solid wall of rubble all the way around and created a coherent fighting force. They should have been fighting for dominance like half of the other groups of survivors she'd seen. So what had united them?

At the edge of her senses, she felt something. Something familiar, but still new. She looked to the west. A dust cloud rose in the sky, far too large and far too fast to be from the shuffle of feet. Her brow furrowed further, even as she felt bits of shrapnel from the next mortar round hit her arm and back. She walked toward the newcomers. Her army followed.

Half a mile later, she stopped and surveyed the approaching convoy. Vehicles in tan and green rumbled toward her. Her scrutiny fell on the lead vehicle. She saw the one she had felt. Her eyes glowed just as Integrity's did, but no army of zombies followed her.

No, she is not of the Fold, my daughter. You will not find an ally here.

It was one of the few times she had felt or heard any kind of strong emotion from the Voice. With a thought and a gesture, she sent the horde at the convoy.

Combat was joined, but the lead Humvee still kept coming. It was untouched by Integrity's horde. Soon it pulled to a stop a few yards away from her. Close enough that she could both see and smell the mortal driver's fear.

The woman in the cupola climbed up and stood on the hood, her eyes glowing a familiar red. "Resist, sister."

Before she had been chosen she would have been a middle aged woman, with pale blonde hair. She wore the digital camouflage of an Army uniform like she'd been born to it. The handle of a sword jutted above her shoulder, looking much larger than a woman of her size should have been able to carry.

"I am Integrity," she said, ignoring the woman's first statement. "Nephilim of War."

The strange Nephilim smiled. "Lydia Black, founder of the Federation of Allied Communities. Integrity, eh? Either your parents saddled you with a bitch of a name, or you did that to yourself."

"What are you? I feel you, but you're different, you're not... whole."

Lydia moved closer to the other woman. "I'm whole. I'm just not wearing the same yoke around my neck that you are. I didn't blindly follow some voice in my head. I didn't turn on my own kind."

Integrity gestured at the humans behind Lydia and peeled her lips back from her teeth. "They aren't your kind! They'll turn on you faster than they'll turn on their own treacherous race."

Integrity turned as a mortar shell fell among her gathered horde, scattering body parts all over the rocky ground. One of the tracked vehicles stopped and turned its turret on a group of her ragers that was running toward it. Its main gun fired. The impacts blew each of the charging beasts apart, one round at a time. As her rager charge was blasted apart, another group of vehicles pulled up beside the tracked vehicles. The machine guns mounted on top of them opened up with short, but hellishly precise bursts that tore through the mass of ferals just below neck level. Integrity could hear the bullets hiss past her.

Lydia smiled at the frown on Integrity's face. "Electronic aiming systems, sister. Even the ragers, can't tear up an Abrams. They might have some luck with the Strykers, but they'll never get close enough. You're not going to win here, Integrity. Not against armored cavalry."

"Why are you doing this?" Why turn on your own kind like this?"

Before she was able to register the movement, she had been

hit. She was up on her feet in an instant, but not before her attacker was there again. She barely ducked under the next punch and ended up dodging right into the uppercut that it had been setting up. She flew back again, this time landing on her back. The scream of her foe was all the warning she had before Lydia's fist hammered into her chest, catching her on the bounce and making the crater she'd made when she landed a tiny bit deeper.

"THEY are my kind!" Lydia roared. "They're YOUR kind, too! We were born human and I chose to hang on to my humanity." Another punch fell, and Integrity felt bones crack under the impact.

"We're more than they are now," Integrity snarled as she caught the next punch and kicked up with her right foot. Lydia went flying and Integrity flowed to her feet, leaping after her. She realized her mistake in midair, as Lydia's leg snapped out and the kick threw her back the way she'd come from. She didn't know where the second kick came from, or the third, but the fourth carried them both clear of the fight.

"How did you do that?" she gasped through gritted teeth. "I am the Nephilim of War."

"I am also an aspect of War, sister," Lydia hissed as she grabbed Integrity by one arm and yanked her to her feet. "And I held on to my free will. I'll always kick your ass up close like this." Her fist blurred again and the scenery changed instantly. When the white cleared from her vision, she found herself back where she'd started. Her rifle was only a few feet away. She scrambled for it.

She heard Lydia's voice behind her. "Look around you, Integrity! I made something that's going to last. You can't say the same. All you've done... is what you're told. That's a half-assed way for someone like us to live."

When she turned to aim the rifle at Lydia, the barrel pointed toward more desert scrub and rocks. The gunfire continued unabated. She felt her force shrinking too fast under withering gunfire from both sides.

"Serving humans is no way to live!"

She pulled her minions away from the humans. As her force disengaged, the firing stopped where they broke contact. The humans were weak to show mercy. But as she pulled her force from the field, another question occurred to her.

Who do I serve?

The horde fled to the east, Integrity's rage held in check by sheer strength of will. More gunfire sounded behind them and she felt more of the horde fade from her awareness. She stumbled as a new sensation flooded through her. She staggered as a wave of dizziness washed through her. Her vision greyed for a moment.

Corey! Her intuition served where knowledge failed.

She reached for the place where he usually was, but felt only a vague sensation of his presence. She called out to him again, but felt only a slight stirring in response. She screamed her rage and frustration as she got back to her feet and began running again.

You must go north and east, daughter. There is an abomination that must be destroyed in the place called Sioux City.

Integrity snarled. "I failed!"

You did not fail me. You were betrayed, as I was. Go, help him.

Dawn never came. The clock said it was nine AM, but the sky was still almost as dark as if it was midnight. Jake stepped out of the camper and looked up at the slowly graying sky. Lightning streaked along the bottom of the low clouds, illuminating the first bits of ash as it fell. Thick spinning flakes showed up black against the briefly lit sky. The first hit Jake's outstretched hand with a noticeable impact. The tiny granules were warm against his skin, almost uncomfortably so. He shook his hand and a small puff of fine grit erupted.

More bits of ash hit him. "This shits' gonna get in every goddamn thing."

One place he didn't want it was in his lungs. He reached into his assault vest and pulled out the large square of folded cloth he carried in his inner vest pocket, next to his personal first aid kit. The shemagh unfolded with a flick of his wrist. He wrapped it around his head and face the way Bowman had showed him. When he was done only his eyes showed. He slipped on the yellow lensed shooting glasses to protect his vision.

In the distance lightning streaked between sky and ground. The rumble of thunder reached his ears all too soon. Another strike and another too rapid rumble of thunder came. If the ash was problematic getting struck by lightning was an order of magnitude worse. That idea was suddenly not appearing nearly as improbable. Jake scampered to the dubious safety of the command bus.

Paul looked him up and down as he entered. "A bit rattled?"

"A little. I prefer to think of it as having good survival instincts, though."

"All the same thing, lad. Though not the usual for an ORBS pilot."

"Ragers I can handle."

Paul could hear no bravado in the words, just the confidence of a man who believed what he'd just said with the utter conviction of one who had done exactly that.

"But even a Titan is no match for a lightning bolt. I don't fuck with the forces of Nature."

"Wiser words have never been spoken, but we've other things to concern ourselves with. Make yourself comfortable until the others arrive; there is coffee in the urn over there and you'll find a bit of breakfast in the mess tins on the table."

The coffee was hot and fresh. The "bit of breakfast" turned out to be steak, scrambled eggs, seasoned potatoes, and thick toast. Jake dug in and tried to ignore the 'last meal of the condemned' vibe he was getting. The rest of the ORBS pilots and squad leaders showed up over the next few minutes, all of them looking a little off balance.

Fipps sat down to his meal with a smile. "Looks like the Orrins made good on those cattle they said they'd send."

Bowman nodded. "Fresh food is the one thing these folks have plenty of."

"For now!" Heart grunted.

"If they listen to us, it'll stay that way." Red Devil grumbled through a mouth full of eggs.

Jake glanced at the big man. "I think they will, Red. And could you please tell me your name?

Sergeant Heart abruptly changed the subject. "So, Paul... I

think we're wondering why you've gathered us all here together."

"Have you figured out who the killer is yet?" Jimmy leaned in eagerly. The joke drew nervous laughter from the squad leaders, but it also discharged a lot of the tension in the air.

"Well, seeing as how there isn't a Great Dane and a group of meddling kids around, we can safely assume it isn't Old Man Jackson in a rubber monster outfit. No, I'm afraid the real culprit is far more disturbing than that. Last night, we received a transmission from a ZOD contingent in South Dakota. They've made contact with a group calling themselves the Freemen and apparently only just in time. They've encountered something new, some sort of... mechanically augmented rager. Some of the augmentations are making them harder to kill. They've requested that we come as soon as we're able. I've considered our larger mission and I feel this has taken precedence over any other consideration. If someone has devised a means to weaponize the infected... we must destroy it."

Jake moaned. "So, we're the only ship in the quadrant?"

"For what they seem to be dealing with, Mister Carter, we're the only ship that exists. Cliché aside, our battle suits are currently the most effective weapon in dealing with *any* feral threat that may arise. And with the eruption... no, I daresay the *super*-eruption of the Yellowstone caldera, we have become the preeminent force this side of the Rocky Mountains in that endeavor."

Bowman tapped the table with his index finger. "This sheriff's got tanks. Well, he's got one tank and a couple of Bradleys."

Paul shrugged. "And he used to have three Bradley Fighting Vehicles. A rager got in close to one and tore the hatches open. The crew didn't survive. Armored vehicles are designed for fighting at a distance. The ORBS were created with victory in hand to hand combat with a rager in mind. For the moment, the threat of the infected appears to be contained in this area. We've educated enough of the local populace to ensure that the knowledge needed to survive the coming changes to the climate can be passed on. We will depart in two days."

Bowman stared at Paul for a few seconds. "If you're right and Sheriff Holder thinks the same way, he's not gonna like us pulling up and moving out."

Paul looked to his sergeants, who both nodded in agreement. "We may have been all too effective in convincing him of that, I'm afraid. We may encounter some resistance to our leave-taking."

Red Devil let out a low whistle. "If he does try to stop us by force then you can bet he's going to fight from a distance and with as overwhelming a number up close as he can."

Fipps set his fork down. "We have to handle this peacefully if at all possible. If we're about to head into a fight with some kind of robo-ragers, we can't afford to lose any of our fighting capability."

Paul nodded his agreement. "And every ally we can claim will be vital."

"Hearts and minds," Bowman added. "Hearts and minds."

Heart looked thoughtful for a moment. "Yeah. That's what we need. Bowman, Sams, you two come with me. I think I know what we need to do. Give us twenty four hours."

She exited the bus with the two ORBS drivers, leaving a group of blinking squad leaders in her wake. Those left behind wondering what had just happened.

The next morning Paul, Fipps, and a trooper sergeant named Quillen were on the front steps of the Knox County courthouse. The pale circle of the sun was clearing the trees and turning the black skies a slightly lighter shade of slate when a trooper trotted up with a piece of paper in hand. Paul took the sheet when it was offered to him. He nodded and scribbled something on it before handing it back to the trooper. The morning light illuminated the two guards on duty at the courthouse doors. One was in a deputy's uniform and the other in Army issue digital camouflage.

"Sergeant Heart sends word that we should proceed."

Quillen nodded and approached the two guards. After a brief verbal exchange one of them stuck his head inside the door for a moment, then returned to his post. A few minutes later Sheriff Holder stepped out. His uniform looking neat as always. A pair of deputies and a pair of soldiers flanked him, but stood a respectful distance back. All of them carried long arms which were pointed down and away from possible targets.

"Gentlemen, it's a bit early."

Paul took a step forward. "We do apologize for the hour, Sheriff. But there is some urgency to the issue. We've received word that some of our colleagues need our help. We'll be breaking camp in the morning. We wanted to give you what notice we could before we left and tie up any loose ends before we did."

Holder's mouth turned down at that. He stood there silently for a moment. "Well, I can't say that's news I'm glad to hear. Anything I can do to convince you all to stay?"

"Unfortunately, no."

Paul looked to Fipps and raised an eyebrow in query. Fipps just shrugged. He and Alexa had worked together long enough that he knew it was better to trust her play than to go off script. "From the beginning, Sheriff Holder, we let you know our stay was intended to be temporary."

"Well, I can't say I'm willing to just let you go either."

Holder motioned at the deputies behind him and their gun barrels came up. They were still not pointed directly at anyone, but not by much. Paul tensed as the expected confrontation started to play out, unsure of how to proceed.

At the sound of car engines, all eyes turned to the road and Scout Two as it led a line of black cars toward them.

"What in the Hell?" Holder glared at Paul.

"I believe an answer will be forthcoming."

Holder's expression sharpened as the other man appeared to relax, sensing that the situation had just changed somehow. As the tall woman got out of the car, she was joined by two of the other battle suit pilots. Holder looked them over carefully. He noted that the one wore his hair cropped short, just like his military contingent. The other was tall and lanky, with properly blond hair. All three of them carried a hand crate that clattered and clanked with each step. The black cars all bore county plates, each one familiar to Holder. After all, he had given them as symbols of status within the county government. The men who got out of them were just as familiar to him as the cars. Each was the mayor of one of the towns in Knox County. At the moment, none of them looked particularly happy.

"Y'all look kinda tense," the lanky one said as he set his crate down. The other two followed suit, and the man with the military cut stepped back with the lanky kid. The woman stayed where she was, her face set in a rather pleasing smile. If he'd seen that smile at any other point, he might have tried to see if things could get more personal between them. As it was, he felt the corners of his mouth lift a bit in spite of himself.

The woman's voice was almost pleasant as she spoke. "Sheriff, I'm guessing you're not happy to see us leave."

Her name came to him from several days before, when she'd introduced herself. "Miss Heart. I'd rather not have you go and take your battle suits with you, no. Knox County is safer than it's been in a long time, thanks to you. It's my thinking that it should stay that way."

Paul smiled. "And it can. ZOD is more than willing to offer you help whenever you need it, as allies. But you must realize that we are only one small part of ZOD. If we do not show up when expected, eventually, someone will come looking. And then, the safety of Knox County will be in serious jeopardy."

"Is that a threat?"

"That depends." Heart's face held a feral smile.

"On what?"

"On if you let us go about our business and how good your people are at jigsaw puzzles. Those battle suits go through parts like crazy in a fight and they take a lot of skilled maintenance just to keep them running. Those boxes there... that's equal to what we've had to replace since we left from Springfield. Here's what your mayors asked for in return for them."

She pulled a sheet of paper from her breast pocket and handed it to the Sheriff. His eyes went wide as he read the list. A slow creep of red rose from his neck to his cheeks.

"That's... exorbitant!"

"I'll admit I might not have gotten the best bargain, but you get the point. You want to take our battle suits; you're in for a fight. If you want to *keep* our battle suits; you're in for a lot more work than you bargained for. But if everyone stays on each other's good side, then you can call us when you need us. We'll handle the busy work and the spare parts."

Holder looked over her shoulder before he fixed her with a

pointed stare. "And I won't have to deal with a group of pissed off politicians. Well done Heart, well done."

"I don't like backing a man into a corner, but I really hate seeing men and women get killed for stupid shit."

Holder glared at her for a moment, then nodded. "I think we've got enough enemies, but a man can never have enough friends. I get the feeling ZOD makes a good friend."

He looked back at the men behind him and nodded toward the door. They turned and headed inside as the group of mayors approached.

"You need help with them?" Heart asked with a glance over her shoulder.

"No, I can handle them. Best you folks get on the road, though. Before you make my day any more difficult."

The sky flashed and thunder rumbled a couple of heartbeats later. Paul looked at the sky. "Looks like we'll be wanting to get ahead of this storm."

"If we can," Fipps said with a glance upward before he turned to the rest of the ZOD members. "Mount up!"

"And they rose up betimes in the morning, and sware one to another."

-Genesis 26:31

Doctor Kilgore looked down at the massive specimen that lay on his table. The surgery had been necessarily quick, but by now he'd had enough experience operating on the things to be both good and fast. This one had been an especial risk with his ability to influence others, but the right combination of sedatives had kept him truly unconscious. As far as Kilgore had been able to discern, none of the infected could regenerate brain tissue. So his sedatives had all targeted the brain functions alone. Now his latest and currently greatest achievement stared up blankly at him. The thing's mouth worked. It seemed to struggle for a word. A sound emerged from the depths of his throat.

"Ssssaa..." it moaned.

"Fascinating! Look at those brainwave patterns, Miss Argent. It's accessing memories and speech patterns!"

"I'm enthralled. What's it mean?"

"It means that where the bulk of these creatures have a cognitive level that borders on being sub-sentient, this one has the cognitive capabilities over a three to four year old. Now granted, I expect those capabilities to degrade as time goes on. Eventually, he'll be as dumb as the rest of them. But until then, I'll have to suppress those thoughts. However, the speech capability... there is something I can do with that. I'll be needing a speaker and a receiver, Miss Argent."

"What are you going to do, turn him into a big walking radio?"

Used to being ordered about, she grabbed the parts he needed and flung them down on the table next to him, a reminder to him that being used to something didn't mean she liked it. Like most social cues, he was oblivious.

"Hmmm...after a fashion."

He bent over the MRI image of the nine foot tall thing's head. "See these readings here in the frontal lobe? Those are on no frequency generated by the human or zombie brain. In effect, these speak to me of something—"

He left the sentence trailing and pulled his gloves off as he wandered over to a file cabinet. For long moments, he rummaged through pages until he pulled out a sheaf yellowed pages. After a minute of sorting through them, he pulled one out and stared at it intently.

He looked up at Miss Argent. "As I suspected. The frontal lobe... there it is. I know that look. What does it mean? It means that someone has already been using this thing as a... I believe the term you used was a 'big walking radio'? And if I can duplicate these frequencies—" he trailed off as he put a new pair of gloves on.

"Then what?"

"My dear, the frontal lobe is where we've always... well, I have always suspected the more esoteric mental powers like telepathy were to be found. If I can duplicate these frequencies, I will be able to do what he did. I will be able to control the infected without needing an interface and I'll be able to do so from a distance."

Argent smiled, but it was a weak thing, easily dispelled by the doubts that suddenly scampered through her head.

The Spider Queen's home was visible from several miles away, the thick threads of her servant's connecting the broken frames of the towers that once stretched across the skyline of Kansas City. Black spots moved across the gossamer looking tapestries of white, her children seeing to the unending task of weaving her web. As Integrity drew closer, she felt the Spider Queen's presence. Whoever she had been before was lost in her new life. Her old name was long forgotten, even her thoughts alien to her once human mind. Integrity sensed her fellow Nephilim's reaction to her presence and smiled. Finally, something seemed to be as it should. Of course, that didn't mean this would be easy. It rarely was with the strong ones.

The sun was setting behind her as she approached the building that she sensed housed the Spider Queen. In truth it was not one building, but two where her webbed palace was suspended between two buildings in downtown Kansas City's ruins. Of course, she had not forgotten that the ground was there. She had decorated the approach to her home with the desiccated bodies of her hatchlings' hosts. The chests and abdomens were riddled with fist sized eruption points, their faces set in the final moments of terror and agony. All around was the hiss of claws on silk and mandibles clacking together.

A pair of pony-sized spiders scuttled toward her and her temper flared. She felt the power within her rise and saw her skin start to glow bright enough that it registered even in the afternoon sunlight. The massive arachnids scuttled back, turning their eyes away from her as she walked between them.

"Tell your Queen she is summoned."

A ripple spread through the gathered creatures. They backed even further away from a spot in front of her. Instinct made her look up. A small figure hurled itself from the edge of the web overhead. It floated down, apparently unconcerned with minor things like gravity. It came close enough to make out a human form. Then it inverted itself and swung down, suspended by a thin strand of web that emerged from its abdomen.

"Who summons the Spider Queen?"

The spiders undulated in response to the fury in her voice. As she came lower, Integrity could see that her form had begun to fit her nature. Glowing white compound eyes now filled the orbs where her human eyes would once have been. Thick mandibles ran alongside her cheeks. An extra pair of chitinous limbs emerged from her back. The lower set gripped the strand of silk she had descended upon with delicate looking pincers, while the upper set seemed to grope toward Integrity, weaving a pattern that suggested a desire to rend the flesh from her bones.

"That which is greater than you or me. You have heard the call."

"It said to wait, so I did."

"I was what you waited for. The time for waiting is done. It's time to move now."

"We go to the north." The Spider Queen murmured, not quite a statement and not far from a question.

"We go north. We are needed."

The hiss and clatter stopped for a heartbeat. The webs became a flurry of movement. In moments thousands of spiders covered the walls of the buildings, flowing north. Integrity allowed herself a smile as she watched an army appear from nothing, its ranks swelling with every passing second.

For a passing moment, doubt shadowed her thoughts. She shook the feeling away. She would be victorious with this army at her back. Once she had released Corey, her army would swell to even greater numbers. She would finally wipe the world clean of the human pestilence.

Her eyes sought the shadowed recesses of the buildings around her, but she dismissed the few remaining shreds of fear that they evoked. The darkness held no terrors for her now.

In one of those shadows, something stirred. The something looked up from the eyepiece of the long scope mounted on an improbably large rifle. Almost five feet long, the rifle was chambered in .50 caliber and its current user had used it to put rounds in targets over a mile away. The Nephilim was just within that range, but her fate wasn't to die today. Nor was it the Spider Queen's. No, her fate was for a different field, a different day.

In the gloom it rose, glowing crimson. Although man shaped and man sized, it was definitely not a man. Even it didn't know exactly what it was. All it knew was that soon enough, the Spider Queen would die by its hand.

Red Devil cursed as his suit sparked and went dead. Nearby, Spartan lumbered toward him. Its right side scored and blackened, sparks flying from its weapons pod. The rager he had been fighting stumbled back, its own skin blackened along its right arm. It looked down at the smoking stump of its left hand for a moment before Spartan's massive main sword blade sliced through its cranium.

"Red, are you okay?" Carter's voice barely penetrated the ringing in his ears. "Red! Talk to me, man!"

Spartan engaged another rager, driving the shorter blade under the boltgun into its chest while it retracted the main sword on its left arm. The rager's fingers bent steel as it fought to free the blade. But with both hands focused on the sword, it didn't see the saw blade coming until it had sunk several inches into his skull. By then, all he was able to do was grunt in surprise and die. Two more ran forward, one engaging Spartan and the other going for the immobile battle suit. It gave the now familiar battle roar as it pulled its fist back to deliver the killing blow.

Even though the suit was inactive, the pilot wasn't. He reached over his head and found the pistol grip of his back-up weapon. He pulled it free of the spring-clips that held it in place. The Ithaca Stakeout shotgun dropped into place. He thrust it forward, through the wider mesh of his cage's navigation window. Instinct guided him more than anything when he pulled the trigger. When the smoke cleared, the rager's head was mostly gone on the right side.

Spartan turned away from the headless rager it had just decapitated and stomped his way toward the immobile battle suit. Red Devil hit the manual release on the cage and waited for it to lift clear.

"I'm fine!" A split second later, the world went white again.

When he could see again he was inside something metal and round on top. Slowly rivets and spot welds came into focus. He lifted his head experimentally. His head hurt and there were afterimages imprinted on the backs of his eyes that came into painful clarity when he blinked.

"Holy fuck, what was that?"

"Lightning," Jake's voice drifted across the aisle to him. "Striking the same place twice, evidently."

Across the aisle from him, the smaller pilot was removing a bandage from over his eyes with the help of a medic in white. Paul's soothing voice caused both men to turn. "Or close enough."

The lean Englishman was making his way to them with Fipps behind him.

Jake blinked a few more times. "What did happen?"

"The second lightning bolt struck Spartan, Mister Carter. Not the Red Devil suit."

"That much juice could've killed us," Red Devil muttered. "Stopped our hearts, fried our insides. How'd we not end up crispy critters?"

"Your suits metal construction acted as something of a Faraday cage for you. Luckily, that same effect protected the more sensitive electronics in the suit's interior."

"But my suit went black. Powered down completely."

Fipps stared at the smaller man. "That was your batteries getting fried and your servos, hydraulics systems and control systems, plus every wire outside the cage getting melted."

"That sounds like a bucket of suck!"

Fipps nodded his agreement. "Well, we're going to have to rewire both your suits and that's not easy."

Paul was not deterred. "Fortunately, the Ash Troopers helped build them so their knowledge of the systems is almost as extensive as mine. What we are going to need is a great deal of wire and electronic parts. Many of which can be found in most cars and buildings."

"That'll only help until the next time we get hit, and judging by what I'm hearing outside, that wouldn't be very long." As if to punctuate Jake's words, a clap of thunder rattled the bus's windows.

"Yes, there is that. We're not sure how long this is going to continue. Doctor Linh believes it may be temporary, a product of the extensive ash fall we're experiencing. In the meantime, we're looking at insulating the suits, which may help them handle more consecutive strikes."

Red Devil gave a low laugh at that, bringing Paul's attention to him. He raised an eyebrow and the big man looked away for a moment, chagrined by the mild rebuke he saw lurking there. "I was just glad no one wanted to put one of those stupid ass lightning rod things on our suits. Be my luck, I'd get a rooster or a cow or some stupid shit."

Jake chuckled at that. "Ain't gonna happen. Lightning rods have to be grounded, like buried in the dirt grounded. I don't think we'd go very far like that."

"Perhaps, though—" Paul said, stroking his chin for a moment. Then he looked up, as if remembering where he was. "I promise you, you won't have to wear a cow or a chicken, Mister Devil. Now, if you'll excuse me Sergeant Fipps here will fill you in on what is happening next."

Fipps smiled as he stepped forward. "Gentlemen, you're going on a scavenger hunt."

Red Devil rolled his eyes. "You've got to be kidding."

Two hours later found Red Devil crouched under an overpass with Jake next to him. The sky was flashing white and thunder was constant.

"Well, he wasn't kidding."

The Native American nodded. "Nope. I just don't remember any scavenger hunts where I had to dodge lightning bolts."

"Yeah, that does put us more on the wrong side of a whack-a-weasel game, doesn't it?"

A lightning bolt struck a building nearby, drowning out any response Red might have given. Another bolt struck the top of the overpass. The explosion of superheated air nearly overpowered the protection their ear plugs gave them.

"Shut up and go!" Red yelled over the next thunderclap. Both men sprinted across the open street. Their feet pounded hard against the ground. The weight of their packs lent force to their steps, but the thick layer of ash made their movement all but silent. A couple of hundred yards later found them pushing the door of a hardware store open to face a double handful of gun barrels.

"What a day! It's raining cats and dogs out there." The rest of the squad lowered their weapons.

Heart gritted her teeth. "You're killing me."

A row of kerosene lanterns on the nearby counter lit the room, and thick rolls of copper wire were stacked near the front door.

"I need you in the back, Carter, stripping wire from the offices. Red, grab computers, card readers, anything more complex than a calculator."

Jake headed for the back of the small hardware store with Red in tow. "So much for a long convalescence."

"That's because you volunteered us once they said we didn't have concussions."

"You would have done the same thing. You're just pissed I said it first."

"Fuck you."

Jake got to work on stripping out the wire from the lights and outlets. The drywall parted under his pry bar with relative ease. Between his strength and the ravages of time he had the conduit exposed in no time. As he tossed the last of the crumbling drywall debris aside, he looked at the outlet and cocked his head to the side. His plan had been to simply tear the conduit out of the wall until he got back to the main junction box, but the way the wires were connected gave him a different idea.

Several minutes later, he was at the main junction box with a screwdriver and a pair of wire cutters. Most of the connections he was able to loosen and straighten out. Those he couldn't prepare properly, he snipped free. Then he followed the lines to the outlets and switches. In a couple of hours, he was pulling the last of the copper wire he could reach free of the conduit.

"Hey, do you hear that?" Bowman asked as they finished coiling the salvaged wire.

Sams looked around. "I don't hear anything."

Red Devil looked up from his pile of electronics. "Yeah, no thunder."

"Maybe these lightning storms are just temporary. Either way, we still need to... well, so much for peace and quiet." Jake finished as thunder rumbled across the sky.

Heart hauled another load of tools to the pile. "Let's take advantage of the break, gentlemen."

After taking a moment to wipe sweat from her forehead, she went outside and pulled a flare gun from her pocket. She pointed it upward and pulled the trigger. The *pop* of the flare was followed by red light flickering into the sky.

Fipps barked orders as Heart headed back inside. "Okay,

boys. Lock and load. If there was anything unpleasant in this town we just told it where to find us."

Bowman grabbed his M4 carbine. "Time to break out the hardware, then."

Jimmy and Red Devil grabbed their carbines. Jake slung his shotgun on its one point sling. Heart closed the door behind her. "Jesus, that was fast. We've got forty or fifty people headed this way. And they don't look like the welcome wagon. Sticks, blades, rocks. I thought I saw a Molotov, too."

Bowman heft his weapon. "Can we fall back?"

"They're between us and the convoy. If we pull out, there's no way they can find us in time. We dig in here and we fight. Our evac should only be a few minutes behind them."

"Your mouth, God's ears."

Red Devil brought his M4 up to his shoulder. "In the meantime, it's time to open a can of whoop-ass!"

"And throw those boys an asskickin'!" Sams added with relish.

"And say macho things." Jake muttered.

That remark broke the tension and got a brief laugh. The enemy lumbered into sight. Dressed in ragged pants and shirts, the plentiful skin that the people did show was almost black with grime. Most carried dented aluminum baseball bats or machetes, with a few crude spears made from knife blades lashed to long sticks. They stopped when they saw the lantern light inside the store and formed a line. A few stepped forward carrying clear, rectangular riot shields and brandishing police batons. The shield carriers looked off to one side and grunted something, but the words were lost against the glass of the storefront. Whatever response they got was positive. A glass bottle trailing flame arced over the crowd and shattered against the glass.

"Carter, fire!" Fipps yelled.

Jake wasted no time in doing just that. He brought the shotgun up and pointed it roughly where he remembered one of the shield carriers had been. Glass shattered outward, sending flaming fragments in the faces of the charging mob along with eight double-aught pellets. The effect was similar to firing multiple nine millimeter bullets through the window, though most of the impacts were in a small area. One of the shield carriers went down along with a man standing beside him. The flaming glass fragments also gave them pause.

Jake pumped another round into the chamber. His next shot was aimed at the second shield man. He went down, his shield now scarred with multiple holes. A few of the ragged survivors batted out small fires on their clothes or skin. For a moment the mob stopped, unsure of what to do now that their distraction had been turned against them.

He pulled a couple of #4 buck shells from his sling and slid them into the tube. Smaller than the double-aught, they would send more than twenty pellets downrange. Jake began furiously inserting the fresh shells into his shotgun as the group outside milled about. "Reloading!"

One brawny man started to charge forward, a baseball bat raised over his head as he let out a yell. Bowman popped off two rounds. The man stumbled a few more steps then dropped like a puppet with the strings cut as two holes appeared in his chest.

The group surged forward at a full run. They let out an inarticulate battle cry as they closed the distance to the front of the store. One leaped through the shattered window. Another threw himself through the still intact one, sending thick pieces of glass flying at the defenders. The entire squad opened fire on them as they charged, but their rounds simply whined off of the heavy shields' front.

Their momentum brought them into the squad's midst. The ORBS pilots were forced to give ground to keep from being overrun. Jake fired at one directly in front of him. He watched as pellets scatter wildly. Red Devil stepped around to his right and put round after round into the people behind him. The big man had to duck when someone got around to his right and swung a machete at his head.

Jake pointed the shotgun at the ground just in front of the shield and pulled the trigger. The shot sent the second #4 buck shell's twenty one pellets under the bulletproof barrier and into the legs of the man carrying it... as well as into the legs of the people behind him. Four of the wild men went down with screams of agony, leaving those behind them exposed. Jake racked another round into the chamber as Red Devil started firing into the mob.

When the shotgun boomed again, two more joined the growing pile of wounded and dead on the floor. On his left, Sams took advantage of the breathing room to put a round into the other shield man's side. The man staggered and angled his shield a little before backing toward the broken windows. The rest of the wild men followed him, with one grabbing the fallen shield bearer's ankles and dragging him back. The downed shield carrier was dragged out, leaving the rest to live or die on their own.

Heart sized up their situation. "To the back door!"

Jake pulled two #4 shot rounds from his sling. He took a couple of the black shelled slugs from the ammo holder on the shotgun's stock as he walked backward, letting Sams guide him and Red Devil. Heart, Fipps, and Bowman joined them as they made it to the door. Heart put her hand to one ear and pressed the mic button on her radio.

"Say again, Heavy One?" Her face looked distant as she listened, then turned ashen.

Sams's stomach lurched when he saw Heart's face. "What's going on, Sarge?"

"The convoy can't get to us. The other teams ran into a horde. And about half of them broke off and started moving our way once they heard the gunfire."

She risked a look at the front of the store, noting that the wild men were starting to regroup. One had taken a green flak jacket from the fallen shield carrier and was putting it on. Others were milling behind the shields, brandishing weapons at the store and yelling.

"Okay, here's the plan. We're going to play decoy, draw these fuckers off from the wire and gear we salvaged then disengage. With any luck the horde will take them out for us."

Red Devil grunted. "Assuming we can stay ahead of them."

Fipps nodded toward the wildmen. "We're in better shape than they are. They won't be able to keep up for very long. Bowman, take Sams and check the alley."

"You got it."

He led the way out the back door with Sams on his heels. As they waited the crowd out front made to move forward, but when Jake put his shotgun to his shoulder even the men behind the shields hesitated.

"We're clear back here!"

"Okay, Carter, you have our six. The rest of you... go!"

The others filed past Jake, with Fipps and Red going last. As Fipps slipped through the door, the mob started to surge forward. Jake pulled the trigger. The gun kicked like a mule as it sent the heavy slug and three triple aught buck pellets toward one of the wild men with a shield. The shield barely slowed the main slug down as it tore through it. The flak jacket didn't help its wearer out, either. Jake saw blood spray against the clear window near the top of the shield, he momentarily gaped as the man behind the shield-bearer went down as well.

As if rendering their best defense useless was their cue, the rest surged forward. Jake racked the slide and fired again, but the hole appeared in one corner of the approaching shield nowhere near anything vital. He backed through the door to find Fipps waiting on the other side. The sergeant slammed the door shut and threw a wooden wedge down on the floor. Red Devil kicked it into place and then swung a small sledge to jam it further in.

"Gogogo!" Fipps pushed them through the small back room and out into the alley.

There was a heavy thump against the door behind them. Jake lifted his shotgun. The twelve gauge boomed followed by the sound of screams filling the air. In the distance they heard the roar of a rager followed by another rumble of thunder, this one louder than before. Heart and the rest were a few yards down the alley. They broke into a run when Fipps, Red Devil, and Jake started running their way.

They cleared the alley just as the wild men broke through the back door. The mob surged left toward them, away from the convoy. The wind started picking up as they ran down the street with the wild men slowly gaining ground. Heart pointed left. They ducked down a side street, but their pursuers were too close to lose them. They hit another street and broke into a sprint, hoping to open the distance between their pursuers and themselves. The wind buffeted them from the side as small ash cyclones started to swirl around them. Ahead of the group two of the little dust devils circled each other for a moment. They merged into a larger one. Another smaller whirlwind was sucked into the growing cyclone. The street began to fill with swirling ash. Heart skidded to a stop as the hungry wind spun in place for a moment then ripped a powerline free as it surged toward them.

"That's not good!" Heart headed left for the cover of a shop.

Jake, Red Devil, and Jimmy went to follow, but pulled up short as a motorcycle bounced end over end between them. Sams cried out in pain as something hit his leg. Red Devil grabbed the wounded Sams by one arm. Jake took the other as they bounded to the other side of the street. As they came close to one of the doors, Red Devil pulled the shorter Ithaca Stakeout shotgun from the scabbard on his back and pointed it at the lock. His gun boomed and the door bounced open. They dragged Jimmy inside seconds before the hellish wind caught them.

The bright flashes from inside the whirlwind caught them by surprise. Even as it illuminated the inside of the store, the flashes heralded tendrils of electricity. Jake leaned over near the windows and watched the filaments of electrical power arc out toward the wild men. They scampered for cover moments too late. Bodies were skewered by electrical bolts or picked up and flung around by the wind.

"God damn! What the hell's stuck in my leg?" Jimmy's voice was high and reedy with pain.

Jake pulled his flashlight from his vest and went to Red Devil's side. Under the light of the LEDs, Jake saw the lacquered end and the gold Chinese characters. He turned to Red Devil and tried to stifle a laugh.

"Well, I guess it could be worse."

"What the hell is it?"

"A chopstick. We're gonna have to immobilize it until we get you back to the convoy. Red, you're a better shot with an M4 than I am. I'll take care of the first aid part, if you want to keep an eye out."

Red nodded and dropped the magazine from his rifle and inserted a fresh one. He went to the window as Jake started to work Jimmy's leg. Outside, he could see the sparking cyclone growing in size as it made its way down the street. A few of the wild men crouched inside another store near the end of the block. He fought the temptation to shoot into the huddled group, knowing that he might make things even worse by doing so.

Jimmy grunted as Jake wrapped his leg. "You're gonna need some more of them slug rounds if we run into any of them ragers."

"I'm down to the two I have on the stock. So we're fine if we only run into a couple more, but I doubt they'll be that accommodating. Now be quiet, I'm trying to fix you up."

Jimmy pulled one of the rounds from the Mossberg's sling. "I gotta keep my mind on somethin' else. Keeps me from thinkin' 'bout bein' hurt, so I don't go into shock an' all."

Jake noticed his comrade's accent had gotten thicker. "Okay, this shouldn't take long."

Jimmy drew his combat knife from his vest and laid it against the side of the shell. "You bein' outta' slugs... that ain't no big deal. See, you make a cut, pretty much all the way around the shell about here, like this."

Jake stopped and turned his attention briefly to the shell Jimmy was holding out, noting the way the cut looked.

"When you shoot it, the front part comes off all of a piece, like a slug. Not somethin' I'd say you wanna' do a lot, but if you really *need* a slug it'll do the trick for ya." Jake had wrapped the leg enough to keep the sliver of wood from moving around, so he took the shell and tucked it into his vest before he pulled out his multi-tool.

At the window Red watched a horde of infected burst onto the street, right in the path of the cyclone. Most were swept up the moment they got into the impact zone, but the ragers stopped short. One of the eight foot tall behemoths was still sucked into the whirlwind and another fell victim to a discharge of electricity that left it a smoking, blackened husk.

The whirlwind started to narrow becoming more distinctly funnel shaped, even though it didn't quite reach the clouds overhead. The bursts of electrical discharges started coming faster and faster as the whirlwind sped up. With a brilliant flash of lightning, the mini-cyclone seemed to burst open with a boom of superheated air. When Red could see again the wild men were nowhere to be seen and the horde was picking itself up off the ground. One of the ragers had a burn across its chest that was rapidly healing. A few of the ferals were not moving at all any more.

As seconds passed, the horde started stalking down the street. Their heads were swiveling left and right, as if they were looking for the people they knew had been there not long before. Red moved back from the window and went to where Sams was propped up against a counter. Jake had finished wrapping the wound so the chopstick that had speared him in the leg wouldn't move. He had even shorn off all but a couple of inches of it to keep the end from catching on things and doing more damage to Jimmy's leg.

Red nudged Jake. "We gotta get out of sight. That horde's coming this way and if they see us—"

Jimmy needed no more encouragement. The two men helped him move around to the other side of the counter, where he wouldn't be seen from the front. "What are we gonna do if one of them pokes its head in here? If we shoot it that'll bring 'em all in here and if they see us, they'll bring the rest of 'em in on us anyway."

"I'll take care of it." Jake pulled his falchion from its sheathe to emphasize his point.

He looked over the counter. "We're in a camping store. I'm going to do some shopping. Can you reload the shotguns?"

Jimmy nodded and took the gun. Jake silently padded around the counter and disappeared into the depths of the shelves.

Long minutes passed as the tread of feet passed the store. Red used the curved fisheye mirror to watch the slow procession of ferals and ragers as they made their way down the street. The beasts were constantly looking, their heads occasionally cocked to one side as if listening. The interminable sound of footsteps was made worse by the soft moan some of them made as they went and the low rumble the ragers uttered. Finally their numbers began to thin and it looked like the horde would pass them by.

Just as Red was about to move, the door was pushed open. A rager ducked its head to pass through the doorway. Three ferals stepped in behind it and a second rager followed. The first rager moved toward the counter. The ferals headed toward the back of the store. The second rager stayed near the door, its head raised and nostrils flaring as it tested the air.

The first rager stopped in front of the counter and knelt

down. Red watched as it put one massive hand to the floor. When it raised its hand its fingertips were stained crimson from Jimmy's recently spilt blood, still fresh on the ground. Slowly its head came up. The two ORBS pilots readied their guns.

A wet smacking sound from the back of the store caught the rager's attention. Red looked up at the mirror to see the feral at the door to the back office slump to the floor. A brief motion that could have been a hand with a knife caught his eye, but it was hard to be certain as another feral rushed the door. There was a blur of motion as it crossed the threshold then it slid feet first into the room while the top of its head bounced back into the store.

In the brief moment of shocked silence Jake burst into the room, his falchion drawn. He ran toward the remaining feral. His left hand snapped upward. Red saw a metal point erupt from the top of the monster's skull. The first rager turned and started toward him. Red stood up from behind the counter with his M4 in hand as Jake drew a long metal spike from his vest and flung it toward the second rager. Spinning under the first rager's grip his sword flicked out and slashed across the back of the creature's leg, almost severing the limb at the knee.

Red heard a wet sound to his right and tried to draw a bead on the crippled rager, but Jake stepped into his line of fire. He watched as his friend reversed direction with his blade in a graceful loop that left it buried deep in his victim's skull. Red turned his gun to the rager by the door, only to find it swaying on its feet with the spike embedded in its eye at an angle. It staggered back into the door, its weight leaving cracks in the glass as it pawed at the spike.

Jake sheathed his sword and started forward. "Shotgun."

Red knew what he was about to do even as he grabbed his own Ithaca and tossed it to him. Jake caught it in midair. He ran toward the rager and leaped into the air when he was a few feet away. His momentum carried both of them through the glass door and onto the sidewalk. Red watched as the smaller ORBS pilot stepped up and stomped the spike the rest of the way into the rager's brain. Jake turned and fired the shotgun. Without a word, he turned and sprinted the way the horde had come from. Seconds later a mass of ferals sprinted past in pursuit.

Red Devil ducked back below the counter to get himself out of sight. Almost a minute later they heard another shot in the distance. Another shot rang out half a minute after that. By then, the street was clear.

Red Devil stood and helped Jimmy to his feet. The pair made their way to the now open door. Heart ran across the street as they tried to negotiate around the rager's trampled corpse.

"What the hell was that about?" she demanded as she took Jimmy's other arm and put it over her shoulders.

"They just about had us. Jake got all of them, but the one... he wasn't dead yet."

Heart got him into the other shop. "We saw. They were heading your way. So Carter went full measure and drew them off?"

Red nodded, his face a stone mask.

Fipps gritted his teeth. "Then let's make sure his sacrifice wasn't in vain. Let's move out."

"But his inwards and his legs shall he wash in water: and the priest shall burn all on the altar, to be a burnt sacrifice, an offering made by fire..."

-Leviticus 1:9

Lungs burning, legs aching, and heart pounding; Jake kept running down the narrow alley. Behind him the ferals were running single file, unable to spread out. The constant jostling also slowed them down, which kept them from gaining on him. All he needed to worry about was not hitting a dead end before he could break contact.

Ahead, the narrow way brightened slightly. Jake took heart. As he got closer to the end of the alley way, he made sure to pace himself until he was almost to the opening. Across the street he could see another tight alleyway, which would help him even more. He put on a burst of speed as he hit the open street. He kept going as he ran straight into the narrow alley on the other side, the street he'd crossed barely registering on his senses. The ferals behind him suddenly seemed to multiply as they spread out, but when they hit the mouth of the other alleyway their own numbers hampered them even more as they struggled to be the first into the narrow opening.

He heard the slap of feet and the grunting of an infected getting closer and closer to him. He took a split second to turn and point the shorter shotgun at the single beast that was closing in on him. The gun boomed in his hand. The right side of the zombie's head turned into red mush. Jake turned and tried to start running again, but all he was able to manage was something a little north of a jog. A side alley opened up on his left and he took it, red brick walls passing by on either side as he looked for his way out.

About fifty yards in, he saw it: a metal fire escape. He put on a final burst of speed and pulled the pry bar from his belt. He jumped and prayed he had the strength for one last leap. The bar clanged as it hit the bottom rung of the extending ladder on the bottom as it caught. He felt himself dangle in midair for a split second. The ladder dropped and he was clambering up it. As soon as his weight was off of it, it drew back up with a squeak and a clang.

He wanted nothing more than to throw himself down and play dead on that first level, but his survival training and his own experience had taught him never to take chances with his own safety. He went up the ladder to the next level and tested the window. He was in luck. It slid up under his hand. He climbed in and turned to cover the room with the Ithaca. Outside he could hear the horde run past, their feet and shoes slapping on the pavement. The windows rattled with each rager that passed below, but there were no roars or other sounds that he'd learned meant they had found their prey.

He kept the shotgun trained on the only door to the room as he looked around. Boy band posters fought with tween cartoon show characters for space on the walls. A single bed with a pony cover took center space in the room. A few stuffed animals, a couple of dolls from a cartoon, and a small stack of books were on the desk. All pf the items vying for space with an older laptop. A child's room. Jake fought down a shudder. Children had been among the first to turn five years ago. Jake had seen several instances where parents had come in already bitten by rabid, mindless kids. His first kill had been a creeper kid in the early stages of turning into a full grown feral.

As he waited, he wondered how it had gone down for this kid and her family. Had she turned at home, or somewhere else? Did she kill her parents... or did they do her in, instead? It wasn't until the last of the horde was long gone that he let himself move to clear the rest of the apartment.

Several minutes later he knew there was no one else alive in the entire building. He carefully lowered himself down onto one of the sturdy looking chairs at the table in the dining area. It creaked but held. He allowed himself a little time to relax. His breathing and heartbeat gradually slowed. He pulled his shemagh off and wiped the sweat beneath it with his shirt sleeve.

Now what?

First order of business was to keep his ass alive. ZOD had always stressed survival as general order number one, barring any other mission. Next thing on his list was to reconnect with the unit. That was going to be easier said than done. He looked out the windows of the apartment he was in. He noted more of the lower clouds that had so far been the biggest source of random lightning bolts. With the new electro-cyclones that seemed to pop up at random, travel on foot was going to be even trickier.

He pulled shotgun shells from his vest and started sliding them into the Ithaca's tube. He stood up and slung the shotgun. He located the kitchen. Even as he looked through the cabinets, he discarded the idea of a quick rendezvous with the rest of the expedition. In their boots with a horde of ragers and ferals on the loose their best bet would have been to cut their losses and haul ass. No one was worth risking the entire expedition over, not even an ORBS pilot.

He pulled cans from the cabinets and checked them for rust or dents, setting two aside for that reason and one that was bloated. What he had left was mostly single serving soups, chili, a couple of cans of fruit, and a few vegetables. He went back to the cabinet and retrieved the jar of honey, the one food he knew would never go bad. With a start on food covered, he headed for the parents' bedroom.

The first thing he found was an open Ruger pistol case and an open box of nine millimeter rounds. The rounds were useless for his Glock or the Judge he carried. For a moment, he debated taking them with him, but decided to leave them there until he had a better idea of what else he had to work with. The closet door stood open. On the top shelf he found a Remington Model 597 with a polymer stock and a scope next to an ammo box. The ammo box yielded three full boxes of twenty two caliber long rifle rounds and a mostly empty one. It also had a half empty box of 7.62 x 59R rounds, a common Warsaw Pact round used in the ubiquitous Mosin-Nagant rifle. The rifle it went to, however was nowhere to be found in the closet, and he figured the owner had probably taken it with them along with more ammo.

His search did turn up a sturdy duffel bag. He dumped the nine millimeter and the twenty two long rifle cartridges into the bag. A yoga mat and a fleece blanket from the living room made do as a makeshift bedroll. A metal water bottle from the kitchen added to his potential water storage. In the back of the pantry in addition to more soup, he found half a case of bottled water. After checking to see that the seals were intact, he poured several bottles into his canteen and the metal water bottle, then stowed the rest in the duffle bag. Finally, he pulled out a family sized can of long spoiled coffee. Lamenting the waste, he poured the coffee out and went to work on it with his knife. He opened several small holes in the bottom and one larger one. He poked three pairs of holes around the sides near the top and midway down, just like he'd watched Jimmy do the first night they were out. He grabbed a couple of wire dry cleaning hangers from the master bedroom to make the pot rest and grabbed silverware from the drawer next to the long defunct refrigerator.

With what gear he could easily scrounge gathered up, he loaded the two magazines for the .22 and rigged a sling for it. His first aid kit was down a lot of gauze, but otherwise intact. He had his water filter, his issue Zippo lighter, his combat knife, mutli-tool, flashlight, and compass. Beyond that, most of what he was carrying was ammo for his shotgun and his pistols.

He hefted the duffel experimentally. It was a little on the heavy side, but he knew that would change over the next few days. There were only a few things left on his mental list that would increase his chances of catching up to the column. Some of those the already knew where to find.

He laid his bedroll down on the floor and stretched out. "All I need now is a little rest, and cover of darkness."

Rest came quickly, but it was all too brief. When Jake awoke it was to the resounding boom of a cyclone dissipating. He sat up, rubbed his eyes, and checked his watch. A little after six. He rolled his bedroll up mostly by feel, then grabbed his gear in much the same way. When he left, it was by the front door. The trip back to the camping store was a long one in the dark, but the intermittent bursts of lightning made the going a little easier. By half past seven he was standing over the body of the rager he'd killed, looking into the shattered frame of the front door. Once inside, he risked using his flashlight with a blue lens. He stepped over the hacked up bodies of the zombies he'd killed and made his way to the cooking supplies. His first find was a set of candles, which went into the duffel right away. The next thing was a small cook set, a fire starter, a rain poncho, a space blanket, a camouflaged tarp, and some paracord. For good measure, he also grabbed a roll of duct tape. He eyed the single tents, but left them on the shelves in favor of the simplicity of a tarp and cord.

He went to the front of the store and checked for maps. The few that he found were water damaged or faded, but at the back of the rack he found a road atlas that hadn't been too damaged to read. He carefully cut out the pages for Missouri, Iowa, Kansas, and the eastern half of Nebraska. South Dakota was too badly damaged to read, so he reluctantly left it in the atlas.

He settled his shemagh back into place so that it covered his mouth and stepped out onto the street. The last he'd known, they had been in a midsized town called Maryville on their way to Omaha. Jake knew the team would still take the extra trip, while he could head straight for Sioux City. His best route was anything that took him north and west, with a big emphasis on north.

For a moment he wished he had a bicycle, but he knew that the thin rubber tires would have rotted after the first couple of years. There were other options for tires if he didn't mind a rough ride, but they required time and resources he didn't currently have. He shook his head and forced his thoughts to other useful subjects, like staying hidden as he navigated toward the university on the northwest side of town. From there he would decide on his route to Sioux City.

ZOD's Survival, Evasion, Resistance and Escape training had pooled the experience of hundreds of survivors into one of the most thorough urban and wilderness survival courses in the post feral world. As Jake crept from the cover of one building to the next, he recalled the two weeks he had spent with SERE instructors after his own two month long solo trek from El Paso to Corpus Christi. Stealth and terrain had been his primary advantages then, but over the years he also acknowledged more and more the role that easily scavenged supplies had played in his survival. He slipped into the broken front façade of an old restaurant, noting that even the salt shakers were gone. The pantry was completely bare, save for a few bloated cans. With no more than a cursory look around, he made his way out the back door and checked the alleyway. Once he was certain it was clear he kept going north until he reached the end and checked the roadway. When nothing moved after a couple of minutes, he made his way across and into another alley.

He stuck to the alleyways for the next few blocks, until he came out between a funeral home and a paint store. Across the way was a bank that took up the half of the block closest to him. The other half was solid buildings. He darted across the street and made his way along the bank's wall until he came to an east-west running alley. He headed west until he got to the next street that ran north, coming out next to an Elks Lodge. The street ran north for a ways, but the next block over the alley ran perpendicular to his path.

He stayed close to the brick Elks Lodge for as long as he could, then darted across the gap between it and a vine covered one story building that butted up against another two story building with a recessed entry way. As he crouched in the entry, he guessed it had been an auto parts store by the raised but faded plastic logos he could see. His choices were limited from there for cover for about half a block.

After a moment's thought, he double-timed it from the corner toward the buildings across the way. An empty restaurant loomed on his left with a line of cars permanently parked on the side of the road. He kept his shotgun pointed more or less in its direction, though his eyes also went to the sunken parking lot on his right about half the time, too. Finally, he made it to the shattered glass front of a little florist's shop. He paused as he looked at the remains of a sign hung above where the door had once been "Local hone…" If the partial word was 'honey' then it was worth checking out. Glass crunched under his feet as he made his way inside. True to the advertisement, there was a box in the back that held six more jars of honey. He tucked them into his duffel bag and made his way back out. He paused at the broken sign that leaned against the cracked glass of the next shop. All he could make out was "…rd's Bait and Bows." He looked inside and saw ruined archery targets and warped bows. While the bows were ruined the thought of straight aluminum shafts, plastic vanes, and razor sharp broad heads was tempting. Part of ZOD's SERE training had covered making a survival bow.

Deciding it was worth the time Jake padded in. In a few minutes he found himself stifling the urge to crow with delight. Below the display he found plastic bags full of plastic vanes, nocks, broadheads, and unopened epoxy. Another box held a double handful of aluminum shafts. Once he'd counted them out, he had fifteen shafts to go with the rest of his find. As he tucked them into his increasingly more crowded duffel, he deemed it worth the space and the extra weight.

Black ash was falling again as he emerged from the bait shop, but it wasn't thick enough to obscure the clock tower on the building a couple of blocks away. Even without a map, he knew he was near the center of town. With the new ash fall, he adjusted his shemagh to cover his mouth and nose, and stuck to the cover of the buildings as far as he could. He crossed the street as quickly as he could. He stopped and waited to see if the movement had attracted any attention.

He looked both ways down the street he had just crossed, noting that the courthouse he was looking at was the county court house for Nodaway County. Which meant the county sheriff and the county jail. In a larger town, he would have expected a line of bail bonds services across the street from the jail, but smaller counties usually only had a handful. Still, the likelihood of finding a nine millimeter pistol had gone up. So had his chances of finding ammunition for both it and his shotgun... *if* he stumbled across the county jail. Searching the city for it wasn't an option.

He moved once he was sure nothing was following him, crossing in front of the court house. The single patrol car he saw parked in front was a burned out hulk, along with the rest of the vehicles. When he got to the next corner he stopped again and checked both ways. He checked his back trail again. Movement to his right caught his eye. He froze in place and waited, hoping against hope that it was just the nonexistent wind. He saw movement again. He heard a sound, soft, short, and deep; something he couldn't be sure was real. When it came again, his heart leaped in his chest. He started toward it, half hoping, half fearful that he'd actually heard the sound of a dog's bark. Sometimes, that meant people. Sometimes, it meant a feral pack. But he'd never heard an infected mutt bark. The dog barked a third time, followed by a low pitched whine, then another bark.

Store fronts went by on his left almost without a glance. He broke into a jog once he got to the Nodaway County Administration Center. Behind the admin center he found the dog and a scene that made his chest ache. Bodies lay outside the county jail, most sporting holes in what remained of the brown deputy's uniforms. All of them had a single hole in their skulls. All except one. The one that was standing up and trying to catch the German Shepherd. When Jake came around the corner the dog looked at him and gave a bark.

Jake's chest went tight when he saw the badge on the dog's collar. He let out a short exclamation as his mind pieced the events together. The sheriff's deputies slowly turning and those who remained having to put their comrades down one by one, until only one man was left: the dog handler. He looked to the dog, and then had to look away as he realized this dog had been coming back here for five years, hoping his human would be... human again. Hoping for something different; his loyalty unflinching, even in the face of the zombie apocalypse.

The feral dog handler turned to face him. Its mouth opened wide as it charged toward him. The Ithaca spoke its lethal one word vocabulary. The infected deputy's body skidded to a stop face first a few feet away. Jake racked a fresh round into the chamber. He turned the body over and pulled the badge from the front of the shirt.

He tucked the badge into a pouch on his vest . "I don't know who you were, but you must have been one hell of a good guy to have a dog that loyal. You're the first zombie I've felt bad about having to put down."

As he loaded another round into the Ithaca's tube, the dog came over and sniffed at the body with a mournful sounding whine. He looked up at Jake and tilted his head to one side. Without a word Jake held his right hand out palm down and fingers relaxed, to the dog. He sniffed at his hand for a moment. He licked his fingers before it took a step forward and put one paw on his arm.

Jake moved his hand forward and rubbed behind the dog's ear. "Wonder what your name is?" I bet they have all sorts of cool gear inside, don't you buddy?"

Jake stood slowly. He headed for the sheriff's office and jail, stopping along the way to pull a set of keys from one of the bodies. The front door was unlocked. He found the door to the jail propped open. He went back into the cell area and saw two bodies with head wounds. The cell doors were all open. The armory door was still locked, but the fifth key on the ring opened it.

Most of the weapons were gone. Only a couple of shotguns and three pistols were left. Jake grabbed one of the pistols and smiled when he saw that they were Glock 17s. He went through the duty belts and pulled a holster and a couple of magazine pouches from them. He pulled his own duty belt off and put the newly acquired items on it before loading up five magazines for the new Glock. He field stripped, cleaned, and oiled the weapon before loading and holstering it. He grabbed the three boxes of nine millimeter ammo that were still left.

The equipment case for the shotguns had one point slings with loops for extra shells, like Jake's own Mossberg. The guns themselves were Remington 870 Police Magnums with pistol grips and tactical lights attached to the pump handles. He opened the ammo cabinet and found several boxes of shells and spare batteries for the tac lights. He sorted through the ammo boxes and found that one box was slugs, and another two were door breaching rounds. The remaining six boxes were double-aught buckshot. When he loaded the shotgun, he got another pleasant surprise: the tube took seven shells instead of just five. Reluctantly, he unloaded the Ithaca and set it aside. Even as small and light as it was, the extra weight was too much.

When he stepped out of the armory, he found the dog looking up at him a few feet away.

"I'm starting to understand why they call it *heavily* armed," Jake said to his new companion as he moved down the hallway. The new weapons and extra ammo added considerably to the weight he was carrying, though the recent conditioning that Heart and Fipps had put him through made it possible for him to carry it without tiring himself out too much.

His last stop was in the office marked "K9 Unit." The single desk was still neat and Jake quickly found his new friend's information in the top drawer.

"Misun."

Jake carefully pronounced it according to the phonetic guide, so that it sounded like 'me-soon'. The German Shepherd's ears perked a that, and his tail thumped on the floor.

"Lakota for little brother. I like that. Okay, little brother, let's get you kitted out." He went through the other door in the room and found himself in a small storage room. A service dog vest and a couple of attachment pouches were stored with a leash, several bags of dog food and a large indoor kennel.

It took a little experimenting and taking in of straps to get the vest on Misun, but the dog stood there patiently as Jake fiddled with the buckles. One of the pouches was a first aid kit. Jake attached to the left side. There were three other pieces that could be attached: a canteen and two larger pouches. The canteen had a folding bowl attached to it, which meant it had to come. One of the pouches was a simple large container, while the other was a food pouch with another folding bowl. Jake pulled the bowl out of the food pouch, tucked it into the larger one and attached it to the vest.

"Now you can pull your own weight."

Misun barked once and turned around. He went to the door and looked back over his shoulder at Jake.

"I get it, you're ready to go. Okay, let's hit the road."

As they neared the door Misun growled and hunkered down, but kept his head up sniffing the air.

Jake looked outside and saw that a handful of ferals had shown up, probably drawn by the gunshot. Using the shotgun on them was likely to draw more and that might include ragers. Jakes rule for dealing with ragers on his own was simple: if you can avoid dealing with them, do it. He unslung the .22 and the duffle bag. He knelt and set the shotgun on top of the duffel.

He drew his falchion. "Okay, little brother. First rule of fighting a group: don't fight the group. Now, watch and learn."

He slipped out the door and went straight for the closest feral, a woman in faded rags. The sword sliced the top of her head off. Before she started to fall, he was moving again. He took two steps, jumped up and brought the falchion's blade down on the next infected's head. When he pulled the weapon free, three more were charging toward him. Jake broke left and cut through a skull. He pivoted and reversed his blade to deliver a chop to the one that was in the middle of the trio. Before the third one could register that he was alone, Jake had covered the distance between them and had the sword lodged in its cranium. He yanked his weapon free and turned to scan for other enemies, but the field was his.

After cleaning the worst of the gore and brain matter from the blade with one of the feral's shirts, Jake sheathed the sword and grabbed the rest of his gear. With Misun at his side, he started heading west again. Thunder rumbled from the north as he made his way west. With Misun to warn him of ferals he moved more quickly, but the looming clouds behind him were still faster than he was. After a few blocks the road he was on turned northwest. Soon he found himself facing the overgrown grounds of Northwest Missouri State University.

"Come on, boy. Let's see if we can find the student union, see what's going on."

He took off at a jog. Clouds loomed above and ahead of him, flashes and thunder coming closer and closer together. On his right rose several residence halls, with trees screening him from view on the left for a hundred yards or so before giving way to a three story residence hall. Finally he saw what he was looking for, the broken, glass edifice of the three story student union. A little ways north was a taller bell tower, which Jake hoped would draw most of the lightning. A few dilapidated bicycles were parked out front; their chains long fused solid with rust, tires nothing more than black dust lost among the black ash.

The glass doors were long turned to glittering shards that crunched under his feet as he made his way in, shotgun up and tac light showing the way. Tables were overturned and trash was strewn everywhere. The few bodies had long since rotted beyond the point of smelling and it looked like there was nothing worth scavenging. The bookstore was a shambles. The commons area looked like a tornado had swept everything around at random, leaving nothing upright save a single chair in the middle of the room. The food area drew Jake's interest. He slipped behind the counters to see if there was anything still salvageable. Only a few bloated cans were left in most of the pantry areas, but in one room Jake found an unexpected treasure: an intact three speed bicycle. The chain was dry but not rusted. The tires were a total loss, but there were ways around that.

"Little brother, we're going to need some tools and a couple of tires."

Two hours later he was back in the student union with a set of pinking shears, two tires, a spool of wire, and a heavy awl. A fire made of broken up tables and chairs burned in the fireplace of the aptly named campus union living room, providing him with enough light to see what he was doing as the lightning storm raged outside. He cut two narrow strips and two wider strips from the bigger tires. The narrow strips were laid along the inside of the tire rim. The wider strip, he laid down on the table and began to poke hoke holes along the edges. Once that was done he wrapped it around the rim and forced the wire through the holes, binding it to the rim to make the outside of the tire. He wired a milk crate to the rack on the rear of the bike.

Once the bike was fixed up and he had a set of spare rubber tire strips in the rear crate. He held up the can of stew and took the folding bowl from the food pouch. "How does some beef stew sound, Misun?"

Misun barked his approval of that plan, so Jake opened the can and emptied it into the bowl, and emptied one of the water bottles he'd grabbed into the water bowl. Once Misun was eating, he stuck the open can of chili close to the fire and waited until it started bubbling before he used a cloth to pull it away from the heat and let it cool down a little. Once it stopped bubbling, he ate straight from the can; that way, all he had to clean was the spoon he'd used.

With dinner done and their dishes cleaned, Jake banked the fire. He laid the yoga mat out and pulled the blanket over himself. Once he'd laid down Misun came over, turned around three times, and plopped down next to him.

"Let me know if someone pays us a visit, okay?"

Misun let out a little sound and laid his head on his paws. Reassured, Jake laid his head down and let sleep and exhaustion take him.

"Wherefore take unto you the whole armour of God, that ye may be able to withstand in the evil day, and having done all, to stand."

-*Ephesians 6:13*

Jake woke up to the sound of Misun's growl. Old reflexes that he thought he'd forgotten years ago resurfaced between one heartbeat and the next. He was on his feet with his Glock out and pointed in front of him. He blinked sleep from his eyes as he turned blindly, the dim light from the banked fire only bright enough to rob him of night vision.

"What is it, boy?"

He fumbled the tac light on. His ears strained to hear anything. Was that the sound of a foot on carpet? Plastic slid over linoleum somewhere to his right. He turned the gun to cover that direction. It was Misun's bark that saved him from the first attack. He turned back just in time to see a dark figure move. He turned the gun on it and pulled the trigger. He got a flash of a snarling face then the sound of a body hitting the ground. Automatically, he trained the tac light on the sound and pulled the trigger twice more when he found his target. The body slumped after the first round and jerk with the second. He spun back to his right just in time to catch a fist to his jaw. He staggered and pulled the trigger, earning a pained cry for his efforts.

"Get 'em, boy!" Jake yelled as he turned the gun back toward the man he'd just shot. The body wasn't moving, but he put another round in it just to be sure. Another bark warned him of an attacker from his left. He managed to get a round center mass.

"Attack, bite, do something!" Jake yelled as he turned back to his right. He got hit from both sides at once and he went down hard.

The two men who attacked him held his arms. When they hauled him to his feet, Misun was nowhere to be seen. They pulled his Glock from his hand and took the other from the holster on his hip. Rough hands searched his pockets. They pulled his vest free of his body before dragging him out of the room.

Out in front of the student union, a semi-circle of men carrying crude torches was waiting. Jake got his first good look at the scavengers. Most of them wore some kind of improvised armor, fashioned from signs and car parts. Their weapons were just as crude, mostly crowbars or pipes with saw blades or jagged metal attached to them. The largest of them stood in the middle, with a belt that was adorned with badges across his broad chest and ample gut. The men all had long beards. Some were patchy and all of them as unkempt as their hair. The big man stepped forward with his torch held high and a thick wooden club in his other hand.

"Ahgot firss dibs onnis shit!" the man slurred, only one side of his face moving as he spoke. Spit flew from the flaccid side of his mouth. Jake grimaced as it sprayed him. The man drew the club back. Jake moved.

While his arms were held tight, his legs were still free and he made full use of them. As the club bearing leader stepped toward him, Jake's right foot lashed out and caught him square in the crotch. As the man grabbed his privates, Jake brought his foot back and slammed it against the side of the knee of the man on his right. The leg bent the wrong way with a cracking sound. Jake's right arm was free. He brought his hand around and hit the man on his left in the throat with his fist. The second guard's gurgle was lost in his companion's screams. It was a small satisfaction as Jake went down under a pile of smelly men.

"Hollim dow. Mgunna smeshis nuss!"

"You caint do that! He got you a good'n, boss, an you wern innat fight. That means this'n goes to the Fire Lady." A low, dangerous sounding murmur rose from the rest of the scavengers. Jake wondered if there was some kind of power struggle happening in front of him.

"She ain' godda know. Sides, 'm boss 'ere. She sesso. Yer jus' wannin some back cuz ah kill yer broth'r."

"Nah, 'em's th' rules. 'Iss here sumbitch made ya drop yer club, put ya onna ground after the rill fightin' uzdun. 'Ere's dirt on yer colors, Rick. 'At means she gets 'er say." The man that spoke seemed to suffer from the same affliction Rick did, but more of his face moved when he talked.

"Shud y'r dem mouf!".

"Ain't shuttin' up! Ain't a man here wha's forgot ya 'come top dawg same way. Ain't a man here's gonna keep his mouf shut. Fire Lady ge's 'er say. 'At's 'e law."

The rest of the men chimed in. "That's the law!"

'Tie 'is dem fee' up."

Moments later, a thick rope made from what looked like woven bits of plastic was tied around his ankles and wrists. He felt himself being lifted over someone's shoulder. Rick lagged behind for a moment, long enough for Jake to see that he was wearing his black ZOD vest.

"Gunna riph yer nussoff 'n shuff 'em dow' yer throa'."

"Well, now that you have me tied up, sure, you *might* be able to pull that off, but you're gonna need to swallow yours back down first."

The world went white, then black.

"Yer pretty stupid."

Jake struggled to focus his eyes. The bearded, gap toothed face that he saw made him regret his success.

Jake's eyes scanned the room for something more pleasant to look at. "But I learn quick. See how I didn't say anything about your looks?"

"I ain't the one tied up. Hey, m'name's Albert. What's yer name?"

"Jake." His hands and feet were still bound, but the room he was in offered plenty of jagged objects to work on his bonds with…if he could get a moment's privacy. One door and a set of high windows, couple with the concrete floor gave him the impression he was in a storage room.

"Good ta' meetcha' Jake. So, you think you could take ole Rick in a stand up fight?"

"Depends on the fight. But yeah, I figure I could."

Albert was fairly bouncing in excitement. "You know karate and shit like that?"

"I've got some training, yeah. Am I going to have to fight him hand to hand or something?"

"Well, maybe. We ain't got no guns right now 'cept the two we took offa' you. You any good with a knife or a club?"

"Kinda."

"Well, here's the deal. When you put ole Rick on 'is ass, othin' him from bashin' yer head in and othing' one in the ole win column know what I mean? And the Fire Lady, she says if a man gets dirt on 'is colors in a fight, an' he ain't dead from it, he better make sure the other fella don't walk again."

"So why didn't you let him?"

Albert's grin made Jake shudder. "'Cuz you made him drop his club. Man's weapon's his honor. That club belonged to the boss before Rick, and to the boss before him. And it was give to the first boss by the Fire Lady. You makin' him drop that with othing' but yer bare hands like that, that's even better."

"I take it Rick's not real popular."

Albert shrugged and scratched his beard. "He's got a few friends. But no one likes them much either. Plus, he's getting' old… and he's a lazy sumbitch."

"Well, that's just un-American."

"Just about. So, you end up killin' Rick, you remember who set you straight. I know who to trust around here and who needs killin'."

"What are you talking about?"

"If you kill Rick, you'll be the boss."

"Oh, just what I've always dreamed of."

"And if I don't?"

"We'll eat you."

"Well, that certainly changes things."

"I gotta run, but you remember Albert when you gut the boss and get that club handed to you." The man went to a side door and let himself out, leaving Jake alone in the semi-lit room. One door led to a lit area, with flickering yellow faint against the narrow rectangle of glass. A low murmur reached his ears, the sounds of life being lived. Shadows passed across the narrow glass and below the door's lower edge.

A few minutes after Albert left the far door opened and three men stepped inside. One carried a torch and a machete. The other two had machetes tucked into their belts. They approached him cautiously. The man with the torch stopped several steps away.

"Okay, get his arms, but be careful. He's tricky." The other two men grabbed his arms and hauled him to his feet.

"I'd love to cooperate guys. Really, I would, but it's like someone tied my feet together."

One of the lead men waved his machete. "Shut your mouth, or I'm gonna cut 'em off."

Jake decided keeping his feet was important, so he didn't say anything else while they carted him through the door and through an industrial kitchen. They set him on his feet in a room that looked like a school cafeteria. People were gathered in a loose circle around a blackened fifty-five gallon drum. A fire blazed inside it and the smoke rose through a jagged hole in the ceiling. Rick stood across the circle from Jake, surrounded by several large men who seemed to share his lack of facial control to some degree or another. Their voices carried over the din of the other conversations and they laughed often.

Suddenly, the room went quiet. All eyes went to a door set in the far wall. Jake looked in that direction and saw a red glow in the otherwise dark hallway. It grew brighter with each passing second. People backed away from the door, leaving a cleared path to the edge of the circle.

The glowing woman who stepped into view possessed a chilling beauty. Her face was an oval of smooth skin that radiated a red light. Full lips seemed black against her skin and dark hair flowed off her shoulders. It was in the eyes that her features turned away from beauty and descended into darkness. While they glowed more brightly than her skin, her eyes were all black and her expression held nothing warm or remotely human.

The scavengers dropped to one knee in unison as she entered the room, even forcing Jake to take the same stance. Her gaze went across the entire gathering. Jake could see where the room brightened where she looked. When it finally fell on him it lingered.

"Who is this man?" Her voice was hard for him to pin down, like a choir singing a dissonant, almost beautiful song that set his nerves ablaze.

Rick spoke up. "Juss a pris'ner."

"And yet," the glowing woman said as she turned her gaze on the scavenger leader, "I hear pain in your voice, and I can smell your fear."

"'At's cuz he knocked 'im on 'is ass an' made 'im drop 'is club," the man who had challenged Rick's authority earlier said with a thin smile creasing the half of his mouth that did work. The Fire Lady's gaze narrowed and the light shining on Rick tightened along with it.

"You know how to address this. Need I remind you of the Law?"

Rick stepped forward. "No, ma'am. I 'uz gonna do like th' Law says, but dey stopped me."

"Fight was over," another man called out. "An' he put ya inna dirt barehanded!"

The Fire Lady turned her gaze back to Jake and stalked toward him, stopping just out of arm's reach. "You were unarmed?"

"They were holding my arms. So I kicked him."

"You were restrained as well." A slow smile crossed her face. The heat of her glow bathed Jake. He felt himself fighting the urge to cringe away from it even as he wanted to bathe in the crimson light she radiated.

"He 'uz done beat." Rick's voice was high and wavering.

"And yet you disgraced my gift to you. You soiled the banner you pledged to me. At the hands of a defeated enemy, no less."

Rick swept his right arm back at the men who had spoken against him. "Ah tried t'make right wi' th' Law! Dey stopped me."

"As well they should have. Now you may make your pride whole before me. Defeat this man in my sight and you may claim all that was his."

"What if I win?"

"Then you may claim all that is under his banner. Free him."

Moments later, Jake was unbound and was being pulled to his feet. Rough hands shoved him forward, into a part of the circle that had widened to make room for Rick.

He could still feel the Judge tucked into his waistband, but he didn't want to pull that particular card just yet. "Don't I get a weapon?"

"Of course you do. You may have any weapon you can take."

That brought a scowl to his face. He glanced at the two men who were flanking him. Both carried machetes tucked in their belts and thick clubs in hand. With his advice to Misun from earlier in his head, he turned to the guard on his left.

"Hey, you know the best way to fight two guys at once?"

The man frowned at him for a moment and shook his head. As his head started to move, Jake spun and grabbed the other guard's weapon hand and twisted it behind his back. As the man struggled and cried out in pain, Jake reached forward with his left hand and snatched his machete. The blade came free of the guard's belt and Jake gave him a shove forward. The man stumbled into his partner as Jake held up his blade.

"Don't fight them both at once!" Jake held up the machete. The Fire Lady laughed and gestured at the two men, who slunk away.

"Very clever, little man. Entertain me more."

From his left the ORBS pilot caught movement. He turned in time to see Rick coming toward him with his club raised. His right arm straightened and brought the tip of the machete level with the leader's throat, stopping him in his tracks.

"And I thought *you* were a fucking psycho."

The burly scavenger backpedaled and swung at Jake's head "Gonna' fuck you up!"

The younger man ducked under the swing and twisted his blade to leave a gash along his opponent's side. Undeterred, Rick came in again with a downward swing. Jake swung the machete up and knocked the blow to one side. He slashed at the scavenger again, though with less success. They circled each other with their weapons held in front of them. Rick's stance was more casual, while Jake held himself in a combat crouch. His left hand held in front of his body, his right hand extending the machete at an angle to block more of his torso.

Rick made a few feints, but was disappointed when they drew no reaction from the man before him. Years of SCA combat had taught Jake how to tell how an opponent's center of gravity stayed relatively stable with a false attack he didn't intend to carry through with. When Rick's weight shifted he attacked in earnest and found his blows knocked aside with precise counters from Jake. When his last attack was met with a swift riposte that left a bloody line down the inside of his arm, the scavenger boss retreated a couple of steps. He held out his hand to one of his cronies and turned to the Fire Lady like a dog asking for permission. She nodded and the man handed his leader his machete.

"Really? Look, I know you're in over your head here. Do you need me to fight you left handed, tie one hand behind my back or something?"

Just as Rick crouched to respond with an attack, another voice cut through the noise.

"Stop!"

The scavenger boss rocked back on his heels. Jake felt a moment's temptation to pursue an attack, but the newcomer's voice carried the same compelling dissonance that the Fire Lady's had. Warily, he turned to face the newcomer.

"Who are you?" the Fire Lady demanded of the woman who stood at the edge of the circle. This woman glowed red as well, with an expression that seemed to Jake both fierce and sad.

"I was called Caroline... before. I am become Morrigan."

"You are not known to me," the Fire Lady said with a look of genuine confusion on her face. "You are Fallen." Jake could practically hear the capitalization of the last word, as if it was a group of things more than an adjective.

"That implies a state of Grace we've never truly enjoyed. Just because you are told something doesn't make it real."

"What do you want?"

"To give you your free will back. You're still human enough

to say no, to defy him."

"I'm not human."

"Makes it easier to destroy them, doesn't it?" Morrigan's words brought a low murmur from the gathered humans. Jake slowly edged away from her. As he started to move, she turned to him and winked before she went on. "That's what you're being told to do, isn't it? Destroy mankind? That's why you tell them to eat their kills. So they slowly kill themselves through cannibalism." The murmurs rose to a collective growl. The crowd surged forward around Jake. He didn't move forward and found himself steadily jostled away from the two glowing women.

"Wha's she tawkin''bout?" Rick's voice rose over the crowd's rumble.

"She lies, Richard."

"Do I? You can barely move one side of your face. Your hands shake so much you can hardly get a bottle to your lips most days. Why do you think that is?" The rumbling of the crowd rose in pitch, but it was lost moments later under the Fire Lady's scream. There was the sound of flesh striking flesh. The red glow shifted, but Jake wasn't sure who had knocked who where.

In the confusion, Jake headed for the nearest door, only to find it blocked by a familiar face pointing one of his own pistols at him. Jake glared at the man. "Albert."

"You gotta take me with you. I don't wanna end up like Rick."

"You believe Morrigan?"

Albert lifted his trembling right hand and nodded.

"Okay, come on. Can you take me to my gear?"

"Yeah."

The scavenger led him further into the building. Behind them the sounds of fighting got louder, resembling nothing more to Jake than a riot. Albert led him through darkened hallways, lit only by intermittent oil lanterns. Soon they were standing before a classroom door. Jake could see random bits of junk strewn on desks and shelves. The little scavenger pulled a set of keys from his pocket and started trying them against the door. Moments later he had the door open and they were wheeling Jake's bike out into the hallway.

"Okay, let's the hell out of here."

Albert led him back along the way they'd come. They turned left down another hallway near the cafeteria. The sounds of chaos and combat covered the soft clicking of the bike's gears as they paced down the hall. Ahead of him Jake saw the lighter squares of night-time darkness against the oppressive black of the interior, punctuated by flashes of light and quiet rumbles of thunder.

Another flash of light came from behind them accompanied with the louder report of a gunshot. Albert stumbled and grabbed Jake's arm as he tried to keep his feet. Jake pulled him forward, into the circle of lantern light. The scavenger's eyes frowned in confusion. When he opened his mouth to speak, blood welled dark and frothy on his lips. As the light dimmed from his eyes, Jake turned to look behind them.

Rick stepped into the light. He was wearing Jake's vest open, his hairy belly glistening with sweat and dark trails of blood. His quivering hand held Jake's other pistol.

"Fuck. Missed."

"I won't." Jake stood and held the machete in his left hand.

"You brough' a knife to a gun figh'?" Rick pulled the trigger again. The bullet hit something down the hall and whined into the darkness. Jake raised an eyebrow and held his blade up.

"You sure you don't want to go back to swords? Seems like you did better with those."

Rick pulled the trigger again and another bullet spanged off of some innocent piece of architecture. He tried a third time, and was rewarded with a shot that buzzed past Jake's left ear as the slide locked back. He tossed the gun down with a snarl and pulled his machete.

"Gonna gu' you, ya sumbitch."

Jake slipped into his stance, left hand forward and right hand back. "Swords it is, but there's something you should know."

"Fuck you!"

Jake caught the descending blade against his own and pressed forward. "I'm not left handed, mother-fucker!"

A gunshot sounded. Rick staggered back and looked down to see the heavy revolver in Jake's right hand. He looked down at himself and saw the bloody hole in his distended belly. Jake extended his arm and pulled the trigger again, putting three pieces of double-aught buckshot next to the first wound for good measure. The scav fell on his ass and grabbed his bloated gut, howling in pain.

While his would-be killer cried and blubbered, Jake holstered the Judge and picked up the empty Glock. He pocketed the weapon then went to the suffering Rick and grabbed the collar of his assault vest and pulled up hard. After a few tries, he managed to dislodge the man's hands from his wounds. He pulled the vest free. Once he had the vest zipped up he undid his belt from under the fold of his belly. He grimaced at the smell of long unwashed skin, but grateful that at least he hadn't bled all over the damn thing.

"Please, he'p me... make it stop!"

"You gave up any right to mercy when you started killing people for that fucking monster back there. You're going to be hours dying and you earned every second of it."

He stood and turned away, leaving the leader of the scavengers wailing in a growing pool of his own blood.

"For he is the minister of God to thee for good. But if thou do that which is evil, be afraid; for he beareth not the sword in vain: for he is the minister of God, a revenger to execute wrath..."

-*Romans 13:4*

12

Misun caught up to him as he left the high school parking lot. Jake stopped the bike to greet him. The German Shepherd jumped around and barked happily for a moment. He pressed up against him, nearly knocking him into the black ash that was starting to build up. Jake knelt and buried his face in the dog's fur.

"Good boy," he said over and over. After a few moments he stood and looked back at the school in the flickering light. Misun barked and moved a few steps down the road.

"Yeah, good idea. There are monsters back there. Best to just leave them behind." His feet pressed against the pedals, and he followed Misun. The roads were still relatively smooth, though riding on the solid, makeshift tires was still no cakewalk. The bike had shocks to take most of the bumps out of the ride, but with solid tires it was still far from easy.

Around noon near the northern border where Missouri turned into Iowa he found an old sign for the Wabash Trace Nature Trail, which took him a few yards off of actual roads. It was mostly asphalt or gravel with weeds growing up in a few places, but otherwise the going was much easier. He found a secluded spot to stop and set up camp just a few miles north of Blanchard.

The hobo stove required only minimal fuel to create a merry little blaze inside it and the two cans of soup that he put on it were bubbling in minutes. He set them aside to let them cool, but kept the fire going to dispel the slight chill in the air.

Once he'd emptied the first soup can into Misun's bowl he finished his off. He took them over to a nearby creek and cleaned them out. Twenty minutes later he had all four cans boiled and cooling near the fire, each covered with a cut up shirt. He used the shirt for a filter as he transferred the boiled water first into his canteen and metal water bottle, then into some of the empty plastic bottles. With his water supply topped off, he doused the fire and repacked his gear. He took a few minutes to reload the spent Glock magazine and give his guns a basic cleaning before he got back on the bike and pushed north once more.

A few miles north of where he'd stopped, the trail veered west, away from the road and through the middle of overgrown fields. He felt his shoulders relax a little as he got further away from the roads and towns, from the places zombies in their various types would be likely to be found. Memories of West Texas resurfaced as he rode along, and the barren places where he'd seen few humans and fewer zombies. One of the more pleasant memories he had was of a group of riders who used camels instead of horses.

Jake hit the brakes on his bike and came to a stop next to a relatively fresh pile of horse manure. "Okay, that's a little odd."

Although it might have been a strange coincidence, he didn't have a lot of faith in happenstance. He pushed the bike to the side of the trail and looked in both directions. Up ahead a tree rose above its brethren. While he wasn't eager to tempt a lightning strike, Jake figured it would be better to do so at the moment than during one of the lightning storms. He crept up to it and began working his way through the lower branches until he found himself high enough to see for a fair distance.

To the west, there was nothing but overgrown fields. If he had to guess, he would have said that the fields he was looking at weren't as overgrown as some others. To the north and east it was a different story. In spite of the gray clouds he could see columns of smoke... most pale, a couple of them darker. Through the brush and trees he could barely make out movement, but shapes eluded his eye. Due north of him was a bridge. He was willing to bet that whoever had a camp set up over there was also keeping an eye on the creek crossing.

The primary concern in his head was whether or not he wanted to make contact with this group. So far, it was almost a coin toss as to whether or not they'd be hostile like the scavs or more like the wild men and Sheriff Holder's people. As close to sundown as it seemed to be getting, the option of sneaking past them in the dark was tempting. He climbed down and headed back to his bike. He was almost convinced that the time lost and the risk of spending the rest of the night nearby but still north of the bridge was the better option.

Misun watched while Jake wheeled the bike off to the west side of the road and concealed it by laying it down behind some brush. As he was working on clearing out a place for himself, the dog let out a soft bark and got to his feet. Jake grabbed the shotgun and crouched next to a tree. He followed Misun's gaze. The dog was looking north. A few moments later, a young woman on horseback rode out of the brush and onto the trail. Her khaki shirt bore several patches and she sported a green neckerchief rolled in a familiar style. She reached up and took off the green baseball cap she'd been wearing to reveal light brown hair that was pulled back into a ponytail. A rifle was in a scabbard at her knee and she wore a knife at her right hip.

"I see your dog there and we seen you up in the tree a little earlier. So we know you're out here. Our Scoutmaster wanted me to let you know if you're not looking to do us no harm, you're welcome to come in and stay the night and have a hot meal."

Jake stood and stepped out onto the trail, the shotgun held across his body and pointed down at the ground. "Your Scoutmaster? As in trustworthy, loyal, courteous, friendly, do a good deed daily and be prepared Scoutmaster?"

"You were a Scout?"

"Troop four-oh-nine, Yucca Council out of El Paso. I made it to Star Scout before I got out."

"Melinda Holt, Scout First Class, Troop nine."

"I'm Jake Carter, Spec Three, First ORBS Squadron, with ZOD."

"We've heard of ZOD. Word is you're decent folks."

"We try."

"Well, the invite's open. If you're interested."

"I'm never one to pass up a hot meal! Let me get my bike." He hustled back to get the bicycle When he wheeled it into the road, he found himself facing five more people emerging from the brush on the other side of the road. Like Holt, they wore the khaki shirts, neckerchiefs and green cargo pocket pants Jake remembered from Boy Scouts. A couple carried rifles and the rest carried either bows or crossbows.

"This is the rest of Fox Patrol."

"They were there the whole time?"

"Of course. A Scout is brave... not stupid. Be Prepared."

"Well played, ma'am. Well played."

"Come on, we'll cut across the field to get back to the camp." Jake followed the group through the brush and across the high grass. As they got to the middle of the field, Melinda stopped her horse and pulled a flashlight from her saddlebag. She shook the light for a couple of minutes then held it up and pressed the button in it. A few moments later, Jake spotted a series of flashes from near the top of the tree line.

"Morse freakin' code. Was that only four letters?"

"I could tell you, but then I'd have to shoot you."

"That would be awkward." Now that he was closer, he could see that the man was carrying a muzzle-loaded gun. He'd spent enough time at Mountain Man rendezvous to know a cap-lock rifle when he saw one. The man's knife was in a handmade sheath and his boots looked like they were also handmade.

When they reached the edge of the creek Jake could see long, sharpened stakes jutting from the far bank. As they approached, a wooden bridge was extended across the fifteen foot gap. Melinda led the way over it and into the camp while another Scout came across and took her horse's rein.

Melinda motioned towards the camp. "Welcome to Shenandoah Lodge."

Inside, the first thing that struck Jake was the unhurried order of the place. Rows of Baker tents sat to the east, each with their flaps open. Inside the ones nearest him he could see two cots with backpacks, duffel bags, and suitcases set on low racks. Most of the tents had wooden chairs in front of them, with a small table nearby. At the end of each row a larger tent was set up with a campfire nearby that was straddled by a tripod and a low spit, with a box on three foot high legs.

Jake recognized the "chuck box" from his own days as a Boy Scout, which he knew would hold almost everything you'd find in a well-stocked kitchen. At the end of each row a small colored flag flew, each with a simple emblem sewn onto it. South of the tents were several one and two story wood and stone buildings, a few still in the process of being built.

"We'd appreciate it if you didn't walk around with your long arms."

Another Scout came up, this one sporting the eagle over a gold fleur-de-lis of a Tenderfoot, the second rank among the Boy Scouts. "You can keep your sidearms, though we'd like it if you didn't wave 'em all over the place."

"Sure." Jake unslung the shotgun and the .22 and handed them to the Tenderfoot. He also unzipped his assault vest and stowed it on the bicycle, which was parked next to the retracted bridge. The Tenderfoot took them to a small log gatehouse on the left of the bridge. The Scout inside looked at Jake and nodded.

While the rest of Fox patrol headed for a larger shade fly Melinda led Jake toward the largest of the buildings, a two story wood and stone structure with a flagpole in front. Double doors opened onto a large open room that held a fireplace on the north wall big enough to stand up in. Melinda took her hat off as she entered the building and tucked it under her arm. A small fire was blazing merrily away. Several men and women lounged on old couches or newer, handmade chairs. Many were playing chess, while a few others were reading.

The main room was open to both levels, but the rear had a kitchen that would have been at home in the nineteenth century. A black wood burning stove with multiple doors and burners took up a good portion of the back wall, with almost blonde colored wooden cabinets and white ceramic knobs. Long trestle tables filled up the rest of the back half on the lower floor. A set of stairs led up on either side of the building to a loft above the kitchen and dining rom. Melinda led him up the stairs to a loft that was part library, part command center, and part game room. A chess game was set up and apparently on hold off to one side. Bookshelves lined two walls, while maps of Iowa, Nebraska, Missouri, and the United States adorned the wall to Jake's right. The back wall had a pair of open double doors that looked out onto a broad balcony. In the middle of the room was a large table the butted up against an equally massive desk that was currently home to a man well suited to both.

The man stood as they approached, his presence larger than his frame. Up close he might have had a couple of inches on Jake, but he still felt like he was looking up at a much larger man. His hair was white, his face weathered but lean. He stuck one browned hand out to engulf Jake's and he hoped the man showed some restraint when he squeezed.

"Scoutmaster Gil Perry, this is Specialist Jake Carter with ZOD."

"Pleased to meet you, son! You out of Springfield?"

"Yes, sir.

"You're a long way from home. Especially with things the way they are."

"Yes, sir, I was wondering about that. How do you handle the lightning storms?"

"Well, the past few days we've just been coming up in the lodge here letting the lightning rods and flag poles handle the bolts."

"What about the whirlwinds?"

"Whirlwinds?" Perry and Melinda asked simultaneously.

"You haven't seen them? Like dust devils, only bigger and electrified?"

Perry nodded. "Wolf Patrol did report something like that up in Shenandoah or Malvern. We figured it was specific to cities. Of course, they also said it sort of shorted out over water, too."

Jake's eyebrows went up at that. "That's good to know."

"Indeed it is. You're just in time for dinner, but we still observe certain traditions here. We're about to lower the flag for the day, if you care to join us." Jake nodded and followed the pair down the steps and to the front porch of the building. A color guard and a bugler approached the front porch, then turned and assumed their places off to one side. The bugler put his instrument to his lips and blew a short call. Scouts trooped in from the line of tents and filed out of the lodge. Melinda stepped off the porch and took her place at the head of her patrol.

"Fall in!" Perry called out. The Scouts lined up in rapid order.

"Atten-shun!" He motioned the Color Guard forward and gave out orders to prepare to lower the flag. Misun came to his feet.

"Lower the colors, Scouts hand salute!" Every hand snapped up.

Jake belatedly remembered to pull his head cover off and held it over his heart, feeling awkward as he stood there as the only stand out. The bugler played a different, slower cadence as the flag was lowered.

"Two!" Perry called out once the flag had been removed from the line. The Scouts lowered their salutes and Misun went back to sitting on his haunches, which prompted Jake to bring his own hand down. He watched as they went through the rest of the ceremony, presenting the flag to the sergeant at arms.

"Thank you for bearing with us and for your respect. You made a good impression on the rest of the troop."

"It's been a long time since I took part in a flag ceremony."

Perry led Jake back inside. "Most people didn't know the traditions before the Fall. It's nice to see that in a man and his dog. Did you serve?"

"No, sir. I didn't but Misun here was a police dog. Closest I came to enlisting is when I fought for my kingdom in the SCA. Now I'm a member of ZOD."

"Which means you fight for all of humanity. Although, ZOD isn't known for its solo operations." Perry led him up the steps to the loft and sat down at the fire place. He gestured at the other chairs, and Jake took a seat.

"No, we're not. I got separated from my unit, I'm trying to rejoin them."

"Where did you get separated?"

"Little town called Maryville, near the Missouri border."

Perry nodded, his face thoughtful. "And you made it here in a day on a bicycle? It's too bad you're already committed to

ZOD. You'd make a good Scout."

"Used to be one. A long time ago."

"Well, your loyalty is with ZOD now. I won't ask you to break any promises. But it does strike me that your entire unit is a long way from Springfield. And ZOD isn't known for dealing with small problems. Is there something I need to be aware of in the area?"

"No. I mean, aside from ferals and ragers, I guess not. Nothing on ground level, at least. No, the ORBS squad was basically brought along to help with security. Our real mission was education."

Perry leaned forward, his eyes bright with curiosity. "Orbs squad? Is that an acronym?"

"Oh, yeah. Outbreak Response Battle Suit. They're designed to fight the big ones, the ragers. Of course they stomp ferals pretty hard, too."

"Battle suits. Fascinating. So, you said your mission was education. Can you tell me more about that?"

"Hell, I wish I could tell you all about it."

"If you aren't authorized to disclose it."

"No. Not so much a problem of authorization as education. It's all farming stuff that I don't know squat about. Basically, it's the whole nuclear winter my folks worried about in the eighties." As he finished, Melinda approached with two more Scouts in tow. She nodded toward Scoutmaster Perry and Jake and the two handed them ceramic bowls filled with a thick, meaty stew, small round loaves of bread, and greens on a metal plate.

"Mindy, you know I don't like it when Constance does this. Thanks, Simon. I'll take my plate back down. Go enjoy your dinner."

"And you know your hands might as well be broken if you set a foot in her kitchen, sir." Melinda set her own tray down and handed them both a mug. Once the food was set, both Melinda and Perry bowed their heads. Jake pulled his hand back from his mug and bowed his head as well.

"For food, for raiment, for life, for opportunity, for friendship and fellowship, we thank thee, O Lord." Melinda prayed.

Perry raised his head with a soft "Amen."

Jake reached for his mug again and took a sip. "That sounds familiar."

"It's the Philmont Grace."

Jake sipped more from his mug and looked up at them. "Cider?"

"Yes, we have a couple of orchards near here."

Perry's gaze focused on the fire. "Although we may have to find a new way to grow them."

Melinda cast a glance at Perry then looked at Jake. "Excuse me, sir?"

Perry's attention returned to the moment. "Sorry. A conversation for after dinner. Do you play chess, Mister Carter?"

"Badly. I'm more of a poker player."

"Not a bad way to spend an evening, either. However, for the moment, perhaps you could tell us what's going on in the greater world outside our little domain. I'm most curious how you ended up on a bicycle, trying to pedal your way to Sioux City."

Jake told him the basics of what had happened in Maryville. He left out the specific modifications they were trying to make to the ORBS, detailing the fight in the camping store and his escape from the scavs instead.

"I'm impressed. Three ragers and a handful of ferals with a sword and a knife. Remind me to keep you out of the kitchen! So, tell me a little bit more about ZOD."

"Well, any more, we're one of the bigger units fighting the infected. We were pretty much nationwide before the Fall. After... well, after that first year people started joining up left and right. Individual survivors and small groups that we'd rescued or helped out mostly. Sometimes we'll get recruits from local communities."

"I'm curious. What one trait do you think makes ZOD so successful?"

"It's two, really. Teamwork and discipline. The other day, we fought a feral elephant. Damn thing tossed my battle suit around like a toy. It took three of us to bring it down. And let me tell you when you see an *elephant* charging at you, you're going to want to run. And you know the guys next to you are going to want to run, too. But they didn't."

"I can imagine that makes it easier to stand your ground."

"Actually, it makes it harder to run." Across from him, Perry tilted his head, looking curious, but Melinda was nodding.

"You don't want to let your people down," she said. Perry smiled at that.

"Yeah, that's the biggest part. When you know they've got your back, you want to be worthy of that, you know?"

"I think there's something else about ZOD that makes you successful, Mister Carter. You innovate and you adapt. Unlike most groups we've run into since the Fall, ZOD has constantly moved forward. From turning baseball bats into lethal weapons to making cars that mow down ferals like wheat, to your own amazing battle suit. ZOD has single-handedly advanced mankind forward in fighting the current threat more than almost any other group. And from what you told me earlier, you have other advances in agriculture and botany to share as well."

"I think that would be a pretty accurate assessment, if I do say so myself."

Perry leaned forward. "So, let me tell you the Scouts' greatest strength. We have taken the skills of the past and kept them and ourselves alive. Almost everything you see around you was made by us using skills we learned either here, or at other Scout camps throughout the United States. As you can see, we have revived traditions not seen in the world for decades. Where my Scouts once spent their free time texting and playing games on their phones; they now play checkers, chess, backgammon, and card games. They know Morse code, some have learned semaphore and many can track game through the rain to its lair. The Scouts and ZOD embody opposite ends of the spectrum, Mister Carter. I can only imagine how effective we would be if we learned to innovate like your people do."

Jake leaned back in his chair and sipped his cider. If this group had the means to produce fresh meat and brew hard cider, it spoke highly of their skills. And there was no doubting their integrity, at least as far as he'd seen.

"Well, I'm not even an NCO. I can take a message to my group, and they can get in touch with our higher ups..."

"I doubt that. But I have another solution to offer. Tomorrow, Melinda will take you to our regional base camp Camp Little Sioux with a proposal I'll write up tonight. I think they'll go along with it. We can at least speak for the Mid-America Council. If things work out well, we can get other councils on board. ZOD isn't the only group out there, Mister Carter. And some of the others aren't as interested in the common good as ZOD is. You're going to need some help. While we're not an army, we are a force to be reckoned with in our own way."

"Well, it's worth a shot," Jake said with all of the confidence of a man who didn't have to make the final decision.

"Excellent! So, how long has it been since you rode a horse?"

"Whosoever shall receive one of such children in my name, receiveth me: and whosoever shall receive me, receiveth not me, but him that sent me."

-Mark 9:39

"It's a lot different from riding a camel, isn't it?" Melinda spoke up as they rounded a curve and slowed to a trot.

Misun loped along beside Jake with his tongue hanging out. "Yeah. Not as smooth, but a lot less side to side going on!"

In the early morning gray, the ash fall was still steady but it seemed to have lessened a little. "It gets easier once you figure out the rhythm. You'll pick that up on the road."

"That's reassuring."

They reined in at the lodge to find a third horse waiting along with all of Jakes gear and his bike on the porch. A Scout with a Quartermaster badge was standing under the awning next to some extra tack. He looked up as they dismounted.

"We got you a couple of scabbards for your long arms," Melinda said as the quartermaster handed her the two scabbards. "And saddlebags for the necessities. We'll put the rest on a packhorse."

Jake buckled the scabbards into place on either side of the saddle. "I can leave the bike if you guys want it."

The quartermaster nodded enthusiastically. "I'll trade you a bow and some arrows and a good hatchet for it."

"Deal!"

They shook on it, and the other man set off while Jake started transferring his meager supplies from his pack to the saddlebags. He took out Misun's folding bowl and filled it with water, letting his companion slurp his fill while he finished packing. The quartermaster came back as Melinda was finishing Jake's lesson in how to tie his bedroll to the back of his saddle. The bow was in a case that attached to its own quiver. Jake lashed it to the scabbard with the .22 in it.

The door to the lodge opened and Scoutmaster Perry emerged as Jake and Melinda mounted. The rest of Fox patrol came out on his heels, looking both excited and a little forlorn by turns.

Perry handed Melinda a folded paper, complete with a wax seal over a ribbon. "I just signaled ahead to Little Sioux that you're on your way. They're expecting you in three days."

"How did you get a signal through? Our shortwave is junk right now."

"Telegraph. Not as easily disrupted... or intercepted. Now, Godspeed. May He watch over you on your way."

Melinda held a hand up to the rest of her team then turned north. "Thank you, sir. I'll make sure they signal you as soon as we get there."

They emerged from the camp through a heavy, planked bridge that crossed the creek at a narrow spot. They turned west and made for the Wabash Trace trail again. Once on the trail Melinda set them to a canter. It was a ground eating pace that got them to the outskirts of Council Bluff by the end of the first day, even with having to take cover a couple of times from lightning storms.

Once they had gotten a few miles north of the cities she took them off their path about half a mile to a small, two-lane bridge that crossed a sluggish river. The aches of riding made getting off his horse almost comical, and it took him a few moments to actually stand upright.

They made camp by the side of the bridge. The site looked as though it had been made for them. It had a circle of rocks and a few short stumps around it, and a stack of wood setting on two thick branches to keep it off the ground. Jake gathered more wood while Melinda cooked a simple stew of cubed meat, carrots, potatoes, and onions dinner in a Dutch oven. After dinner was cleaned up, Melinda brought out a folding game board and proceeded to beat him soundly at chess. Their game was lit by the flickering light of the campfire and the occasional strobe of lightning across the constant cloud cover.

"Tomorrow night, we'll play backgammon," she promised as she stowed the pieces and folded the board back up. They banked the fire and laid down in their bedrolls, but sleep seemed elusive.

"What did you do before the Fall?"

"Built houses. What about you?"

"I was in college. Majored in agribusiness. When it happened, my husband and our son were on a camping trip with Gil. My son... he killed his father and Gil had to put him down. Most of the older boys in his troop survived. When he got them back home—"

"Home was worse than where he'd just 'escaped' from?"

"Yeah."

Jake took a deep breath. "I was on the road, coming back from seeing my folks for my mom's birthday. It was late at night No one was on the road and I hit a deer. Smashed my radiator, tore up the front of my car, damn near killed me in the process. Couldn't get a signal on my phone, so I started walking. Took me three days to get to El Paso. By then... it was Hell on Earth."

"That was Omaha, too. Gil gathered up as many people as he could in the chaos and we headed east into Iowa until we found the camp."

"So, how did you guys hook up with the rest of the Scouts?"

"Oh, that was bound to happen. Once we got things kind of settled and we weren't worried about starving to death or getting eaten by ferals we sent patrols to the scouting camps and found the other council members. It was pretty much a given that someone was going to go to the camps. So we left trail signs all over the place directing folks to go to rendezvous points if they hadn't already gone to a camp. We set up the telegraph a couple of years ago. Though, until the other day we've been using low powered shortwave radio for most of our transmissions. Little Sioux even has a two hour radio show they put on every

Friday night."

Jake raised an eyebrow. "A radio show?"

Melinda propped herself up on her elbow. "Yeah. They do a couple of serial shows, music, news, and an instructional program."

"Serial shows? Like *The Phantom* and *Little Orphan Annie*?"

"Yeah. Only right now, ours are *The Detective Brown Mysteries* and *Galaxy Star One*. They rotate a new series in every few months. A little something for everyone, I guess. They do printed versions after each episode in *Scouting Life*."

"You have your own magazine? Where do you find the paper?"

"We make it."

Jake shook his head. "Of course. I should have figured that."

"It's okay. I was as surprised as anyone else when Little Sioux sent us our first copies."

Quiet settled after that and eventually sleep found them.

Breakfast was oatmeal with dried apple slices and cider. Misun wolfed down his portion of left over stew. Sniffing around he marked the campsite in the name of ZOD before they returned to the trail. They used the same ground eating combination of gaits, stopping only to have a lunch of peanut butter and honey sandwiches between thick slices of coarse bread while they took shelter from a lightning storm. Late that afternoon, they stopped near another bridge.

Melinda dismounted. She handed him the packhorse's reins and edged her horse forward a couple of steps. "Go ahead and get a fire going. Cut up some of the meat and vegetables and we'll make Turtle Wraps tonight. The foil is in the bag next to it, with the spices."

Jake tied the packhorse next to his. "You're not going to use the Dutch oven?"

"Not for dinner."

She smiled at him before riding back the way they came and turned up a side road. Like the previous night, the campsite was as good as made for them. By the time Melinda made it back

Jake had built the fire and had the beef cubes and vegetables sliced, spiced, wrapped in foil, and ready to lay in the coals. She dismounted and brought a canvas sack with her. She left it beside Jake along with two smaller cloth bags. When he opened the larger sack, his eyes lit up as he saw the dozen or so green apples. The smaller bags held blueberries and strawberries.

"There's an orchard up the road there. I figured we'd have some apple cobbler for dessert and some fresh fruit with breakfast."

"I am all for that! So, you guys travel this road pretty regularly? This is the second campsite that looks like it's regularly maintained."

"This is our supply route with Little Sioux, yeah. We passed two other campsites along the way for the trip back to Shenandoah Lodge. That's why we haven't run into any infected along the way." As she was speaking, she had been mixing ingredients together and began stirring in earnest as the batter thickened.

"Makes sense." Jake began slicing apples. He got more water when he was done.

"So, was there anyone before the Fall?"

"There was a girl I'd just started seeing. She lived in Lubbock, Barony of Bonwicke. I met her at an event. Thing is, I can't remember which one. We called each other a few times and we were going to stay together at Crown Tourney."

"What's Crown Tourney?" Melinda put the Dutch oven on the coals and used her camp shovel to lay some on the lid.

"It's where the best fighters in the kingdom fight for the right to be king for six months. Anyway, we never made it to Crown. The end of the world happened first."

"Do you miss her?"

"I barely got to know her. I think that's what makes it worse. There's so much about her that I just don't know. Everything was all about survival after that and then ZOD was pretty much my life."

"Fox patrol is like family to me. So if it's anything like that, I get it."

"Yeah, something like that. I don't always like everyone, but we'd all die for each other." He buried his hand in the fur behind Misun's ears and rubbed gently, making the dog tilt his head into his hand and kick his leg a little.

Melinda lifted the lid of the pot. "Smells like dinner is done."

Jake used the shovel to get the three foil packets out of the fire and set them on a rock. Misun's portion was all meat and drippings, which he opened first and set aside to cool while he got the other two meals onto their plates. When the meat was cool enough to eat without scorching his tongue he dumped Misun's into his bowl, then waited until Melinda had said grace to set the bowl down and start on his own meal.

The cobbler was bubbling and hot when they pulled it off the fire. The green Granny Smith apples gave it a tart flavor that made Jake's mouth water. After they finished cleaning up, Melinda pulled out her game board and flipped it over to show the backgammon side. It took a little bit of a refresher, but Jake remembered the rules quickly enough. With the dice favoring him he won two out of three games, but declined to play a fourth.

"I may not be a genius, but I'm smart enough to know when not to push my luck."

She unrolled her blankets. "Yeah, quit while you're ahead."

They hit the road as early as they dared after another breakfast of oatmeal. This time with sliced strawberries mixed in for flavor. The wind was turning cool as they approached a turn in the road and Melinda motioned for Jake to stop. She pulled her flashlight out and shook it to charge. She repeated the flashing sequence she'd used outside of Shenandoah Lodge. Moments after she finished another light flickered back at them from the top of a steep hill and she continued up the road. Almost a mile later they came to the camp entrance and Jake let out a low whistle. A stone wall stretched between two ridgelines. When he looked along the ridge, he could see where the hills had been shaped to present a steep face all along their length.

"That's incredible! How did you guys manage that?"

"Camp shovels," Melinda quipped, then laughed as Jake rolled his eyes. "Okay, would you believe trained gophers?"

"No."

"Didn't think so. Truth is, the trick is dynamite. Lots of it.

And someone with an engineering degree."

"Do we knock, or say the secret password or something?"

"No, that's what's odd. These gates are never closed unless there's an emergency. Usually, the kind of emergency that would make them close the gates is out here pounding on them." A head popped up over the gate. After a few moments it opened just enough for one horse at a time to get through.

A Scout motioned to them from just inside the gap. "Hurry up, get inside."

They urged their horses forward, and the gate closed almost on the packhorse's tail.

"Why are the gates closed, Brad?"

"Council's orders. I'll stable your pack horse. Head up to the watch tower, the Region Head wants to talk to you." Brad gave a slight head tilt toward Jake, which he took to mean that he was why they were heading up to talk to the Region Head.

Jake followed as Amanda headed further into the camp. She turned her mount right and started up a trail that led up the side of the second ridgeline back, the tallest one he could see. As they got closer to the top, he could see a tall metal tower built on the crest. An older man was waiting at the door to the building by the base of the tower. He wore a Scout uniform that had more patches and insignia on it than Jake had ever seen. Melinda dismounted quickly and rendered a salute, which the man returned casually.

"Who are you?"

"Specialist Three Jake Carter, First ORBS Division, Springfield ZOD. Who are you?"

"I'm Regional Scoutmaster Samuel Claypool, mister, and I don't appreciate your tone."

"My apologies, sir. I was following the example I was given. I assumed you exemplified proper etiquette here." Beside him Melinda turned her face away, but not before he caught the smirk she tried to cover with her hand. Claypool started to turn red then stepped back and looked at Melinda's reaction.

"Your point is well taken, Mister Carter. If not exactly appreciated. Are all ZOD members as insubordinate as you are?"

"No, sir. Just the ORBS pilots."

"Well, I hope we can—"

He was cut off by a long horn blast. A trumpet began playing from another direction and Claypool's face went ashen.

"Infected."

Melinda's face went pale as another series of notes sounded. Her eyes went to Jake. "Ragers."

A familiar sounding series of notes went up. Melinda scrambled back into her saddle with Jake a heartbeat behind her. They galloped down the trail and came out into the main valley of the camp to find it in a state of controlled chaos. A steady line of Scouts was racing toward the gates on one side, while another line, mostly younger and older Scouts, were heading further into camp. Jake and Melinda bounded out of the trees and exploded through a gap in the line of fleeing people, then raced alongside the other line. They pulled up at the gate to find Brad directing defenders to positions.

"How many?" Jake demanded.

"About a dozen of the smaller feral ones, and three of the big ones. Now get clear, we have a group coming in. We need to open the gates!"

Jake backed up and pointed his horse's nose toward the gate.

Melinda sidled up next to him. "You're not going to do what I *think* you're going to do, are you?"

Jake opened the scabbard on the shotgun and slung it at his side. "Oh, I probably am."

The gate opened and he slapped his horse's rump with his reins. Misun barked and charged out with him. He thought he heard Melinda's voice behind him as he hit the opening, but he didn't give it any more thought. The incoming group was to the north. He turned that direction and galloped past them, counting six horses and nine packhorses heading the other way as fast as they could. The first feral was nearly fifty yards from the end of the line. Jake drew his falchion with a tight grin. A slight nudge to his horse's flank made it veer left just far enough that he could swing at its head. The impact nearly tore the blade from his grip, but he managed to keep his hold on it and rein his mount in.

Another feral was closing fast. He drew the shotgun as he spun his horse to the right. The thing's head fell under the bead and he pulled the trigger, sending brains and bone chips flying.

His horse shied a bit at the sound of the gunshot, but settled as he pumped another round into the Remington's chamber and sighted in on a new target. His second shot staggered the beast, but it took another shot to drop it. By then his mount was getting too skittish to shoot from, so he slid out of the saddle as he inserted a new shell into the tube. Without a rider, the horse bolted back toward the camp, leaving Jake to face the rest of the horde.

"Swords cut him not, nor may fire burn him, O son of Bharata, waters wet him not, nor dry winds parch. He may not be cut nor burned nor wet nor withered; he is eternal, all-present, firm, unshaken, everlasting. He is called unmanifest, unimaginable, unchanging; therefore, knowing him thus, deign not to grieve!"

-Krishna; Chapter 2, verses 23–25

Jake stuck the falchion's point into the dirt and shoved another shell into the tube, then brought the gun back up to his shoulder, all in a matter of seconds. The next feral dropped when he pulled the trigger, and the next. It was a matter of firing, pumping a new round into the chamber while he shifted targets and firing again.

"Dual kill, Tri-Kill, Quad-Kill, Penta-Kill, Off-Kill-ter, Spec-ta-Kill!" he yelled, letting the shotgun dangle by its sling as the last round dropped the seventh feral. "Shotgun killing spree!"

He drew the Glock from his vest. It took most of the magazine to drop the five remaining ferals. He holstered the pistol as the ragers came into sight. Thus far, he'd had the advantage of dealing with the ferals in a line strung out as they'd chased the Scouts. The ragers came in a group. He unslung the shotgun and stripped out of the vest, knowing that he needed every ounce of speed and agility he could get. As he picked up the falchion, he looked up and pulled a bit of dirt from the point.

He tossed the bits of earth into the air. "If I die here, then let it be said, by earth and sky, that I lived my last moments well."

The ragers slowed and spread out. Jake went into his combat

stance. "At least one of you fuckers is going down!"

They started to move. Jake bolted right. His sudden change of vector caught them off guard. The gunshot that rang out and the bullet that caught the middle rager above the left eye turned momentary confusion into disorder. The left most rager turned, thinking to deal with the woman riding toward them. Its left leg was yanked out from beneath him and he ended up sprawling as the horse trampled him. Bones splintered under its weight. He spat blood as he rolled to his feet in search of his original antagonist. Misun was already out of reach, barking and darting in and out of reach before the rager could lay a hand or a fist on him.

The middle rager shook its head and wiped blood from its eye, only to have a round puncture a lung as Melinda rode past. Jake had darted under the right hand rager's swing and had severed the Achilles tendon on its left leg, bringing it down. It had rolled away as he went for the head and now he found himself trying to stay out of its reach as it grabbed for his blade. When it stretched its hand out again Jake swung fast. Four fingers tumbled on the grass. His next swing severed the hand at the wrist. As the massive infected grasped at its wounded limb with its other hand he took it off, too. Jake jumped over the waving stumps, turned in midair and spun the falchion so that it was point down when he landed on his opponent's back. There was a wet crunch as he pinned its head to the ground.

Misun was struggling to stay out of range as the second rager joined the one he'd been tormenting, deciding to ignore Melinda. Jake drew the Judge from his waistband and pointed it at the left hand rager's back. He pulled the trigger five times, sending three double-aught rounds tearing through the monster's spine and organs with each shot. One shot hit something important in the spine and the rager flopped to the ground, unable to move anything below its shoulders.

The third stopped and focused on Jake, making its final mistake. The right side of its head erupted as Melinda put a .308 round through its left ear, taking the shot the moment it was still for more than a heartbeat. Jake stepped up and pulled the nine millimeter Glock from the holster on his hip and took deliberate aim before putting a round between the last rager's eyes.

Melinda rode up at a gallop and sent dirt flying as she skidded to a stop nearby. She slid from the saddle with her rifle still in hand and stormed up to Jake.

"You are an idiot! What were you thinking? Running out here like this risking your life, facing more than a dozen infected on your own?"

"Well, I wasn't exactly alone."

"You *weren't* thinking, that's the problem! Did you just *assume* I'd ride out to save your ass? Do you really think you're *that* important?"

"Actually, I figured I'd run at some point."

"Of course you didn't, you... wait... what did you just say?"

Jake wiped his blade on the grass before he sheathed it, then stood and smiled at Melinda, who still fumed nearby. "I figured I might end up getting killed, but I figured I could thin them out enough to make them manageable for you by the time they did reach the gate. I planned on killing as many as I could then drawing one off to chase me or something. I was still going to let you guys have a little of the fun."

Her lips thinned as she clenched her jaw. She walked toward him. Just when he figured she was going to punch him, she reached for him and drew him into a fierce but short kiss. In spite of his surprise, Jake found himself returning the kiss almost immediately.

"Damn it, I'm so—"

"Horny? Confused?" Jake rubbed his fingertips across his tingling lips. "It's the adrenaline. Is this your first time getting up close and personal like this?"

Melinda's voice shook. "Yeah, we usually just shoot them from a distance or run and fight them from the walls."

"Which is probably the smarter way to do it when you're fighting ferals, but ragers—"

"We've seen what they can do to walls and buildings." Melinda made her way to her horse, her pace unsteady.

Jake picked up his shotgun. He knelt down and patted Misun. "Good boy. I'm going to have to find you some treats or something."

Melinda whispered as the gate came into sight. "I would really like it if you didn't tell anyone about me kissing you."

"No, of course not. My father used to tell me that a good man let a woman's smile do the talking. 'If you have to brag, you're not worth her time,' was how he always said it."

Melinda's face flushed a little pink. "Thank you."

"That being said, it was one hell of a kiss. Thought you should know that."

"Thank you. You're a good kisser, too. Now, shut up." The gate opened as they approached and they were hustled inside.

Claypool was fuming inside the compound. "What in the hell was that, Mister Carter?"

"That is why I'm an ORBS pilot, sir."

"What the hell is that?"

"Outbreak Response Battle Suit. They're designed to fight ragers. In other words, I'm the guy who runs *at* the things other feral fighters have the good sense to run away from. Besides, between Scout Holt and me we killed all fifteen of those damn things. So you're welcome."

Jake turned and walked further into the camp. Scouts moved aside as he approached. Before long he reached a building with a sign on it that read "Welcome Center." With a sigh, he sat down on the bench by the front door. A few minutes later Claypool rode up on a bay horse, leading Jake's roan by the reins.

"Follow me, please. There is something I need you to see."

Once Jake had mounted up, Claypool led him back up the trail to the lookout tower, then dismounted and started the climb up the steps to the top. Once they were at the top, the Regional Director handed him a pair of large binoculars and pointed west.

"What am I looking for?"

"Movement." The answer seemed too simple, but he put the lenses to his eyes and started scanning the fields.

"Further out." Claypool suggested.

When he focused on points further away he noticed movement almost immediately. He turned the knob and saw a group of ferals come into sharp relief. Then a pair of ragers. Seconds later he saw another group, this one a line of ragers goaded on by a woman riding some kind of creature.

Jake handed the binoculars back to Claypool. "What the hell?"

"We've been seeing two or three groups a day for almost a week, but some of our camps and lodges in Illinois and the Dakotas report groups moving south in the past couple of days. I believe you'll come to the same conclusion we have."

"Somehow, someone is mobilizing an army of infected. We'd heard rumors of a new kind of infected, Nephilim, that have special powers. It's pretty crazy. Some people say they can control the dead, others say they control bugs. Nothing we could verify."

"Until now and they all seem to be going toward Sioux City, Mister Carter. The same place you said you were heading. You can understand my concern with getting the Scouts involved with your group, if you've somehow become a target for all of the ferals in the US."

"We were headed to Sioux City to check out something else. Someone's making undead cyborgs or something. We were on our way to help out a group called the Freemen."

"Yes, we've heard of the Freemen. Be careful when you deal with them. Now, I understand you're wanting to get back to your unit. You can rest here tonight and leave in the morning. I'll be talking to the rest of the Council tonight and we'll figure out what course of action we want to take where ZOD is concerned."

"Sir, I can't speak for ZOD as a whole. We've never demanded anyone help us. If you want to that's great, but no one is asking you to if you don't want to. If you want to send someone to observe I'm pretty sure that would be okay, too. If not, I'll head out in the morning and maybe we'll send someone out later on to do something official and make nice. Truth is, if it was me, I'd say you guys would do better to sit this one out."

"Why is that, Mister Carter?"

Sensing he'd stepped on some toes, Jake paused for a moment before answering. "Well, from what I've seen, your people are like Rangers. Highly trained light infantry. You don't send special forces in against tanks. That's what I think this is going to be, a major slug-fest. That isn't your style, but it's ZOD all over. Especially the ORBS division."

The older man put binoculars down and headed for the stairs down. "You may have a point. You're welcome to stay as our guest as long as you need to. I'll let you know what our decision is in the morning and... thank you for helping out today."

"You're welcome, sir. Anytime."

Jake listened as the Scout leader walked back down the steps. He picked up the binoculars again. It was rare that he got this kind of view. Turning his attention to the other four points of the compass he noted several dark columns of smoke to the east and a lightning storm heading toward the camp from the north. Though it looked to be hours away, he still didn't want to stay on the highest point around any longer than he needed to.

Jake woke slowly, his thoughts fuzzy and his eyelids heavy. Vague memories of dark dreams hovered at the edge of his memory, but without the usual terror that usually accompanied their rare recurrence.

Melinda's voice came from the darkness. "Who's Holly?"

"Holly? How do you know that name?" Gentle fingertips stroked his cheek and he became aware of the warmth beneath his cheek.

"You talk in your sleep." He turned his head and saw her face looking down at him, her features softened by the flickering light of a dying fire.

Jake realized he had his head in her lap and that she was sitting in his bed with her back to the wall. "Damn comfortable beds."

He knew he should have been uncomfortable with the situation, but he was reluctant to move. The bunk bed was the most comfortable bed he'd slept on in a long time, even more so than the beds in the Army Depot barracks in Corpus.

"You were moaning and thrashing. Then you called me Holly when I tried to calm you down. Was that ... her name?"

"Yeah, I haven't said it out loud in years." He sat up and rubbed his face.

He turned to her. "You'd probably better go. People are gonna talk."

She moved her legs and laid down beside him, pulling him down to her. "They already are, I'm sure. Let them."

She kissed him and any thought he had of arguing with her vanished. They were slow and hesitant at first, both years out of practice. But the pace suited them and they spent the rest of the night sating long denied hunger.

Jake woke up first in the gray hours before dawn and padded to the kitchen once he was dressed. The kitchen in the small guest cabin was well stocked and by the time Melinda stumbled out of bed, he had hot oatmeal and blueberries waiting. He admired her long, lean legs as she came in wearing only a lengthy shirt.

Once they had eaten and were dressed, they went down to the open stage area along the main route through the camp with Misun loping beside them. Morning assembly was still a ways off, but no one wanted to miss the day's announcements since everyone knew that the Regional Scoutmaster Council had met last night.

Most of the Scouts were quiet, many still looking like they weren't fully awake. One group caught Jake's attention, louder than the rest and slightly separate. All of them wore the same patrol patch, a wolf with its head turned up and mouth open. After a few minutes the one wearing the patrol leader patch on his left arm, headed their way, with a trio of larger men in tow.

The leader sidled up to Jake. "So you're the one who thawed out the Ice Queen of Troop Nine."

Jake tilted his head and gave the man a long look before he answered. "And you must be the guy who's business that isn't."

In his ZOD gear Jake stood out, especially since he was the most heavily armed person there. The belligerent Scout looked him over, his eyes lingering on the two visible pistols and the sword. He turned away with a dismissive wave and took a step to the side so that he was facing Melinda.

"Slut."

If he was planning on elaborating on the statement, it was lost when Melinda's fist slammed into his jaw. He spun and hit the dirt face first. For a few seconds he didn't move. The three men with him moved forward. They stopped as Jake stepped in front of them with his hand on the hilt of his falchion.

Jake tapped the handle of his sword. "I'd think twice."

The largest of the three puffed out his chest. "There's three of us and one of you."

Jake smiled at him. "True. We can wait if you need to go get more guys."

"We don't need more guys."

Melinda stepped up beside Jake. "Yeah, you do."

The trio exchanged glances, their will faltering. One of the trio backed away. "I ain't messin' with them. Not after yesterday."

At the mention of their previous day's exploits, the other two went pale and took a step back.

One of the larger Scouts shrugged. "Ah, Tommy deserved that."

They grabbed their fallen leader who was moaning and trying to regain his feet, and hoisted him to something more upright before hauling him back to the rest of their group.

"That was one hell of a punch."

"He deserved it. Tommy's been propositioning me since the first day we met. According to him, he's slept with half the women in the Scouts. The other half are sluts. Somehow, I'm not getting his logic."

Their laughter was cut short by the bugle call to assemble. They took their place at the back of the formation for the day's flag raising and Pledge of Allegiance. Finally, it was time for the day's announcements and a hush fell over the assembled Scouts.

Claypool stepped up to the podium and looked out over the group. "I'm sure everyone has heard about yesterday's attack and the response to it."

Claypool paused as a low murmur spread through the ranks of the Scouts. "What yesterday's events have made clear to the Council is that even now, the world is still changing. The challenges facing mankind are greater than any one group of people can face alone, even a group as exceptional as the one gathered before me. To that end the Council of Scoutmasters has decided to send envoys to ZOD, to explore the possibility of a partnership between our two groups. We will seek two more volunteers to accompany Scout Holt with Specialist Carter to rendezvous with the ZOD contingent currently bound for Sioux City. Before that can happen, there is another matter of business that must be addressed. The Council calls Scout First Class Holt to come forward."

Melinda gave Jake a wide eyed look. She stepped out of formation and went to the stage. As she walked up onto the stage, another Scout called the formation to attention.

Claypool was stone faced as he stood in front of her. "Miss Holt, in recognition of your service as a Scout, your leadership and bravery as exemplified by your actions before this camp, the Council has recommended that you be promoted to the rank of Star Scout. You are no longer just a Scout, but have joined a smaller group, a group that is faced with the greater responsibilities of leadership. The Star Scout lights the way for those who follow and is a steadfast beacon for anyone who is lost and seeking their way."

Melinda's eyes were wide as he handed her the new insignia of her rank and shook her hand.

Claypool smiled. "Scouts, salute! Two! At ease! Dis-missed!"

Another Scout came up to Jake as the rest began to disperse and gestured for him to follow. He led Jake to a building nearby and ushered him into a room with Claypool and several other men and women wearing the more elaborately decorated Scoutmaster shirts and white bordered green neckerchiefs.

"Mister Carter, may I present the Mid-America Scoutmaster Council. We'll make this brief, since you'll be facing enough delays as it is. Miss Holt will be acting as our representative, but we also want to give you a copy of our diplomatic packet to make sure that our proposal makes it to ZOD's leadership one way or another."

One of the women stepped forward. "We feel that ZOD and the Scouts have a great deal to offer each other."

Her hair was a steel gray, and her narrow face was set in a determined look. A couple of the men near her frowned, but she pressed on apparently either oblivious or uncaring of their reactions. "Both in material and combat support, and in knowledge. And we've seen the writing on the wall. The infected are no longer the only threat to our survival as a species. The world itself has turned against us. It's time we began to stand together."

"I think you all are right. Things are getting worse in some ways, but I'm just a battle suit pilot. My idea of handling a problem is to go looking for it and hit it as hard as I can. I'll get this to the folks who need to see it." He picked up the packet of papers and tucked them into his vest before leaving. For a few moments, silence followed his departure.

One of the men smirked as Jake left. "That was the man who killed fourteen infected yesterday? He certainly doesn't look like much."

"And what do you think such a man should look like, Tim?" the woman who had spoken asked with an amused grin.

"Bigger. And taller."

"We tend to see men like him only from behind and from a distance. The only time we usually see them up close is after they're dead. And dead heroes always look bigger than life."

"Fear thou not; for I am with thee... I will strengthen thee... I will help thee... I will uphold thee with the right hand of my righteousness."

-Isaiah 41:10

Finding where ZOD had been wasn't hard. The wrecked hulk of ZRV Three and Scout Two marked the edge of a corpse-strewn battlefield on the outskirts north of Sergeant Bluff, just before the Sioux City limits. The Zerv was still smoking, a pyre for its crew. Scout Two had been peeled open like a sardine can, but the bodies of the two person crew didn't seem to be in evidence.

Jake walked among the feral and rager corpses, noting blast damage and the savage rents in unhealed flesh caused by his fellow ORBS pilots. Many of the ferals along the outside edge of the killing field had the narrow but jagged cuts caused by saw-axes, or the slight concave impression of war clubs. ZOD troopers had joined this fight early on, Jake guessed. Probably buying time for the slower battle suits to deploy. There were other wounds with flaps of skin hanging outward, long tendrils of flesh and viscera stretching away from the bodies that Jake couldn't identify. Misun sniffed at the dead briefly then came back to his human's side.

"They went west."

"How can you tell that?" The question came from Scout Second Class Harper. The boy was a lanky city kid from Omaha, he'd been eager to join the expedition and prove himself, which Jake had found funny given the outspoken, "issues with authority" act he usually put on.

"Because that's where the bodies go," Jake replied, pointing to the scattering of infected corpses stretching out from the rest of the field. "If you ever need to find ZOD, follow the trail of zombie corpses. Most times, they'll be at the end of it."

"Y'all ain't very subtle, are you?" Tenderfoot Hoskins gaped. She had been a newer recruit, coming from closer to Iowa City. But she was one of the best marksmen Jake had ever seen with the heavy Mosin-Nagant M91/30 PU Sniper rifle she carried.

"Subtle isn't our job."

Melinda folded a laminated map and stowed it back in the map case she carried. "If they headed west, they'll have to take Highway 129 across the river."

Jake said as he looked around again. "Then we'll check that out. Okay, Scouts. What is wrong with this battlefield?"

Harper spoke up after surveying the scene for a couple of minutes. "No ZOD bodies. If they got bit, they'd be up walking around. And what's with the big holes in these other bodies? It's like someone ripped something out of them."

"Mechanized ferals. The same motherfucker who is making the cyborg zombies must have collected our dead."

He went to his horse and pulled the pry bar from his saddlebags. He walked over to the misshapen wreck of Scout Two. After a couple of minutes of work, the latch on the trunk gave way, and he had access to the contents.

Inside was the standard contents of any ZOD vehicle's supply load out. Scout Two had two M4s and two Glock 17s mounted to the trunk lid, with a case of ammo for each kind of gun. Two survival packs, a first aid kit and a pair of machetes.

Jake pulled out one of the M4s and loaded a full magazine into it. "Load this stuff up."

As the Scouts emptied the trunk and loaded the contents onto their two packhorses, Jake checked the front of the vehicle. The radio had been crushed against the dash and the microphone cord had been snapped.. Brass and blood littered the seats, so at least the crew had gone down fighting. Beside the car, a rager's body sported multiple bullet holes to the head, so Jake could count at least one last kill to Scout Two.

Once everything of use was taken, Jake mounted back up and they followed the trail of dead ferals. As Melinda had predicted the trail led to Highway 129. Bodies stretched halfway across the river. Thunder rumbled overhead and Jake looked back toward Sioux City.

"Looks like Dr. Frankenzombie has range problems."

Melinda thought for a moment. "If we could find another side of his range limits, I bet we could narrow down where he is a little bit."

"Oh, I think we're going to get plenty of chances to test the limits of his range. But I think he's going to figure out how to boost it pretty damn quick."

"How do you figure that?"

"This guy had to go tinkering with ferals, trying to make them 'better' somehow. He's not going to leave well enough alone." That raised some eyebrows, but it got no argument as they pressed on.

An hour later, Melinda laughed as she handed her binoculars to Jake and pointed at a ridge line to the north. "You're right, ZOD isn't subtle."

Through the lenses Jake saw a line of construction vehicles, bearing a logo that had been marked out under a crude version of the ZOD insignia. From what he could see they were creating an earthen wall in the old Roman style, by digging a ditch and using the displaced earth to create a wall. The Romans had done it to create temporary bases, using man-power alone. ZOD had taken the idea and industrialized it, using bulldozers to build an earthwork easily a mile long that encircled a ridgeline. A massively built central structure acted as a gate to the fortified area using entire trees as the outer wall, backed by concrete drain pipes set vertically. If Jake was any judge they were probably filled with rubble or dirt and partly buried.

"They better get that done quick."

"Why?" Jake focus was still on the hastily built fortification.

"Smell that? It's gonna rain soon."

Jake pulled his shemagh down and sniffed the air. Sure enough he felt the humidity in the air, the odd sensation in the back of his nose that usually meant rain.

"We should be kinda quick ourselves. 'Cuz we're about to have company." Jake turned around to see what Harper was talking about, and let out a low curse. Behind them was a line of infected that stretched back out of sight.

"Let's move, people!" Melinda barked. No one hesitated, and all four broke into a gallop for the fortification's gate. Misun kept up, a feat that still surprised Jake. He pulled into the lead to make sure his ZOD uniform was visible.

Their approach got someone's attention, because the construction vehicles stopped what they were doing and turned to face outward. People started to appear on the top of the earthen walls and a pair of battle suits emerged from the gate house. Jake recognized the first one to emerge as Bowman's Ranger. The second one was no ZOD design. Easily half again the size of an ORBS, it was also more heavily armed and it moved faster and more fluidly than Bowman's battle suit. Both arms ended in gun mounts and a pair of pods stuck up over each shoulder, with a set of stubby little tubes jutting from the back. Where the ZOD units had angled cage style cockpits, this one sported a smooth oval bubble. Jake could see the pilot's helmet and shoulders, but nothing else. The new battle suit pointed both arms at them as they approached and Jake could see multiple barrels.

"Stop and identify yourself!" a woman's voice demanded from the speakers under the cockpit bubble. "Or you will be fired on!" Jake reined his horse in held his hands out.

He turned his horse to one side. "You've just got all manner of options for killing folk, don'tcha? I'm Specialist Jake Carter. Springfield ORBS Division."

"Jake?" Ken Bowman's voice came from Ranger's PA. "Is that really you?"

Jake smiled. "In the flesh! How'd the upgrades work, Ken?"

Seconds later, Ranger's pilot cage swung up and Ken Bowman emerged with a grin splitting his face. Jake dismounted and the two caught each other in a quick hug before stepping back to look the other over.

"Upgrades worked great and Paul's geek tank came up with another cool idea."

"Mister Bowman, please stand back," the other battle suit

pilot said, her voice crackling with anger. "Your people told me Carter was missing and presumed dead in Maryville a week ago."

"Chill out, Lieutenant! The brass might have thought he was dead, but we weren't so ready to write him off. ORBS pilots don't die that easy. So, who are your new friends?"

"Well, Ken, let me introduce you to the representatives of the Mid-America Council of the United Scouts."

"Like the Boy Scouts?"

Melinda rode forward. "Only coed… We rescued your boy here outside of Shenandoah. If it hadn't been for us, he'd never have made it this far."

Jake took on a feigned expression of horror. "It was terrible. It was snowing and raining at the same time, I was being chased by wolves. And there were pirates."

Bowman threw his head back and let out a booming laugh. "Because pirates make any story more interesting. You can stand down, lieutenant. Only Carter would know that joke."

The other battle suit turned and headed back inside the gate. Jake looked back over his shoulder. "We better get back inside ourselves. We may have some uninvited guests soon."

"You have no idea, kid." Bowman turned to get back into his battle suit.

"So, who's the new girl?" Jake asked when they got back inside the gatehouse. Ranger and the other armor moved to one side and Bowman exited the armor again. Jake and the Scouts dismounted near them and watched as the other armor's pilot emerged from the back of her armor. Nearly six feet tall, she was lean for her size, but even in her pilot's suit, Jake could see muscle rippling with each move. When she turned and pulled her helmet free, blonde hair in a tight braid slid across her shoulder and fell down to hit the middle of her back. Blue eyes blazed as she approached. Jake steeled himself for an unpleasant conversation.

"Where's your salute, mister?" Bowman shook his head as his hand came up in a perfunctory salute, which the newcomer didn't return.

"Lieutenant, it's a little early for that." Bowman voice was sharp as he brought his hand down. "Specialist Jake Carter, let me introduce you to Lieutenant Hannah Carter, formerly of the Federation of Democratic States. Major Blakefield has *allowed* her to retain her former rank and all courtesies due an officer. Going forward, she is to be rendered such courtesies."

Carter took a deep breath and her pale cheeks went a little pinker. "But I think the lieutenant was about to tell you that you needed to report to the major for debriefing, so you could be informed of the changes in our chain of command."

"Yes, Mister Bowman, see to that, if you would. I have the gate." Lieutenant Carter turned and stalked back to her armor.

Melinda glared at the other woman's back. "Is she always this sweet?"

"Usually, she's a little easier to get along with. But she still thinks she's the top dog here and it bugs her when she remembers she's playing second banana to ZOD. Come on, let's go talk to the major. Looks like you've got as much to tell us as we have to tell you."

Inside the walls, the layout reminded Jake of the Army Depot down in Corpus Christi. The construction vehicles coming in through the gate turned to their right and headed toward a fairly well organized motor pool area. Tents were set up in neat rows on the right of the path they were following. On the left Jake could see the ORBS parked and the bigger vehicles from the ZOD caravan set up as a sort of headquarters area. At the far end of the road he could see stacks of boxes and crates, some protected by rain flies and others covered with tarps. Bowman led him to the converted bus that had served as their mobile HQ. Jake found himself looking at a sea of familiar faces.

For a few moments, he was swamped with hugs and happy smiles as his friends and squad mates rushed to greet him. Finally, he found himself face to face with Red Devil and Jimmy.

"Red! You got him out! Glad to see I didn't go through all this for nothing." The big Ojibwe nodded slowly and took his hand in his bigger paw.

"Mihko Machayis."

Jake blinked and frowned. Red Devil smiled. "It's my name in Ojibwe, brother. You earned it."

"Thanks, brother."

"I see you found you long lost twin." Mihko pointed down

at Misun.

Jake laughed. "His name's Misun. It means little brother."

"I can see the family resemblance." Mihko knelt down and said something that Jake didn't understand. Misun immediately trotted over to him.

"*Gib laut!*" Mihko said. Misun barked in response.

"What the hell is that? I could barely get him to come to me, much less speak or sit or even attack."

Mihko laughed. "He's a police dog. They learn their commands in German. I worked with a dog handler when I was on the force, he taught me the commands."

"I need you to teach them to me, if you don't mind.

"Sure thing, little brother. But, hey, aren't you out of uniform?" The rest of the squad smiled or chuckled at that. Jake looked down at his uniform then held his hands out.

"Am I missing a button or something?"

Major Blakefield smiled as he walked toward him. "It's that rank insignia,"

Jake put his hand to the curled edge of the rank tab. "It is a little worn."

Paul reached out and took the curled edge between his fingers and yanked it free from the Velcro backing. "It's wrong. You're no longer a specialist."

As the major pulled the tab free Jake's heart sank. He felt the edges of his world start to crumble, fearing he'd done something wrong.

"You've been promoted to Chief Warrant Officer Two, along with the rest of the ORBS squadron." The major pressed a new insignia to the tab, a green bar with two black squares in the middle. The inside of the bus erupted in laughter.

Jimmy slapped Jake on the back. "You should have seen your face!"

"So, what does that mean?"

Bowman chuckled. "We're more than NCOs and not quite officers. Basically, you salute an officer first, enlisted salutes you first. We'll go over the courtesies later."

Blakefield let out a slow breath. "Yes, there will be time for that later. "First, I need to debrief Mister Carter and our guests. For now Sergeant Fipps, please stay. Everyone else, please excuse us."

The bus slowly cleared out. At Paul's prompting Jake introduced Melinda and her fellow Scouts, then recounted the events from the point where he had been separated from the rest of the squadron.

Once he had finished and had answered the follow up questions, Paul stood and headed for the door of the bus. "Come with me. Sergeant Fipps, please take Miss Holt and her companions to the quartermaster and get them billeted. Also, brief them on the escape routes we have in place. If things go poorly for us, I don't want them to get caught up in the aftermath of our conflict."

Paul led Jake to the top of the earthen wall and walked along it silently until they were once more at the gatehouse. Once there he sent a runner down to get Lieutenant Carter and waited, his gaze on the open field before them.

"Do you see that?" he asked after a moment, pointing to a low plume of smoke in the distance. "It's what's left of a pyre. The bodies of the fallen."

"Who fought here?"

"A combined force." Lieutenant Carter's voice came from behind them. Jake turned and gave her a salute.

"The Federation came to honor an agreement with the Freemen, to help them defend the settlement here against this Kilgore person. An armored task force under the command of my uncle, General Mason. We thought our Valkyries would make short work of the ferals and the ragers. We did okay against the ferals, but the ragers... we were losing a Valkyrie to every rager we killed, it seemed like. We thought it was a matter of firepower, but after seeing your ORBS I think we took the wrong approach altogether. Anyway, we thought we had a chance until the Titan showed up."

Jakes face scrunched up in confusion. "The Titan?"

"Biggest infected we've seen yet. At least fifteen feet tall, massive arms and legs. I watched one throw a battle tank around like a lawn chair. It tore every Valkyrie we sent at it apart like they were made of tin foil."

"How did you kill it?"

"We didn't. We ran. Every Valkyrie pilot, every Gun Captain, every officer. They took every transport we had, turned tail and ran. Declared our obligations met and just... left. They abandoned the enlisted and the work crews. Expendable, they claimed. So it's still out there."

"And there are more coming?"

Blakefield nodded sadly. "This wall will only hold them for so long. With more like Sammy out there with who knows what kind of powers we can't afford to stay on the defensive, but we don't have the manpower to launch an effective assault. Hell, we don't have an objective to assault in the first place."

Jake pointed across the field. "I think we're about to get the option to let them dash themselves against our defenses."

Three ferals and a rager were marching across the field, the rager holding a large speaker. When the quartet of infected got to a point about fifty yards from the wall the rager held the speaker aloft. At that range they could see the metallic additions to each infected's body.

A tinny, slightly nasal voice boomed through the speakers. "Freemen and Federation forces, I am Dr. Kilgore. You are interfering with a preexisting agreement between the inhabitants of Jackson and myself. Withdraw immediately and I will not assault your forces. You have until tomorrow morning to comply with my demands. If you do not, you will be destroyed. This is your only warning."

As the message was being broadcast, a bearded man in jeans and a black t-shirt walked up. He carried a rifle on his shoulder and a pistol at his side. "You folks considerin' surrendering?"

Both Blakefield and Lieutenant Carter shook their heads.

"Me, neither." With that he casually unslung his rifle, took aim through the scope, and fired. The rager stood there for a moment then pitched face forward. The ferals looked down at the corpse and took off at a run, going back the way they came.

Thunder rumbled overhead, and the English engineer smiled. "That should send the proper message. It seems we've another group of storms on the way. That should play merry havoc with his mechanical feral men."

"It'll be good to get back into the fight."

Lieutenant Carter spun on him, her voice hot. "Not so fast, Boy Scout!"

Blakefield cleared his throat and stepped between the two. "Well, about that. There have been a few changes, you see."

"Am I not an ORBS pilot anymore?"

"Your status hasn't changed, Mister Carter. It's that we've made some modifications to your battle suit. Until you're qualified on it, you're out of the combat rotation. Perhaps Mister Bowman should take you to see for yourself. Lieutenant Carter, you will stay at your post." The Valkyrie pilot scowled at Blakefield and turned to go. Jake saluted and waited for the major to return it before he headed down the inside slope of the wall to find Ken Bowman.

"What did you guys do to Spartan?"

"Oh, great. They didn't tell you? No, of course not and they told you to ask me. Come on." Bowman led him deeper into the camp, to a cleared area to the rear where the six ZOD battle suits and their rigs were set in a circle. Each of the rigs had a crew in front of it, welding something to the front bumper. With the exception of Ranger and Spartan, all of the other ORBS were beside their rigs. Bowman led Jake to the trailer behind Spartan One, where the front of the battle suit was open.

"Jake!" Danny called from the far side of the battle suit. "I'm glad your back!" Danny and the rest of the crew gathered around Jake, taking turns shaking hands or hugging him as they chose.

"What's wrong with Spartan?"

Danny's face lit with a broad grin. "Nothing! Hell, she's better than ever! We got her insulated so the lightning strikes don't hurt her so bad, beefed up the servos in the legs and we just got a new control system installed! This new Fed neural system makes our old feedback system feel like a slug!"

"Danny, slow down, you're techno-babbling at me. What are you talking about? What did you do to my armor?" Danny stopped and took a deep breath, moving his hands up and down while he tried to calm himself.

"Okay, so the Fed armors use this neural interface system. You know how prosthetic limbs use nerve impulses? It's the same principle. Their systems use a harness that goes down your spine and uses your nervous system to control the suit. It takes a little calibration, but once you get set up... Jake, this thing will move just like you do. Have you seen how that damn Valkyrie moves?"

"So why the hell am I sidelined? And why did you even go messing with Spartan?"

"Oh, that. Well, Spartan was the only suit without a pilot and Lieutenant Carter wanted a melee capable suit. And well... we thought you were dead."

"How long to get me up to speed on the new control system?"

"A couple of days? We have to do the neural mapping and calibrate the suit to you."

"Not good enough."

As the sky darkened toward sunset, it began to rain. Multiple strikes hit the lightning rods erected along the wall and near the center of the camp, creating a bizarre strobe effect every few minutes. Jake made his way to the HQ bus in his rain slicker, noting the ZRV and Scout One parked near the gate. Inside the bus Major Blakefield, Lieutenant Carter, the rest of the ORBS pilots, and the man Jake had seen earlier that day on the wall were waiting. Jake peeled his rain gear off and hung it over the railing with all of the other coats and slickers. He slid into a seat next to Heart. Misun padded over to him, still dry and now bearing a new insignia on his collar; a silver bar with three black squares on it.

"Hey, what's with the rank bar?"

Mihko and Bowman exchanged a knowing glance before Bowman answered. "Military working dogs are always a rank higher than their handlers out of respect for the dog. Chief Carter, you're working with Chief Misun."

Jake got to his feet and snapped a quick salute. "Congratulations on your promotion, little brother."

As his hand came to his brow, the rest of the squad came to their feet and did the same. Misun brought his paw up momentarily and the rest of the squad dropped their salute.

"Who taught him to salute?"

Mihko shrugged. "Probably his previous handler."

They took their seats again and Major Blakefield turned to a whiteboard that had been set up behind him.

"Very well, let's begin. Mister Carter, how goes your unauthorized training on your battle suit?"

Jake gave Blakefield a steady look. "Too slowly."

"Keep at it, I'm sure you'll get the hang of things in no time. For those of you who weren't with us in Omaha we discovered something that might allow us to make these electric storms work for us, doubly so with this rain. We discovered several weather balloons in our explorations. Using Ben Franklin's experiment as a basis, we intend to send out our remaining light vehicles to deploy a series of them where we believe tomorrow's battle will be fought. Once deployed, they should draw electrical strikes and conduct the current to the ground. The standing water should allow us to expand the area affected. The ORBS should handle this just fine. If it becomes imperative that we move into the area on foot, we have the means to either retrieve them or release them in place. We will deploy the balloons, then the ORBS, then heavy combat vehicles, and last our infantry forces. Lieutenant Carter, I believe you had some other resources to offer?"

"Yes, sir. When our Gun Captains left, they took almost all of the artillery and shells. We do have a mortar and about a dozen shells. If we need to retreat, we can use them to good effect. Also, with Spartan in reserve he can cover our retreat if it comes to that." She looked at Jake with narrowed eyes at the last part.

"This Kilgore fellow is expecting us to wait for him to attack. We've been monitoring a slow buildup of mechanized ferals on this side of the river. If we take the fight to him, we believe we can overcome the numerical advantage he currently seems to have. We also don't think he's had time to make the changes to insulate his creations from the electrical shocks, so that we may be able to make short work of his forces."

Heart raised her hand. "What about the second force Chief Carter reported?"

Blakefield looked grim. "We expect that we'll have to engage them as well. Kilgore's force is the bigger threat due to its more organized nature, even if it is the easier to eliminate. So our plan is to deploy the balloons once Kilgore's forces take the field and eliminate his control over them. At that point we should be facing one large, disorganized contingent of infected. And that is what ZOD is all about. Between the armored construction vehicles and the battle suits, this fight is winnable."

Lieutenant Carter glared at Paul. "Aren't you forgetting about the Titan?"

"No I have not. We have a plan for that."

"This thing beat over a dozen battle suits, how are you going to bring it down with the half dozen we have?"

"Tactics, Miss Carter. Tactics and teamwork. Your battle suits went at him one at a time. If and when he takes the field, we will not be making that mistake. We will deal with him as a team and rest assured your fallen brothers and sisters will be avenged. Now, if things go wrong the Scouts have offered refuge at their nearby camps. Squad leaders will have locations and directions. ORBS pilots will get as far away from the field as you can before scrapping your armor and proceeding to the scout camps. Are there any questions?" After a moment of silence from the group, Blakefield nodded. "Very well, then. The field team will deploy at four AM. Dismissed."

Jake filed out with the rest of the squad leaders and pilots, but instead of going back to where the rest of the armor was set up he headed for the billets. After asking around, he ended up at the tent the three Scouts shared.

Melinda greeted him as soon as he announced himself. "Come in out of this mess!"

"You guys should head out in the morning. Things could go seriously sideways here, and this isn't your fight."

"Well, I have to send Hoskins and Harper ahead to make sure the camps know what's going on, but you're an idiot if you think I'm going to ride out of here one minute before I have to. Or you forgot your Scout Law and Oath. Besides, it's one thing to tell people where the camps are. If you need to bolt, you're going to need someone to show you the best way to get there."

"Damn it, Melinda. I have enough to worry about without adding you to the list."

"I'm going to ignore that because I figure it comes from a good place. A stupid, sexist place that I ought to lay you out on your ass for, but a good place. I'm a grown up, I can make my own choices. But if I don't inspire you to be at your best, then fuck off. Now get the hell out and get some rest. Morning is going to come way too damn soon."

Jake shook his head and clenched his jaw, biting back what was on his mind. "Fine. Just... be careful. Remember, brave not stupid, okay?"

He turned and stepped out of the tent. For a moment, all he could do was breathe slowly and shake his head again. Once his heart stopped racing as badly, he started to walk away, the cold rain as strong a motivator as anything. He stopped when he heard Melinda call his name. He turned back to her in time to get caught in her embrace. His arms went around her as she pulled him down into a kiss that set his blood on fire and left his lips tingling.

She finally pulled back and looked up at him. "Brave, not stupid, goes for you, too."

"I don't think either one of us knows where that line is."

"It's one of your best qualities." She kissed him again, then turned and headed back for her tent, pausing only long enough to give him a smile and a good look at how the rain had made her t-shirt cling to every curve of her figure. Suddenly, going back and training with Spartan's new system held a little less appeal. He shook his head to clear it and turned back toward his rig. He had to survive the next twenty four hours before he could think about that kind of thing.

"A prudent man foreseeth the evil, and hideth himself: but the simple pass on, and are punished."

-Proverbs 22:3

Integrity looked out over the plain and fought the emotions that stirred in her breast. Anger at the human who had taken Corey from her was supposed to be foremost, but something kept trying to encroach on it. She promised herself as much the absent Corey, she would have him back and Kilgore would begin to understand new levels of pain and regret.

"It feels empty, doesn't it?" a voice spoke from behind her. She whirled, but found herself facing only thin air on the hilltop. "That place in your heart that you're trying to ignore." Again, she found herself facing empty space. "I know that feeling. Every day. Thanks to you."

"Who are you?" she snarled.

The voice taunted her from the darkness. "You don't remember and that pisses you off."

"My wrath is *not* to be taken lightly."

"I savor it and the pain you're feeling. I was going to kill you. I was going to watch you die with battle on the horizon, because I knew it would be the worst way possible for you to go out. But this... this is better. You're suffering and I'm not going to get in the way of that."

"What do you want?" Integrity ears strained to find her tormenter. She whirled to face a hooded figure.

"To kill you on your best day."

Lightning flashed as she lunged for him and he was gone. His laughter created a soft echo in the darkness. Integrity looked out over the field, the empty place in her heart suddenly sharper now that she remembered what it was. She cursed the mysterious figure and the frail brittleness of her humanity on the heels of that.

Movement on the field caught her eye and she smiled. "Spider Queen... dinner is served."

The electronic voice synthesizer squealed out the same name for the umpteenth time "Sammy."

The oversized rager smiled at the sound of the name. He said it again, almost singing it to itself. It repeated it and Kilgore turned to the dangerous woman beside him.

"Miss Argent, would you please deactivate that thing's voice synthesizer? This interference is getting worse, and I can't afford any distractions."

She went to the control panel and pulled up the menu for the voice synthesizer, but her fading humanity, the part of her that was still a woman named Patricia, rose up within her. She turned and went to the huge form and squatted beside it.

"Are you Sammy?"

The thing's eyes focused on her. "No. Not Sammy. Sammy friend. Sammy help... me."

"Do you remember your name?"

"Sammy help me... remember. Sammy says... Corey. That's me. Where is Sammy?"

"Miss Argent!"

She stood and went to the control station and pulled up the control menu. RLV-001A, his entry read. She entered the main menu and erased the impersonal designation. She typed "Corey" in its place before she disabled the voice synthesizer.

"Bastard." She wasn't sure if she was cursing him for what

he'd made her do to the rager, or what she'd allowed him to do to her.

"There! Something made that area of the forebrain light up. So whatever you did, you inadvertently helped. With that new interference blocked, I can deal with this Freeman unpleasantness. And whoever they've enlisted to help them. I'm afraid we'll need to scout about some more to find a new source of food."

"What about Jackson?"

"Oh, no, they've become far too troublesome. The only thing they're good for now is to serve as an example. I can't let them survive. Who knows who they'll try to ask for help from next? It's best to just replace them."

Argent shuddered and wondered if she needed an exit strategy of her own.

Jake flexed his legs, then straightened quickly. The sensation of being airborne lasted a microsecond, but Spartan's feet splashed mud for yards around.

"I got air!" he crowed, then looked at his mud splattered team.

Danny's face broke into a grin as he wiped mud from his cheeks and forehead. "Damn, Jake. I never seen one of these things move so smooth! How did the legs handle the weight?"

He checked the new screen on his right and ran back the performance logs. "Went yellow for a split second, I think. Yeah, short spike. Nothing the new servos couldn't handle, it was the compensator motors that had trouble with keeping up."

"A couple of days to familiarize yourself with the way she moves and I think Blakefield will put you back to combat ready status."

"I'm combat ready now."

"Ain't our call to make, Chief."

He popped the release on the cage and watched his breath mist into the air. "Yeah, I know. Doesn't mean I have to like it. Or agree with it. Time to muster up, either way."

Danny began to unhook the charging cable and the telemetry

lead while Kim loaded up the two bolt magazines on the right arm's gun mount. The other battle suits were approaching the front of their rigs and the crew had disconnected the trailers. Next to the Spartan rig, Mihko's crew leader watched as Red Devil was loaded onto the newly attached platform on the front of the vehicle.

Stocky and olive skinned with graying black hair and a thick moustache, Phillip Garza had earned his Chief's rank the hard way. "Wish we'd had those a couple of years ago. It's gonna make insertion a cinch."

Only the Spartan rig still carried its payload on the trailer, because the Valkyrie was too big to carry on the front of the truck. The six vehicles started as the battle suits were secured. Jake got the thumbs up from Danny before he pulled forward with Valkyrie in tow. Jake climbed into the ORBS cockpit and pulled the cage down. He fired up the motors. Once she was powered up again, he reached back over his shoulder and grabbed the neural interface and plugged it into the harness. His back tingled as the leads read his neural impulses. He knew the strip that ran down his spine was passive. He knew it couldn't actually send energy to his spinal cord, but to him it made his skin tingle.

Once the last of the rigs had pulled away and headed toward the gate Jake fell in behind them and walked toward the base of the wall. As he stomped along he heard the soft tap of something hitting the cage and bits of ice fell into the cage as rain became sleet.

The rigs lined up behind the two black cars and Jake walked in behind them. Once everyone was in place the gates opened and Scout One and ZRV One sped out into the darkness in a spray of mud. The gates closed again and silence fell. For several minutes nothing happened. Scout One reported its first payload dropped off, with ZRV One reporting a few moments later. The second and third drop off were equally uneventful and everyone began to breathe a little easier. Then the radios came alive.

"Jackson Base, Scout One, heads up. Three ragers headed your way!"

"What the hell is that? There's something out here with us."

"The ground is moving."

"That ain't the ground... oh my God... it's... fucking bugs everywhere!"

As the first screams started Jake popped the cage on Spartan and unhooked himself from the neural relay. He ran to the trailer for his rig. He grabbed the bug sprayer bottle that they used for bonfires and a can of the biodiesel fuel the rig ran on. He hastily filled the sprayer's tank. Once it was full, he grabbed the blowtorch from the tool box and opened the back of the trailer area. Misun barked a greeting and Jake feigned surprise.

"Danny, did you hear that?"

Danny's voice echoed back to him from the front. "Hear what?"

"Misun just ordered me to go help those guys out there. Right little brother? *Gib laut?*"

Misun barked again. "See, he did it again."

"I'll be damned. He did. Go, you stupid son of a bitch. You wouldn't want to refuse a direct order from a superior officer."

Jack slammed the door shut. He raced back to Spartan and plugged himself in. The front gates shuddered as the first rager ran into it at a dead run. Jake turned and took Spartan up the slope to the top of the wall. Troops were scrambling to hack at the hands of a rager that had jumped up and grabbed the top of the wall. The men moved away when they heard the battle suit come up behind them. Jake stomped on the rager's hands and it fell into the darkness. As it disappeared into the inky blackness, Jake pulled the armor's NVGs into place and switched them on.

Blakefields voice crackled over his radio. "Spartan, what in the hell are you doing?"

"Following orders, sir!" Jake jumped off the top of the wall.

He prayed all the way down, until he landed on something big and squishy. With a quick sidestep, he brought the battle suit's foot down on the rager's skull. He turned to face the two who were pounding on the gate. The first one never heard him coming, and he brought the thick blade under the bolt gun down through the top of its skull. The second one turned toward him and Jake flipped the battle suit's light on. As it recoiled at the sudden assault on its eyes, he extended the sword blade on the left arm and thrust up under its chin. He stepped back as it slumped to the ground.

"Gate's clear. Looks like I'm the closest ship in the quadrant. Heading out to assist Scout One and ZRV One. Try to keep up." He turned away from the gates, and started walking.

He built up speed, until he pushed off a little harder with his back foot and got airborne for a split second. He landed on his lead foot and pushed off with it and stayed in the air a microsecond longer.

Spartan ran.

Lightning lit the field and Jake's heart nearly stopped as he saw what the two vehicles were fleeing from. The field was covered in a writhing mass of spiders. Where there weren't spiders, there was web. And among the spiders were things that were horrible combinations of spider and human. The ZRV slowed and then stopped as its wheels got mired in the mud. Jake watched in horror as one of the spider hybrids pulled the driver through the window and plunged thick mandibles into his midsection. As he spasmed, he drew his pistol and emptied it into the back of his killer's head. The swarm covered the car seconds later, only to be consumed in a fireball as it exploded.

Jake sprinted past the burning wreck to where Scout One was also stuck. The swarm of spiders hadn't gotten into the car yet. He moved behind it and gave it a nudge with Spartan's knee. It was enough to send the vehicle skidding ten feet forward. The driver hit the gas while the car was still moving and used the forward momentum to get them going again.

Jake heard an elated voice over the radio. "Scout One's clear! We're headed for the gate, but we're covered in bugs!"

Blakefield's voice came back. "Understood Scout One. We'll take care of you. Just make it back to the gate."

Jake turned and started the slow process of running, only this time he managed to get to full speed in fewer steps. The weather balloons loomed ahead, by then just silk covered lumps in the field. He skidded to a stop in front of the center lump.

"Jackson, this is Spartan, I'm at the first weather balloon. It's covered in webs. How do I deploy it once I clear it?"

Blakefield's voice answered him, his words tight and clipped. "Spartan, once you clear the box, there will be a manual deployment handle on one side. Turn it, and the balloon will deploy.

That should also deploy the rest of the balloons in series. Then you are to return to Jackson base immediately. All ORBS are to deploy immediately. Open the gate."

"Okay, we got us a bug problem. Let me show you fuckers how we handle bugs down Pecos way." He popped the cage open and pumped up the sprayer then grabbed the blowtorch and hit the striker on the nozzle. A yellow, billowing flame erupted from the nozzle and he held it a few inches in front of the sprayer. When he pressed the lever on the sprayer the bio-diesel caught, He directed the impromptu flame thrower across the spider covered lump. Thousands of spiders were crisped in his first pass and the web began to smolder. He released the pump and let the gout of flame die. He directed a stream of fuel over the web itself. Once it was well soaked in diesel, he brought the blowtorch around and pointed the spray though its flame.

The result was a pyromaniac's wet dream made real. The diesel went up with a low *boom* as it caught, but didn't explode. The resulting fumes made the fire expand that much faster. A ring of fire rolled upward as the web popped and whistled, peeling away in layers as it burned. More spiders were consumed in squealing masses as the fire went deeper, undeterred by the sleet. Once the area in front of him had stopped burning, Jake slung the sprayer tank across his back and jumped down. A few quick passes with the blowtorch revealed the handle he was looking for.

He swore under his breath as he picked up the broken handle. "Uh, Jackson. We have a problem. The handle is no longer on the box."

An unfamiliar voice came over the radio. "Pry it open. That'll break the release spring free and still deploy it."

Jake turned and looked back at the light of the walls. His pry bar was still in his saddlebags. Reluctantly, he reached for the handle of his falchion. The tip slid into the narrow seam along the top of the box, and he leaned back to get more leverage. The box still held.

"Gonna need some help out here. This is definitely not a one man job."

"Red Devil's on the way, brother."

"Ranger is en route to your twenty."

"Mauler on the way, kid."

"Hang tight, Thunder's coming."

"Samson's on the way to save your bacon, buddy!"

"Valkyrie, responding." Jake took a moment to look back as the six vehicles charged toward him, an expanding feeling filling his chest at the sight of his squad mates heading his way. Suddenly, one by one, the vehicles stopped, their noses dipping.

"This is Bison Four, we're stuck. Red Devil, deploy, deploy deploy!" A chorus of similar calls came in rapid succession and Jake turned to look back to the east. A line of ferals and ragers was visible in the dim light. They were still a couple of hundred yards away, but advancing inexorably. He planted his foot against the box and pushed as hard as he could, but only succeeded in slipping. When he tried to pull his foot back, it only moved a few inches before the strands of sticky silk stopped it.

"All I need now is a fucking bucket to get the other one stuck in!" He tried to draw the falchion free. It grated a few inches and stopped.

Blakefield's voice came over the headphones. "Who the hell was that?" "Close those damn gates up!"

Ranger gasped. "Was that a damn horse?"

"Hot damn it was!" Samson piped up. "Ride, girl, ride! Jake, looks like help's on the way. You just hold tight, we're right behind her!"

Jake looked back and saw Melinda riding his way. Her head was down over her horse's neck. He drew his combat knife and sawed away at the strands of silk that held his pant leg. One by one they separated. He pulled his foot free as she reined her mount to a stop behind Spartan.

"You're helpless without me! Well, are you gonna help me save the world or what?" She grabbed the grip of his sword.

Jake couldn't help but grin as he put his hands next to hers and they both leaned back. The lid groaned and opened with a resounding *ping!* They fell back in the mud and watched as the weather balloon inflated in front of them.

"You need to get the hell out of the area!" Jake picked himself up off his butt and pulled Melinda to her feet.

"I told you, I can take care of myself." Her face was just as defiant as it had been hours before.

Jake shook his head then pulled her to him and kissed her hard for a second. He pointed to the rising weather balloon. "You're brave, not stupid. Your horse isn't insulated against a damn lightning strike like Spartan is."

"Gotcha. I'm out of here! Good luck stormin' the castle!" She raced to her horse and galloped back toward the wall.

Jake watched her go for a moment then unslung the sprayer tank. He climbed back into the cage and hit the transmit button on his radio. "Balloon's up. Shouldn't the other ones be going up, too?"

Blakefield sounded tense over the speakers. "The webs must be holding them shut."

"I can fix that."

Jake turned the blowtorch off. He pulled the leg covers closed. He took the sprayer nozzle and pulled the lever, sending a wide arc of diesel in front of him until the tank sputtered and went dry. He tossed the tank to one side, reconnected the neural link, and closed the cockpit up. He took a few steps back and he felt the hair on the back of his neck start to prickle. He reached up and slid the night vision goggles out of the way. He yanked the helmet's dark green visor down. In the slowly graying dawn, he could see the approaching horde of mecha-infected almost a hundred yards away.

"Might want to put your shades on, boys and girls. I think it's about to get a little bright."

Lieutenant Carter balked. "They're still too far away!"

"Then let's ask them to come a little closer!" Mihko giggled.

"What? How?"

"Politely." Jake pulled the trigger on the bolt gun and sent an explosive bolt sailing into the approaching mass of infected.

Body parts flew as the feral he hit blew to pieces. The other ORBS opened fire with their long range weapons. As if waiting to see what the rest of the squad was doing, Valkyrie bent its legs at the knees and leaned slightly forward before it opened fire with one of its guns, and demonstrated what superior firepower really meant. The ORBS used man-portable ranged weapons. The smallest weapon the Valkyrie used was its fifty caliber machinegun, which it employed to send even more parts flying as its rounds passed through bodies and left massive damage in their wake.

Heart beamed as the line charged forward. "I think they got the message! Now all we need is for Mother Nature to—"

Lightning exploded over her ORB. Even diffused through the wire, it was almost more than the suit could handle.

When Jake could see again after the flash every light on his control panel was yellow, with some slowly dropping to green. The diesel had caught as well and the fire was spreading quickly across the webbing. The ferals closest to them were lying on the ground and their cybernetic parts were glowing red hot. Further out more of the infected were on the ground and only a few were stirring. The fire was spreading to the left and right, consuming webs merrily.

"Cooperate." Heart finished.

"Oh my God." Jimmy whispered as the conflagration picked up speed.

In the light of the fire, they could see that Kilgore's ferals stretched clear across the field to their left. To the right were unaugmented infected, their ranks interspersed with the spider hybrids. The fire reached the boxes with the next set of balloons and they popped open as the webs burned away, already half inflated.

"Valkyrie. Those spiders probably don't heal like the infected do. You got anything for 'em?"

Her response to Jake's question was to spin the torso of her battle suit and extend the left arm. A tube on the underside of the arm spat fire as she swept it in a slow arc in front of her. A line of small explosions lit up the morning, sending spiders and zombies flying. Most of the ferals got back to their feet, but the spiders remained on the ground unmoving. The high-explosive grenades added to the inferno sweeping the field and in moments the right side of the killing field was almost completely ablaze. The rest of the balloons deployed, rising quickly into the air.

The rest of the balloons worked exactly as planned. Lightning bolts hammered the line they had strung across the field, ran down the cables, and the impurities in the thin layer of water conducted the charge across the field. Mechanized and normal ferals alike jerked and fell. Most of the remaining spiders were either fried or killed outright. The hybrids fell with the ordinary infected and most stayed down. When they could see again, the squad saw that many of the mechanized monsters stayed down.

Bowman let out a low whistle. "So far it's worked exactly like it was supposed to."

In the middle of the field one of the ragers, larger than any the team had ever seen before stood, parts of its body smoking. It was close enough that Jake could look it in the eyes and some part of him recoiled at the intelligence he saw there.

"Sammy!" the rager called out, then repeated the cry.

It coughed and gurgled. Jake raised the bolt gun and centered the thing's right eye in his sights. He stopped as his finger began to tighten on the trigger. It reached up to the still smoking metal device embedded in its throat and pulled it free, spitting blood once it had the offending piece free. It gurgled then roared incoherently. Jake moved the bolt gun's sight away. More lightning struck the field and the ORBS and Valkyrie stayed put, not wanting to risk a direct strike. There was silence as the balloons fell. Two glowing figures appeared in the smoke and steam that rose from the field. One was a pale red, the other emitting a white light. The massive rager lord stood and went to the red glowing woman. It knelt in front of her. The red woman spoke briefly to the rager while the white glowing one went from hybrid to hybrid, occasionally reaching down to scoop up ash from the ground.

The white glowing woman snarled. "My children! They killed so many!"

"Yes, Spider Queen. Kill them."

The Spider Queen smiled. The expression was wiped away when she suddenly lurched as part of her chest erupted. Glowing blood splashed on the ground and spilled from her lips. One of her strange insectoid eyes burst and something ricocheted off one of the battle suits.

Bowman let out a sharp gasp as the glowing woman fell, her light fading as she died. "Son of a bitch! That came from the *other* side of the field."

The red woman turned and screamed. She ran to the rager

and jumped on its back. The massive rager leaped into the air and landed several yards away. The pair fled to the east.

Fipps laughed. "Looks like some of the piss has gone out of the storm; let's go kick some rager ass!"

"Major, we're advancing. You can send in the armor." Blakefield's response was lost in a burst of static and the rest of the team moved forward. With the full squad it was mostly clean up, especially since about half of the unaugmented force was heading east after the glowing woman.

As they neared the river they left the battlefield they had prepared, and found themselves among trees.

"Stay together." Mihko warned as they lost sight of the open field.

The thick trees made that harder, but they managed to stay within sight of each other until they emerged from the woods to find themselves facing an abandoned strip mall. Several mechanized ferals and a dozen ragers stood between the red woman and a gas station at the end of the mall. The red woman whirled to face the squad, her face a rictus of hate.

She snarled in the dissonant double voice Jake had heard the other two glowing women use. "I grow weary of you."

There was a crashing sound behind them, and they watched as fifteen feet of rager titan emerged from the tree line. She motioned at the group. "Kill them!"

Valkyrie turned and opened fire with several guns, blowing bits of muscle and tissue off of it as she walked forward. Fipps started yelling over the radio to fall back, but the ORBS moved too slowly to maintain any kind of distance from it. Mauler was closest to it. The gigantic beast wasted no time in grabbing the heavy battle suit by the arms and tearing them off. It lashed out with a heavy foot, kicking it back twenty feet into Samson. As the Titan turned toward Valkyrie the Fed battle suit skipped back out of reach, never letting up the stream of fire. It raised one arm to protect its face and turned its attention to Red Devil. As the massive hand descended on the battle suit, Mihko activated the pneumatic axe and four fingers fell to the pavement. The titan roared and backhanded its tormenter, sending Red Devil flying as well. When it turned its attention to Ranger, Jake charged.

"Leroooy Jenkins!" He brought his blade down across its wrist.

The massive hand fell to the asphalt and Jake ducked beneath the forearm to fire an explosive bolt into the thing's side. With its attention on him it missed Ranger and Thunder coming up behind it, but it noticed when they cut its hamstrings. The infuriated backhand caught both of the battle suits and sent them tumbling back, with Thunder landing on top of Ranger. By then, Red Devil had made it back into the fray. He brought its heavy axe blade down into the meat of the titan's right shoulder. Undeterred it grabbed Red Devil and flung it at Valkyrie, which knocked both suits tumbling. Jake stayed out of easy reach and kept firing explosive bolts into it until the magazine went dry. As the last bolt hit it, it got to its feet and faced Jake.

Already, bones were forming under new flesh where its right wrist was regenerating before Jake's eyes. Samson's weapon arm emerged from under Mauler and Jake held a moment's hope. He stepped in and took a swing at the titan, leaping back as it tried to grab him.

For a moment the two faced each other, trying to guess what the other was going to do next. In that moment of stillness Jimmy shoved Mauler off of his suit and opened fire, sending 7.62 millimeter rounds into the side of the titan's head. Jake held still hoping to see the giant go down, but all it did was wince and turn its face away. In a move too quick to react to, it grabbed one of the Mauler's discarded arms and threw it into the middle of Samson. The jackhammer punched through the roll cage, leaving only a foot or so sticking out of the hole.

"Jimmy! Okay, motherfucker. You want to play? Let's play my game." Jake turned to face the titan.

On asphalt Jake found that he could break into a jog almost immediately. He bolted forward with the sword blade extended, held down and back. His left arm was positioned forward and raised to attack. The titan put a hand out to grab for him as he came to the edge of his reach, but Jake sidestepped and converted his momentum into a slice across the thing's midsection. It doubled over, both hands covering the loops of intestines that tried to spill free. As it coughed blood and snarled in his face Jake activated the saw on the left arm and brought it around in an uppercut that put the blade in the middle of the titan's chest. The blade bound up in the breastbone and Jake found his arm trapped.

The two played a gruesome tug of war, their faces only a couple of feet apart. The titan's eyes narrowed and Jake knew the tide of the fight was about to change. Intuitively, he yanked his left arm out of the battle suit's control harness. The move saved his arm. The titan hit Spartan in the middle of the chest, nearly caving in the roll cage and ripping the right arm off completely as it sent him skidding across the concrete.

"Spartan, try to hold its head still!" Jake heard over his comm.

He tried to get his bearings. "I'm trying to keep it from ripping mine *off*!"

To one side he could see Red Devil next to Valkyrie, one arm dangling useless at its side. The claw of the other gripped the longest and thickest barrel on Valkyrie's right arm mount. Before he could get eyes on the titan, it had hands on him. The massive rager reached down and grabbed the edge of the roll cage. With a roar, it pulled and the cage started to bend. Jake grabbed for the shotgun mounted under the dash and got his hand on the grip just as the mounts gave way. The Ithaca slid free of the scabbard as the titan pulled the cage away. Jake pointed the gun at its face.

The compact twelve gauge boomed in his hands. The blast caught the titan just above the upper lip, blowing its nose away completely. It reared its disfigured head back roaring in rage and pain. Jake pumped another round into the chamber. As it turned its face back to him, he extended his left arm and put the bead on the barrel right under its left eye before pulling the trigger again. Blood and bone chips showered down on him. He pumped another round into the chamber as the titan pulled its head back and turned the ruined eye away from the source of its pain. Which suited Jake just fine. He let go of the pump with his left hand and shoved the barrel against the side of the titan's face just below the right temple and pulled the trigger. The blast and the double-aught buck blew an inch wide hole in the orbit of the right eye socket, continued through the nasal cavity, and left a three inch gap in the left side of its face.

The titan reared back and screamed in agony. Jake dropped

the shotgun across his chest and slid his right arm back into the control harness. "You killed a friend of mine! Your life got a lot shorter!"

As the titan straightened Jake lifted the battle suit's legs and planted them in the middle of its chest. Blind, hurting, and confused it grabbed the legs and held them tight. With a thought he flexed his feet and Spartan's stabilizer spikes fired sending eight stainless steel, inch and a half thick and three foot long spikes through the titan's chest. Jake brought the right arm up and extended the sword blade. The point caught it at the base of the throat and he flexed his arm to lock the hydraulics.

"If you're gonna do something, do it now!"

"Incoming." Valkyrie's voice sparked across the radio with an eerie calm.

There was a loud boom and twenty millimeters of depleted uranium barely slowed down as it passed through the cranial cavity of the titan. The lead casing expanded and deformed as it went through the thick bone plate of the forehead and delivered a hydrostatic shock to the brain that blew most of the skull backwards for several yards. Jake turned his hips and retracted the stabilizers, letting the body slide off to one side.

Slowly, Jake crawled out of the wreckage of his armor. He had the shotgun cradled at his side as he stood in the chill morning air and surveyed the damage. Heart and Bowman were helping Fipps out of his armor. All three were bloody and Heart limped while Bowman favored one arm. Fipps' right arm hung useless at his side, obviously dislocated. Mihko and Hannah were leaning on each other as they stumbled toward him. Heart looked inside Samson. She stood and shook her head before heading over to the titan's corpse.

The glowing red woman emerged from the abandoned gas station. Her eyes were blazing, a rifle cradled in her hands. She stopped in her tracks when all six survivors pointed gun barrels at her. Her eyes went to the titan's corpse then back to the gathered warriors facing her. She turned her back and walked away.

Jake slowly lowered his weapon. "Brothers and sisters, the field is ours. I declare this day officially saved."

"Immediately after the tribulation of those days shall the sun be darkened, and the moon shall not give her light, and the stars shall fall from heaven, and the powers of the heavens shall be shaken."

-Matthew 24:29

EPILOGUE

Kilgore felt like his lungs were on fire as he burst into his lab. He'd lost count of the number of close calls he'd had after he'd fled his temporary headquarters. But he'd finally lost the glowing woman and her hulking rager minion. Once he was sure they were no longer on his trail, he had gone straight back to the lab. He paused long enough to catch his breath, then headed toward his sanctum.

The moment he entered the room, he knew something was wrong. Drawers were opened that he'd locked and the carpet that he had used to cover the floor safe was rolled up on one side of the room. The safe itself was open and empty. He went to the computer and stopped short when he saw the gaping hole where the hard drive had once been. Who could have done this? It couldn't have been Miss Argent. He'd asked her to buy him some time to escape. The loyal simpleton that she was, she'd agreed. It had to be one of the Fed scientist or maybe one of his old colleagues who had also survived the fall of Man?

Either way it was inconsequential. There was no greater asset in the room than the very brain of Martin Kilgore. He shrugged into his coat and grabbed his emergency pack. He headed for the little storage room he'd hidden his means of escape in.

The door opened to reveal the little electric car still in place.

A quick walk around revealed that nothing had been disturbed. He tossed his bag into the back seat and loaded the survival gear he had squirreled away in as well. Once that was done, he pulled the spare set of solar panels out from behind the empty locker by the main door and lashed them to the roof. It wasn't until he went to grab the keys that he found something out of place.

"You honestly thought that I'd let you order me to my own death?" Miss Argent voice came from his right.

He dared a look and found her sitting in the unused, darkened office that overlooked one side of the loading area.

"To buy you time, at that. Did you borrow that from a movie script? Or was it just a generic line you'd always wanted to use?" She got to her feet and walked toward him, the gun barrel she held on him never wavering.

"Miss Argent, I'm... I'm glad you made it back in one piece!"

"You're really going to try this? Do yourself a favor. Don't." She lowered the gun and pulled the trigger.

Searing pain lanced through Kilgore's calf, and he fell to the floor. "That's better. Now we know where we stand. Well, where I stand and you crawl."

"But... why?"

"Self-preservation, Martin. Simple dog-eat-dog self-preservation. You brought ZOD, the Federation, the Freemen and now this glowing feral-controlling chick who has a soft spot for the biggest rager I've ever seen down on your ass. I'm loyal, but I'm no zealot. So, good luck and thank you for loading the car up for me."

Something crashed elsewhere in the complex and Kilgore let out a whimper. "Please, don't abandon me!"

"That's the sound of all the terrible things you left me to face back there. This is what karma feels like. I just wish I could stay to see what they do to you. But I can live without it. Good bye, Martin." She stood and turned on her heel.

He watched her go silently, suddenly aware of the shape of her legs, the curve of her hips. Suddenly aware of just how remarkable a woman Miss Argent was. He struggled for a moment to recall her first name. "Good luck, Patricia."

"Piss off!"

The car pulled out silently, leaving him to face his fate.

Integrity found him by the coppery scent of his blood. He had crawled out of a delivery door and half a block away before she caught up to him. She grabbed him by his good leg and dragged him back into the factory she had followed him to, relishing his screams until he had passed out.

Now the scent of urine was mixed with blood, which she could smell even through the bandage she'd wrapped around his wound to stop the bleeding. She strapped his hands to the table and tilted it upright. His eyes fluttered open, and he let out an inarticulate cry when he saw her standing in front of him.

"You owe me a great deal of suffering."

They were just outside her grasp. Even as battered as they had been she sensed that Death favored them, at least for today. Between them and the Spider Queen's death, she had been denied enough. "I have decided you will serve me. Did you know that the further away from the heart an infected bite is, the longer and more painful the process of turning becomes? I'd bite you myself, but I have less of a claim on your suffering than my Corey does. You do remember Corey, don't you?"

The scent of urine grew stronger as Corey stepped around from behind the table and bared his teeth.

The ORBS squadron stood on the wall as the grim procession bearing Jimmy Sams body arrived at the gate. Their cheeks unabashedly wet with silent tears as they gave him honors, all hands up in a smart salute. As one, they brought their hands down as Samson's rig passed through the gate. All activity ceased when the truck passed, heads bowed, hats removed, a hundred silent gestures of respect.

Caleb intoned softly. "Through me, my brother lives on. Brolo."

The rest of the squad joined in. "Our brother lives on. Brolo."

"Though I think one of my brothers is about to get himself ripped a new one." Mihko nudged Jake as Major Blakefield walked up the slope toward them. Jake nodded and steeled himself for the expected ass chewing as the major stopped in front of him. He saluted and went to attention.

"I thought I told you... no, *ordered* you to reserve status."

"Yes, sir, you did."

"So, who, if anyone, authorized that little stunt you pulled today?"

"Chief Misun gave the order to help Scout One and ZRV One, sir."

"Chief Misun?"

"Hairy little dude, about this tall, wet nose," Jake offered, putting his hand down to the middle of his thigh. "Doesn't say much."

"I'm... familiar with him. I believe I'll have a talk with him about overstepping his authority. Given that you were following the orders of a superior officer, I believe I can overlook your actions today. To think, I've lived to be countermanded by a dog. In the future... let's just not *have* any future incidents like this, shall we?"

"Yes, sir."

The major turned and walked down the slope, leaving the ORBS pilots to their vigil. As they watched their armor being carted in on their rigs, dark gray flakes of dusty snow began to fall. Winter had come to the world.

CHARACTERS

Ami Taylor- Wife of Daniel Emery Taylor.

April Simpson- Reporter/Anchor for FOX2 in Saint Louis. www.facebook.com/AprilSimpsonTV

Arianna Lamb- Damsels of Dorkington member.

Artez Hardin- Saint Louis Police Officer.

Benisha Abe- American living in Japan, home for a visit.

Billy Tackett- Top horror artist in America. www.BillyTackett.com

Blythe Renay- Damsel of Dorkington member.

Chloe-AKA-Adrastea (Latin for inescapable)- little girl brought into room 425 in Maryville. First child to be taken in the Rapture.

Corey Phillips- CEO of Black Pigeon Press and owner of "Gameday." www.blackpigeonpress.com

The Damsels of Dorkington –Group of entertainers famous for their skits and comedy on the convention circuit. www.DamselsofDorkington.com

Dani Burke- Woman that comes in and lies down next to Frank Fradella right before the 4th seal is opened.

Daniel Emery Taylor- Actor from Road Trip and Return of the Swamp Thing. danielemerytaylor.com

Danielle Nevin- A nurse at Anderson Hospital and last person to be Raptured.

David Dyer- Owner of St Louis Science Fiction/Fantasy convention named "CON-tamination."
www.Con-Tamination.com

Dean "Midas" Maynard- X-factor TV personality caught in the Apocalypse in Memphis.
www.deanmidasmaynard.com

Doctor Josh Poos- Doctor working with the CDC on the Abaddon Virus.

Frank Fradella- Old man in Anderson Hospital that is visited by an angel and given the power of the coming Rapture.

Hometown Comics- Comic Store located at 110 East Vandilia, Edwardsville IL 62025 www.hometowncomics.com

Irma Cassorla- A CNA at Anderson Hospital in Maryville, IL.

Jeff Yenzer- Damsels of Dorkington member.

Jim O'Rear- Actor trapped at Con-tamination in Saint Louis. www.jimorear.com

Kirby Krackle- Awesome band with many genre songs.
www.KirbyKracklemusic.com

Matt Hill- Actor (Raphael from Teenage Mutant Ninja Turtles). www.Matt-hill.com

Pete Koch- Former Oakland Raider and Heartbreak Ridge actor. www.PeteKoch.com

Peter and Angie Mayhew- Peter played Chewbacca in every Star Wars film. www.PeterMayhew.com

Private Shane Nettleton- A man awaiting military trial for killing a captured insurgent that tortured and killed a civilian by cutting his head off on video. Shane has been relocated to a reserve unit and is out on bond, put up by his unit and internet fans.

Randy Roach- High School graduate on his way to the science fiction and fantasy convention in Saint Louis named Con-tamination.

Rebecca Hultz- Shane Nettleton's girlfriend.

Ryan Roach- Former EMT and church musician on his way to the science fiction and fantasy convention in Saint Louis named Con-tamination.

Sara Delp- School Teacher at Troy Middle School.

Sheree Speckman- Lab tech working with Doctor Poos.

Sinjin Oleszczuk- Z.O.D. member of the Double'O First Cosplayer. Runs CCG website for advanced looks at MMOs for their subscribers.

Stephanie Schofield- Z.O.D. member of the Double'O First cosplayer.

Steven Tibbs- Professional rapper and Biz Markie collaborator. www.StevenTibbs.com

Terry Naughton-Disney animator and Abyss Walker Artist. www.TerryNaughton.com

Tori Bilderback- Stranded in Memphis, TN while on vacation.

Z.O.D. (Zombification, Orientation, and Defense)- A nationwide cosplay group dedicated to edifying the public on how to survive a Zombie Apocalypse.

About the Author

Ben Reeder's parents claim they found him in a pineapple patch in Hawai'i and brought him home, which was their way of telling him that he was adopted. He grew up in South Texas reading Tolkien, Asimov, and Robert E. Howard. Ben has always loved telling stories, and in high school, he wrote pulp style action adventures for his friends. Ben has been filling notebooks and hard drives with stories and ideas ever since.

After graduating from Calallen High School, Ben joined the Air Force to see the world. The Air Force had other ideas, and he ended up in Kansas. Since serving his country, Ben has had a myriad of jobs. He has worked in a video arcade, on a farm, selling ads, a clerk in a convenience store, scanning medical records, and has been a manager and in a New Age bookstore.

Over the years, he learned archery and sword fighting in the Society for Creative Anachronisms, became a solitary Wiccan, plus he has learned a little bit about a host of other religions, trained to be a massage therapist, has attained his second level in reiki and can list a dozen other skills that have no particular use outside of an historical recreation event or one of his stories.

Currently, Ben lives in Springfield Missouri with his girlfriend Randi, and a pride of cats, led by their little gray queen, Dora.

Other New Babel Titles

Core Series
"The Plea of Apollisian"
"The Trial of Innocence"
"Darrion-Quieness"
"The Death of Kings"
"Tides of Winter"
"Return of the Father"

"The Sword from the Sky"

Core Series Collector's Books
"A Prisoner's Welcome"
"The Breach of Crowns"
"Exodus of the Strong"

Other Novels
"The Wererat's Tale"
"The Wererat's Tale-Of Rat's and Men"
"The Wererat's Tale-Ring of the Nonul"
"The Wererat's Tale-The Collar of Perdition"
"The Wererat's Tale-Tiers of Valdore" 2016

"White Wraith"
"White Wraith-The Journey"
"White Wraith-The Lock of Requ" Summer 2016
"White Wraith-Maelstrom Serpents" 2017

"The Forge of Feasts" Dwarven Cookbook
"Walk the Abyss" Abyss Walker Anthology

"The Apocalypse of Enoch"
"The Apocalypse of Enoch I-Rapture"
"The Apocalypse of Enoch II-Scourge"
"The Apocalypse of Enoch III-Desolation"

The Apocalypse of Enoch World Setting
"Children of Enoch I-Dark Harvest"
"Ash Fall"

Graphic Novels
"Orcs and Generals"
"The Apocalypse of Enoch-Rapture" Kissell Studios 2016
"Vindicated Inc" Kissell Studios

For additional NBB titles, visit: www.newbabelbooks.com

Go to www.Zod001.com and Join for Free!

Peter Mayhew

Matt Hill

Daniel Emery Taylor

Jim O'Rear

Steve Tibbs

April Simpson

Terry Naughton

Billy Tackett

Pete Koch

James Fipps

Alexa Heart

www.ingramcontent.com/pod-product-compliance
Lightning Source LLC
Chambersburg PA
CBHW071006280626
47160CB00015B/1410